Best Climate Change Stories

An Anthology of Original Short Fiction

Ron Sauder

Editor

Best Climate Change Stories

Ron Sauder
Editor

SECANT PUBLISHING

Salisbury, Maryland

Contents

Foreword

This anthology, *Best Climate Change Stories*, is the product of a collaboration between an independent bookstore and an independent book publisher, both of us based in a rare, beautiful, and vulnerable piece of American coastal geography called the Eastern Shore.

Book Bin, the book's sponsor, is located on the Eastern Shore of Virginia, and Secant Publishing, the book's publisher, is located some sixty miles to the north on the Eastern Shore of Maryland.

In both cases, the "Eastern Shore" refers to a 200-mile-long peninsula that divides the waters of the Atlantic Ocean from those of the Chesapeake Bay. Bounded by the states of Maryland and Virginia, the Chesapeake is renowned for its abundant harvests of blue crabs, oysters, and rockfish; its picturesque waterfront towns and marinas; and its seminal role in the formative years of American history. On the Atlantic coast, the Eastern Shore is known for the NASA spaceport at Wallops Island, the Chincoteague ponies, and Ocean City, a major resort that swells into Maryland's second largest city in the summer beach season.

And now, the Eastern Shore has added a new dimension of importance – that of canary in a coal mine.

A combination of land subsidence, sea level rise, and storm damage has literally erased a series of populated islands in the Bay. Still more are threatened with oblivion. Tangier Island, in Virginia waters, and Smith Island, in Maryland, cling to their proud maritime traditions in the teeth of ongoing erosion and flooding.

On Maryland's Eastern Shore, large tracts of desolate ghost forest have been created by saltwater intrusion on the sprawling Blackwater nature preserve and migratory flyway, while thousands of acres of salt marsh have been lost to rising waters. An oxygen-deprived dead zone appears and blooms every summer in the deeper waters of the Bay, threatening the web of life down to its very roots.

Some of these processes are geologic, some meteorologic, some anthropological – but all contribute to an increasing awareness of climate change and the inexorable power it is exerting on the quality of life many remember from just a few decades ago.

Whether inspired, overwhelmed, *im*pressed, or *de*pressed by these local examples, we (Philip Wilson from the Book Bin and Ron Sauder from Secant) decided to join our very finite forces and hold a worldwide contest to explore the *human impact* of climate change – not through science or journalism, but rather, the power of literary art. What are people feeling, we wondered? How are these trends playing out around the globe at the psychic level – whether individual or communal? We wanted imaginative interpretations of human experience, not numerical analysis or political advocacy.

Philip and I were joined by Karen Gravelle, a bestselling author who also lives on the Eastern Shore, and the three of us proceeded to advertise, promote, and eventually, sort through a gusher of entries from all over the world. (Special thanks to the contest directories at Reedsy, Duotrope, Almond Press, and ChristopherFielden.com, among others, for helping us to get the word out.)

We set no limits on location in time and space, or even on genre. We wound up with a cornucopia of stories running the gamut from humor to horror, suspense to satire, science fiction to social realism.

In the end, there were thirty-four surviving stories from thirty-four authors, hailing from nine countries and ten American states. We could have doubled the total without diminishing the richness and liveliness of the finished anthology, but we felt duty-bound to hew close to the total of thirty we promised would see the light of day.

The most torturous responsibility of the judges turned out to be picking three prize winners, again as advertised. Many, if not all, of our entries were deserving, but in the end we settled on:

o *Noah's Great Rainbow*, by New York writer A. A. Rubin, Gold Medal. In this societal projection of the near future, geoengineering has taken place to protect the Earth from runaway heat death. It has worked – too well. All over the world, skies are darkened, and a spiritual pall has fallen over humanity. What can one painter do?

o *Desert Fish*, by Maryland writer K. M. Watson, Silver Medal. A solitary refugee girl has survived her family's trek from Central America to the great American Southwest, where she is rescued by an older woman whose people claimed the land before the Europeans came. The two of them bond over small, fragile fish who survive improbably in seeps and springs of water. How is that even possible? And how long can it last?

o *Beyond the Timberline*, by Viennese writer Olaf Lahayne, Bronze Medal. A Swiss and Italian duo, ascending the Alps into white-knuckle territory, are startled by the discovery of a pine tree growing above its known range – enabled by global warming. As each climber proudly claims it for his own country, will he pay attention to what this rare sprout may portend for the frozen crag?

Lest anyone consider *any* of these fictions far-fetched, here are just a few true stories ricocheting around the media-sphere in the summer of 2024, as we prepare to go to press:

In the annual *hajj*, or pilgrimage to Mecca, more than 1,300 Muslim believers have died, succumbing to extreme temperatures of more than 120 degrees Fahrenheit.

In California, a trial run to "brighten clouds" with sea salt particles, thus enhancing their reflectivity to the sun's rays, has been called off due to environmental concerns. But researchers and private funders supporting the work vow to keep trying.

Meanwhile, Mexico City is nearing "Day Zero," when the last aquifer is tapped out and the last drought-stricken reservoir runs dry. One of the world's largest metro areas, boasting more than 22 million residents, may soon be unable to pump its own drinking water.

Scientists have been startled by new readings showing that the "Doomsday Glacier" on Antarctica is dissolving at an unexpected rate, undercut by warm water inflows at its base. The loss of this one glacier alone could raise sea levels by two feet worldwide.

One could go on and on, but you can write your own Google Alert and call up as many examples as you can bear to read.

Before the numbness of repeating headlines sets in, dive into our short stories for psychological insights and illuminations. We owe a debt of gratitude to these word artists who have plumbed their hearts and spirits to explore this defining issue of our day.

Enjoy. Or perhaps more aptly, read and reflect. We thank you for taking the time.

Ron Sauder
Editor
Salisbury, Maryland

Beyond the Timberline

Olaf Lahayne (Bronze Medal Winner)

After the two climbers have reached their destination, they spend some minutes panting and crouching against the trunk of a solitary tree, one from the left, the other from the right. Standing upright, they wouldn't be able to lean against the tree anyway: even while sitting, the branches start right above their heads, and the whole plant is barely three meters high. Nevertheless, after taking a breather and putting down their rucksacks, the duo marvels at the meager tree for a while. At the same time, they are careful not to step back too far, as the rocky protrusion, in the middle of which the tree is rooted, forms a roughly equilateral triangle with an edge length of some five meters. On one side, the ledge is confined by the almost vertical flank of the mountain, while in the opposite corner, a boulder taller than a man is balancing on the edge of a yawning chasm. On the other two sides, the plateau falls steeply into the abyss.

Finally, the younger man breaks the silence: "*Si, senza dubbio: Un cirmolo*. A ... a pine?"

The older man nods: "Yes, indeed. A *Swiss* stone pine, to be precise. Well, if a tree can grow that high in this region, it *must* be a Swiss stone pine."

"Si, *certo*. Call it a Swiss stone pine if you like. Ma... here!? We are at an altitude of..."

The Italian takes a calculator-like device out of his rucksack and activates it. "*Dio mio: Quasi 3,000 metri!* That is definitely the highest tree on Monte Cervino."

"The highest tree on the *Matterhorn,*" the Swiss corrects. "And most probably the highest tree in the Alps, if not in Europe. It's a record! But with global warming, the timberline will soon be at even higher altitudes. In any case, this Swiss stone pine probably owes its sheer existence to that boulder over there: the rock is just small enough to stay on that ledge, yet large enough to protect the plant from wind, weather, and discovery. So it's true what the German helicopter pilot said: there *is* a tree up here. Thank God we decided to take this detour."

Meanwhile, the Italian caresses the bark of the pine. "*Bellissimo!*"

After a while, he notices that his companion has taken out a camera and is taking photos of the tree from all sides: "*Cosa vuol dire?*"

"Well, isn't it obvious what I'm doing? I have to document this find for the WSL, the Swiss Federal Institute for Forest, Snow, and Landscape Research. After all, this is the highest tree in Switzerland!"

This infuriates the Italian: "*Assurdo!* Didn't we start climbing the mountain in Italy?"

"Sure," admits the Swiss, adding GPS data to the image files. "But as you know, according to our binational agreement, in the vicinity of the Matterhorn, the border between Switzerland and Italy runs along the watershed. The watershed is on the ridge, and that's where we are now. That is why we are in Switzerland."

"*Assurdo!*" the Italian swears again. "The watershed, and therefore the border, is the line where it goes down on both sides. Behind you, I mean. The tree is *un vero italiano!* What about the GPS?"

"The signal changes back and forth across the border. It's not accurate enough."

The Swiss man calmly puts his equipment into his rucksack, which he leans against the boulder next to the Italian's baggage. Then he looks down into the abyss behind him, then to the other edge, one step behind his colleague. "It seems to me that the plateau is descending towards me. That means the watershed is behind you—and so is the border. The tree is Swiss."

"No, no, no!"

"But of course."

This goes on for a while. Finally, the Italian takes his water bottle out of his rucksack. "*È facile come bere un bicchiere d'acqua!* If the water flows towards me, then the watershed is on your side, and it's an Italian tree. *Altrimenti-*"

"Otherwise it's in Switzerland," continues the Swiss. "Well, you will see."

He watches intently as the Italian unscrews the bottle. The alpinist begins to pour the contents beside the tree, but only a few drops come out. "*Maledetto!*"

The Swiss smiles gloatingly—until the same thing happens when he tries to empty his own bottle. "*Gopferdammi!*"

At a loss of what to do, the two men look at each other for a while. Then the Swiss has an idea: "Well, I have to take a leak anyway."

The Italian looks at him questioningly. But when the other man unzips his jacket and then his trousers, he understands and does the same. Simultaneously, both men start to water the pine tree. Then they stand back and watch what will happen to the yellow, slightly steaming puddle around the slender trunk. But instead of flowing to the left or right, the liquid quickly disappears into the cracks in the rock. "*Maledizione!*"

His colleague is about to add another Swiss curse but hesitates and raises his hand in warning. "Is it possible that the permafrost is already melting even at this altitude?"

"*È assolutamente impossibile. Ma-*"

A rather discreet crack in the rock below them interrupts the Italian. Instinctively, both men retreat from the tree. Immediately, a loud crash follows; a crevice opens across the rocky ledge, parallel to the mountain flank and directly under the tree. For a second, the boulder lingers; at that moment, both men jump over the widening chasm toward the mountain flank. No sooner have they landed than most of the ledge is plunging into the depths behind them, along with the boulder, the rucksacks, and the tree. For a minute or so, as the men are pressed against the rock, they hear it crashing, rumbling, clattering, and rolling beneath them.

At last, it is quiet again. As soon as he is sure that the remaining two or three feet of the ledge are stable, the Italian turns to his companion: "I hope you have your... What do you call your radios for such accidents?"

"You mean the REGA emergency radio?"

"Exactly! Where is it?"

The Swiss nods toward the abyss, whereupon his companion turns even paler: "*Maledetto!*"

American Mangroves

Paul Briggs

Arney shook her head. "This forest is dead."

Two men with shovels looked at her funny. One of them gestured up at the green leaves, the sound of birds and squirrels around them.

"Look around, not up," said Arney. "No saplings. No trees any younger than ten, fifteen years. Those are the first to go. After that..." She pointed southeast. A sparse line of bone-white loblolly pine trunks still stood between here and the encroaching Atlantic.

Chet scratched his sandy hair. "So... are we planting here or down there?" Arney could only imagine what Chet's ancestors would have thought of him being part of a work crew headed by a Black woman, but she was the one who'd taken the dendrology course.

Some of them need to go up here. That way, even if another Cat-5 or 6 hits South Carolina before next spring, our work won't all be washed away.

"The small white mangroves," said Arney. "They're labeled LR." Arney was about to explain that this stood for *Laguncularia racemosa* but decided there was no point showing off. "Put 'em wherever there's sunlight and give 'em a three-foot circle of mulch. Everything else goes in the ghost forest." She picked up her own shovel and headed for the line of dead trees.

No need to worry about sunlight here—the branches of the dead trees had mostly fallen off, leaving what had been forest floor naked to the sun. Salt-tolerant wax myrtle shrubs already grew amid the chunks of debris washed up last year from what had been Charleston. Left to itself, this land might become a salt marsh... or might get washed completely out to sea in the next hurricane. Best not to take any chances. There was a spot about midway between two trunks that looked like a promising place to start. Arney set her shovel on the damp ground...

... and found oyster shells.

Seashells. Under a foot of dirt. That didn't happen by itself. This was a grave.

The woman Arney's mother had named her for—Arney Savage, who had labored at the plantation called Gowrie on an island in the Savannah River, owned by Charles Manigault in the 1830s—wasn't an ancestor. Arney Savage was no one's ancestor, at least not biologically. Cholera had taken every child she'd ever given birth to. Those children were almost certainly buried somewhere on that island, but whatever stones, seashells, or wooden posts she had marked their graves with had long since been buried under leaf litter and silt from some flood or other. Their gravesites were as lost to time as their names.

And that, in a nutshell—or a seashell—was the story of this part of South Carolina. In the antebellum era, the Lowcountry had been the kingdom and prison of the Gullah. Their ancestors had been stolen and shipped here in chains precisely because they knew how to grow rice in the swamps. The reason they had a name for themselves—two names, actually, Gullah and Geechee—was that in the antebellum era, they had held more autonomy than almost any other enslaved population.

The bad news was why. During the summer, the Lowcountry had been infested with so many deadly diseases that white plantation owners and oversees didn't want to risk their lives by being there. Cholera. Malaria. Yellow fever. One planter famously said, "I would as soon stand fifty feet from the best Kentucky rifleman and be shot at by the hour as to spend my night on a plantation in summer." Arney's ancestors, on her mother's side, hadn't been given that choice. And her ancestors were just the ones who'd lived long enough to have children of their own.

If she dug down another three or four feet, Arney knew she'd find bones—perhaps of a child, perhaps of a man who'd died at thirty, perhaps of a woman who'd be as old as fifty. And where there was one grave, there were bound to be many more. *What a way to discover a new cemetery.*

Among the first signs in the fossil record of humans acting distinctly human were graves dug by Neanderthals or early modern humans. It was a way of saying *These people mattered. We haven't stopped caring for them just because they're gone.* The Gullah had hung on to that basic need in the face of plagues and state governments that were equally indifferent to their humanity. Some of their cemeteries had been continuously maintained from the late eighteenth century to the late twenty-first. Others were still being rediscovered.

Arney reached for the phone on her arm. At some point she'd have to let everyone know. How much would they care? This was the 2060s, not the 1960s or 1860s. Society had gotten a lot better at treating everyone as though they mattered equally.

The bad news was that mattering equally wasn't the same thing as mattering a lot. It was a hot, muggy autumn in South Carolina, but down in Antarctica, a too-warm summer was coming. Sometime early next year, the Thwaites Glacier was finally going to collapse. The ocean would rise another few feet, swallowing the salt marshes and eating into the unprotected earth beyond. In the face of that, would they hold off on protecting the remaining coastline just to dig up and study some more graves? Graves from a culture that was still alive and could speak for itself?

Arney looked out at the ocean. It had swallowed all those who died on the slave ships, and now it was coming for the graves of the survivors. In the same way, it had swallowed the passengers of the *Titanic* and the *Lusitania*. It was on no one's side. It did not care.

And the people buried here? They never got justice. The bulk of their lives was stolen for the profit of others. And yet they chose to survive, in a place where dying would have been as easy as walking into the ocean. They chose to keep their own children alive in a place where that was a near impossibility.

Arney suspected that her understanding of the lives of the people buried here was not much clearer than that of Chet or any other white man. But their own community—exploited, plague-ravaged, trapped between the Devil and the deep blue sea more literally than anyone else in history—must have meant more to them than anything.

Arney looked at the trees. These were no invasive species. They were American buttonwood and white, black, and red mangroves from Florida, and like any mangroves, they would survive the saltwater intrusion and hold the land in place in the face of the worst storms. Left to themselves, the changing climate would have let them spread this far north in their own time—perhaps fifty years, perhaps a hundred. Trees weren't known for speed. No reason not to help them along.

And planting things on gravesites was one of many African traditions her mother's side of the family had kept going.

It was a farm-raised black mangrove sapling. *Avicennia germinans*, just over a year old. Arney carried it from the truck to the little hole in the ghost forest, planted it herself, and staked it. In another ten years, the high-tide line would be just below here. By then it would be a good, strong tree, one of many.

A little closer to the coast would go the red mangroves, *Rhizophora mangle.* Given a full Carolina winter-in-name-only to spread their roots into the surrounding soil, these trees would be ready to stand on their own by spring.

There was nothing like a mangrove forest for protecting the land from the ocean.

The sea brought us, the sea shall take us back. But not today.

2100, Remnants of a Thriving World

B. E. Saunders

The boat lurched. As one, the crowd stumbled forward with murmurs of surprise. I gripped the handrail and tried to ignore the spasms shooting up my back. Old and frail, I should find my daughter, take a seat, and rest, but I couldn't turn away, for I could feel it; I would never see Bangladesh again.

Even with the sea breeze, sweat trailed my face; my body was slick with it. My sari clung uncomfortably to my skin, but the heat did little to stop the nervous chitter of the people pressed in around me. Their hands extended toward the shore of Dhaka, waving frantically to those left behind, and with strained smiles, they sang their hopes that they would soon follow.

The boat pulled into motion, slow at first. The foul hoard of floating plastic knocked and scraped its sides as if Dhaka and all its accumulated history were holding on to its prow, willing us to stay.

I remembered the first time I laid eyes on our capital city when I was just a young girl, fresh from our drowned rice paddies on the coast. I had never seen so many people. Like us, they were running from the floods, from the storms and the waves, to find sanctuary in an overflowing city of migrants, where at least there was fresh water and money to be made. But the relentless, ever-rising tide had finally reached Dhaka's edge, and the time had come to succumb to the waves, one way or another.

"Luck be with us," I whispered. A man beside me, all bushy beard and eyebrows, looked down his broad nose at me and nodded grimly.

"And with them." His voice was thick as if holding tears, and yes, he swallowed hard. He waved to the shore again. I followed his eyes, but the throng was too crowded for me to guess who he was leaving behind. Not for the first time, I gave silent thanks that my daughter and grandchildren were here with me. At least we would end this together, whichever way it came about.

The boat picked up speed, revealing the extent of the slums. Crammed together, the makeshift huts sprawled the coastline. Six decades I had lived there. I did not know why I had survived when others I loved had not, for the raging fires that roared through the streets, the riots, the outbreaks of cholera, had all claimed so many. Too many.

We were so far out on the water now that the huts had bled into one, and my throat burned, my knuckles were white from clutching the rail, and I felt the wail rise within me and escape to join the chorus of mourning from the other passengers, who had all lost their homes, their heritage, and maybe they too felt the same fear as I, that we may never reach our destination. Calmer days than these had morphed into cyclones that shredded houses, flooded cities, and sunken ships. And those days were more frequent than ever.

I wondered if we had already sailed over the land I once called home, where a lifetime ago, everything had changed. My little brother's cries echoed in my chest as I remembered our mother cradling us on the bed. Though she cooed and shushed, her body trembled with every roar of the wind that shook the walls, and when the water entered and quickly climbed, she hoisted us both high on her hips and waded outside. Under the dark, thunderous sky, we watched our house collapse, and the waves devoured it all.

It was strange to think that if things had been different, I would have reared my own children there. We would not be leaving our nation, our home, our identity for a refugee camp I did not want to spend the last of my days in. If things had been different, we would have been given aid sooner, the land would still be thriving, the great war for the world's fading resources would not have ignited, and I would be drifting asleep each night knowing that my family was safe. If things had been different, if people had made changes when those changes mattered, none of this would have begun.

A small hand, more bone than flesh, laid across my own. Blinking through tears, I looked down to see Mishti had wriggled her way through the crowd. Such a little thing, all arms and legs, her cheekbones too prominent, but we were all paying the price from the strict food rations.

"Nani, Maa said to find you."

"And found me you did, but I will stay a little longer." I squeezed her hand in my own thin, wrinkled fingers.

She nodded and leaned her head on my arm, and together, we watched the coast of Bangladesh shrink until it was swallowed by the horizon, and there was nothing but the rise and fall of an endless, churning sea.

Adaptive Solutions

Karly Foland

Our daughter, munching on a celery stalk slathered in peanut butter, is young enough to believe the world is as it always was. She's unaware of how miraculous her arrival was, how her parents' bodies overcame air that scorched skin and water that blackened teeth to produce a new, perfect thing. For years we hoped, but nothing happened. Until, unexpectedly, it did. But with mounting pressure from antinatalists, we toggled between joy and despair and agonized for months about whether or not to bring her into this hot, tempestuous world. Indecision led to inaction led to her. So, old and exhausted and terrified, we stumbled late and uncertain into parenthood.

Half a dozen years later, my stomach knots up still. A curious adventurer, she's in the wrong time, an era hell-bent on stifling her spirit. She belongs to an age when tiny worlds full of curious creatures blossomed in every puddle and under every rock. When kids ventured far beyond their compound walls to catch slick toads, flee squawking geese, and peek at fluffy newborn bunnies nestled in hidden burrows. She senses she's missing something but can't grasp what. Children's books no longer feature the hijinks of talking sheep, loyal canine companions, or moral lessons from families of bears. Big hairy mountain gorillas, prowling orange tigers, ancient spotted sea turtles—they're all mythical creatures to her. We might as well describe dragons and unicorns to her crinkled brow. So when she asked her father and me what a pet was, our heads swiveled to each other. We grimaced and our eyes searched each other for the answer to where in the world she learned about pets. I cleared my throat and spelled it out as simply and nonchalantly as possible to avoid frightening her. *Animals we'd keep inside our homes, as ...* I glanced back at my husband, unsure how to describe the cats and dogs of our childhood, before they went their own way. *Friends.* She gasped, her eyes, hazel like her father's, wide and watering. Animals hadn't been our friends for decades, certainly not in her lifetime. They had no role in her life: not to cuddle at home, not to admire in zoos, not to eat for nourishment. They were just out there, unseen, experiencing the world as we could not. And responding to misguided approaches with a clear message: *You're not welcome here anymore.*

The animals changed slowly, at first, in ways that broke the hearts of those paying attention. Shifting hibernation and migration practices, declining cognitive and sensory abilities, broken mating rituals ... across all species, the rising temperatures and fickle precipitation patterns disrupted their internal ways of making sense of the world. Then, new changes appeared more rapidly and in ways that froze the hearts of those paying attention. *Adaptive solutions,* the zoologists labeled them in fearful bewilderment. We accepted humanity had set in motion forces leading to our own downfall. But we hadn't anticipated that those same forces would reshape the structure and function of the brains of the entire animal kingdom. Or in such unexpected ways. At once conspiratorial and defiant and aloof, they flew and galloped and crawled out of our lives. To some we said no, stay, we need you to provide for us. But they never did again. The fiercest prisoners fought back with growls and claws and fangs and broke free. The weakest sat in their fields and coops and chose passive resistance, even at the threat of execution, over servitude. Desperate humans clutched their horses and parakeets and hamsters and begged them to stay, to comfort them as the world burned. But each stared back, eyes brimming with menace and melancholy, chilling the souls of their now-former owners, who opened cages and pens and stepped aside.

My own orange tabby, lazy and plump and addicted to the comforts of indoor life, tore up the screen on our back door when I was seven. He strutted out, tail up, and disappeared into bushes behind our house, never looking back. Our border collie, ever loyal, stayed two more years before her anxiety and distrust of humanity drained her natural verve, and she, too, fled. Carrying only her well-worn tennis ball in her mouth, she dashed off with the neighbor's golden retriever. In a final attempt to convey her motivations, she tore our thermostat off the wall. It ran at full blast for years as heat wave after heat wave engulfed our once-temperate region. Her brown eyes pled with us, *You're making it worse.* Our pets' abandonment gutted me. The weight of humanity's guilt crushed my innocent heart, and I grew militant in my climate activism. I forced composting, vegetarianism, and bike riding on my still-skeptical parents. They threw cash at bootleg breeders to appease me with designer pets with untainted genes. But they floated through the house like lobotomized ghosts. So I snuck out one night and walked them into the postage-stamp-sized park at the bottom of our hill. Once sprawling and verdant, encroaching development deteriorated it into a paved, trash-strewn wasteland. But it was the best I could do. As the yellow grasses snapped underfoot and under paw, their comrades emerged from the shadows and led away the last pets I'd ever have.

My last salient, joyful memory of nature was rocking on our front porch with a cold glass of lemonade next to my grandpa, dazzled by the fireflies dancing over the tall grass. Now, few remain. Several years ago, I glimpsed a small swarm through our compound fence. I inched closer, but as my fingers grazed the metal, they flickered out and vanished into the darkness. They refuse to share their beauty with humanity's unappreciative eyes anymore. My daughter cackles at her father and me for telling tall tales of these little flying sparks of lightning; she can't fathom such marvels exist. A little drunk on our last bottle of dark rum, we once went on a storytelling spree crescendoing in our pathetic mimicry of the electric buzzing of cicadas. She fell out of her chair, gripping her side in delight. We long for her to enjoy the same summer ambiance we once did, but her days are so much quieter now. An eerie void has replaced the buzzing and chirping and trilling of insects I once, unforgivably, found irritating.

One night, I awoke with a start. Something had finally pierced the silence. I nudged my daughter out of her nest of pillows and carried her outside. She rubbed sleep from her eyes as we crept to the center of the yard. There, under haze-smudged stars, we listened to the hoots of a distant owl. She'll never see one, but it comforts me to know they still exist. I described their big eyes and swiveling heads but she yawned and rolled her eyes. She reminded me she's not a baby, and declared that she was old enough to know something that sounds so sad could never look so silly. I wanted to offer up the contrasting beauty of the common loon's plumage with its mournful wail as a counterpoint but remembered it's just something else she'll neither hear nor see. I couldn't bear to reveal that they faded away after coal-sullied air dirtied their lungs and overheated their homes until it all became unlivable. We humans knew about this but didn't stop it. So instead, I put her back to bed and wept for what we lost, for what we never appreciated when we had it. My husband held me close and his body trembled with mine. We share sorrow over how we deprived our daughter of a life with other species. How do we explain this to her? How do we apologize when there's no making amends?

Our day-to-day lives are so busy, so focused on teaching our daughter how to thrive beyond survival, that I often pretend none of this pain exists. But it sits there, deep inside, building like a volcano, until tears erupt from my eyes. In these moments, I turn from my daughter and busy myself with mending clothes or pickling vegetables. But she always notices and wraps her small body around one of my legs and squeezes. *I have her,* I tell myself. *What other creatures could I possibly need?* But I can't help it. I miss them. I miss them so much. I long for the warmth of a purring cat on my lap, the love of a dog wagging its tail so hard its entire backside shakes just because I stepped into the room, to giggle at a red panda's adorable antics at the zoo, to taste the butterscotchy flavor of goldenrod honey and to bite into the tangy creaminess of manchego cheese. The creatures of this earth want nothing to do with us, give nothing to us, and no longer abide being captive, no matter how gilded the cage.

Now we're the ones in cages. Stuck on compounds, hiding from predators, both animal and human, rationing everything because the lean times are longer and more frequent than the plenty times. This is no life for our child, one of the few in hundreds of miles. Others had better sense than us. I dream her generation will find a way out of this. But when I dare to hope, my heart races like I'm a rabbit surrounded by hunters, desperate to run but unable to discern which direction is safe. I know it's too late. The world is moving on, healing itself, and will do anything to keep us from interfering. I can't blame it, though it terrifies me. Not for me, but for my daughter. She played no role in the mess we're in, but she'll suffer for it. *I'm so, so sorry,* I whisper into her hair as I cradle her at night.

Plants became my last connection to the earth. With dirt-caked nails and pollen-stained hands, I guided seeds to satisfying meals, bulbs to cheerful decoration. This sliver of peace soothed me and returned me rejuvenated to the responsibilities of parenthood and partnership. Until, on a stroll through our orchard, the trees thickened and darkened. Sunlight no longer dappled their trunks, and their shade cast a hostile, unnatural coolness. Birds and squirrels chattered on the branches, and leaves rustled in response. I dropped my basket of peaches, and synchronized heads turned toward me. They fell silent, then scattered. That night, a great tearing shook the walls and I burst outside as thick roots ripped up from the ground and set upon the lawn like massive spider legs. The oaks and maples paved the way, then the apple and cherry trees. By the end of the month, they all were gone. The animals had shared the secrets of adaptation. With such knowledge, of course they chose to leave us behind.

Inspired, our crops followed suit. Thickets of hawthorn and firethorn sprouted like a fence around our fields. The tomato plants and bell peppers in my small garden sunk into the earth. Three days later they popped out on the other side of the brambles and spikes. The plants in our greenhouse, cut off from the soil, from the tremors and signals of their fellow kind, remain unaffected. But I removed the potted rose bush from my daughter's room and set it outside the compound. Just in case. It's only a matter of time before they find a way around—or through—us to freedom.

Maybe the plants and animals will give my daughter the chance to prove she's not like her forebearers. That she understands stewardship and harmony. That she has already adapted to the needs of this new order and doesn't deserve the same ending as the rest of us. They have to, or I'll never forgive myself for forcing life upon her. I scream these pleas into the wind every night.

Awakened

Cindy Diggs

It was the yelling that woke me up. A tall man was standing and yelling. His frizzy red hair stuck out, struck out in all directions like it didn't know which way to go. His temper was hot, erupting into bellowing bursts of fiery energy and anger.

"This is not my fault!" the Spirit of Fire yelled. "Do you know how hard I worked to create the element of fire?" He continued ranting, "I made it for YOU! To warm your bodies, your homes, and your food. I gave you the spark that keeps you alive, keeps your heart beating. For years untold, I carefully managed my fires, teaching you humans how to harness them and use them wisely. Now, look what you have done. You destroyed the things that kept me in line. You unleashed me, unchecked, out of control. This is your fault."

Fire glared at the small human in front of him. The man, covered in soot, pleaded for an explanation, a reason, an apology. But, and most of all, he desperately wanted a promise of no more pain and destruction.

"I lost my home, my family, all my belongings. I stand here, alone, beaten and burned. Most of my village is gone, life forever lost, and you can't promise me that you will stop your attacks," the man cried, overwhelmed by his emotions.

I shook my head to get oriented. *Wait, is this a dream?* I looked around. I was in a forest glade. Animals lined the perimeter, silent and still, watching and listening. There were strangers I didn't know, all upset, some angry, some sad, some faces unreadable. A tall and beautiful woman sat behind a big wooden table made from an old, majestic tree. She had Elemental Spirits on both sides of her.

Fire then turned to one of the female spirits. "And what about you?" he sneered. "You're no help anymore. When the forest was set ablaze by one of my lightning bolts, you used to quench the flames with your downpours."

The Spirit of Water lowered her eyes, holding back tears. She was a small woman with flowing blue robes and golden tresses. Her voice, usually calm like a bubbling brook, was now gushing with anguish and sadness.

Water raised her head and spoke, "I don't know what to do anymore. There is drought where there once was water. My oceans are too full, and they threaten the land. And my beautiful creatures, those of river and sea, how I mourn for them. Mankind kills and pollutes my virgin waters. My lakes and rivers are evaporating faster than I can refill them." Water paused, worry and anger wrinkling her old face. She turned to the Spirit of Wind.

"And HE is not helping," Water stared at Wind and spat accusations. "His ferocious blows are only stirring up my water with tornadoes and hurricanes. He dries out the fields, killing the crops the humans need to survive," she spoke. She started to speak again but stopped in mid-sentence. All eyes turned.

Mother Nature had stood up. Her stern and serious glances at each Elemental Spirit demanded silence. She looked exactly as I imagined her: a living spirit. Long brown hair, green robes adorned with flowers, a face not old but not young. Normally mild-mannered, she took her responsibilities very seriously. She was comfortable with her immense power and shimmered with it now. Even the birds were silent.

Her glance softened. She had met with her co-creators—the Elemental Spirits of Fire, Air, Water, and

Earth—several times over the most recent centuries. Their relationship stretched back for millennia. Each Element was needed to create human life, to supply the oxygen, the blood, the bones and flesh, and the Spark of Life. She supplied the Life Force. The committee then turned their attention to creating the planet Earth, a complex, intertwined, and interconnected, abundant collection of beauty and Life.

The Creators had observed the slow and steady harm the growing number of humans were doing to the Earth they created. They observed how the natural processes of decay and rebirth were getting out of balance, destruction faster than recovery. The careful planning of the powers of the Elements, each contributing to the life forces of this planet in a coordinated manner, maintaining the balance, were now out of balance. Mother Nature cleared her thoughts and cleared her throat. She addressed everyone and everything assembled in the glade with tender focus on the group of humans standing before her.

"Everyone, please listen," she started. "I know this meeting is long overdue. Tensions and emotions have built and intensified. But please hear me. We are in this together now. I know we all have different views and perspectives, but finger-pointing and blaming will not help. We have an emergency to solve together. Chaos will not solve anything," she finished, exhaling a deep sigh.

Another human asked to speak. Mother Nature nodded her head in approval. She listened intently. An elderly woman stood supporting herself on a cane, still trembling. She spoke in a sad but firm voice. "My town was flooded. A big hurricane came through. The newspeople told us to evacuate if we could. I had nowhere to go. The water came under the door. I grabbed my purse and picked up my baby cat, Ginger. The water was rising fast. I didn't know what to do. Thank God, a neighbor came by in a small boat and rescued us."

She took a breath and continued to speak. "The water was terrible, moving fast. I was afraid we would overturn. Other people paddled in canoes loaded with belongings. What they had thought to bring, I don't know. How do you decide? We passed a cat in the water. He was soaked and hanging on to something sticking out of the water. He was trying to stay afloat, but with most of his body in the moving water, he couldn't pull himself up, only his tiny arms desperately latching on. I held my cat tighter. I could only cry for that cat. There was nothing I could do." The Spirit of Water murmured a heartfelt apology.

The Spirit of Air jumped up then, agitated. Turning toward Mother Nature, he blew out his frustration, huffing and puffing. "Do we really need to listen to this dribble?" he blustered. "I know I blow hot and cold, but these people have to take some responsibility for their actions. In the beginning, we came together and created a miracle. A lush and beautiful planet filled with a variety of life-forms. We all did our parts and kept our promise to work together to maintain this paradise." He glared and pointed. "THEY ruined it, and now THEY want us to fix it?" A gale-force wind suddenly threatened to blow everyone down, but it went as quickly as it came. Wind was making his point.

But Mother Nature would have no more arguments. She stood as tall as a Redwood in her stance, the force of her resolve spreading out across the glade and beyond like a shield of maternal protectiveness. She said again, "We are here to work together. We are together. We are One."

It was then that a piercing howl broke the silence. Everyone started and looked up and around. A man came forth from behind a large gray wolf, greeted by an outcry from the animals surrounding the glade, forgotten until then. I had noticed the forest animals earlier—birds, squirrels, mice, a fox, and deer. Now they stepped aside. Coming forward to us, other animals entered the center of the glade. Did they suddenly appear, or were they there the whole time, ignored and overlooked?

Koala bears, polar bears, giraffes, rhinos, and an elephant stepped forward. Shadows and outlines of countless other creatures filled the background. The human man, his hat adorned with antlers, feathers covering the sleeves of his woolen coat, and his feet bare, strode forward. "I have many names, but here I am called Lord of the Beasts," he said with pride and purpose.

The Lord, looking first at the Spirits and then the humans, declared, "I speak for my creatures. They have voices that have gone unheard. They communicate but remain misunderstood. Some sacrifice their lives for the benefit of man, others are slaughtered, without reason."

The wolf howled again, this time a long, mournful cry. The Lord, touching his heart, continued, "My heart bleeds each time their blood flows. My breath stops at the moment theirs does. I feel crushed under the weight of so much pain and suffering. I—we—plead for help from all of you before all my precious creatures are gone." He bowed his head in respect to Mother Nature.

She returned the gesture to the Lord and her eyes lingered on the animals in front of her. Lifting her head, she peered into the distance, encompassing all there was, with sadness in her heart, as they were her beloved creatures, too. "Yes, we must save our animals as well as humans, the trees and the plants, all living things, as we are all connected to each other," she reminded everyone.

Lastly, the Spirit of Earth stood and turned toward Mother Nature, asking, "May I speak?" The Spirit of Earth was, naturally, a female spirit, a slight variation of Mother Nature. She wore a hooded green robe with pride. It seemed to be delicately covered with leaves and vines. She turned her big brown eyes toward the humans and held out her arms as if to embrace them.

She began, "First, I would like to tell you all how much I can feel your pain, just as I feel the physical pain of my beloved Earth crumbling under the strain of what some humans have done to it. I know not all humans have sought to destroy me with their insensitivity, ignorance, and greed. But those who have, have done great damage indeed. I am not sure I can heal myself at this point and need to ask for your help." She sat back down.

A tall, thin, well-dressed woman stepped forward. "I want to help," she said, lifting her chin. "I really do. I have been trying in any way I can."

"Bullshit!" a gruff man shouted. "With your pretty clothes and dainty hands, I doubt you've done an honest day's work in your life." He motioned, and a few others came to stand with him. He continued with anger and disgust in his voice, "You rich people hide out in your fancy houses or take your private jets out of danger while the rest of us suffer from what your indulgent lifestyle has cost us."

"That's right," agreed another man, dressed in dirty work clothes. "You rip apart the earth, searching for more gold, diamonds, and gems to drape upon your body and more oil to run your fancy cars and planes. Mother Nature and Earth built a strong planet, sturdy and stable until your digging sabotaged the very foundation of this planet."

The gruff man was about to speak again when he saw Earth stand up, pressing her hands to her face, looking out past the two men speaking. She silently walked around the big fallen tree of a table, toward the men, and then past them.

Out of the forest, behind wisps of smokelike haze, came more women and men. Each human carried another human, some small, some large, all lifeless. The bodies of children, wives, husbands, mothers, and fathers were held seemingly weightless by those who had loved them in life. Earth walked among them. She pushed back the muddied hair of a dead woman and wiped her face off with the hem of her robe. She gently lifted the bloodied and mangled body of a child from her mother's arms to kiss the cold cheek, bringing the child to her breast for a moment before returning her. She walked among them, between them, touching some gently, just sharing an understanding look with others.

"I call to anyone willing, come with me," she said, loud and clear. "Your loss will not have been in vain. We'll return to the earth for rebirth. That's something I can still do. Like the seasons of my earth, these souls can be reborn in the womb of my fertile soil." Earth turned and walked toward the smokelike haze from which the people had emerged. Those who chose followed her until they were seen no more.

Mother Nature stood again, calling back the group's attention. They waited for her to speak but she stood silent for quite a while, her thoughts unknown, her face unreadable, but there was pain behind her eyes. She spoke, "There will not be an easy solution to this crisis. As we have seen and heard, the problems are many and varied, and emotions are high."

"It doesn't matter whose fault it is," Mother Nature continued. "The humans came to us for help. The creatures of the earth, too. I will have no more arguments. We will come together in peace and love and use all of our combined power and wisdom to try to save this planet of ours, to save ourselves. I ask each of you to pledge to help in any way you can."

Then, to my astonishment, Mother Nature looked straight at me, straight through me. I thought I was invisible. I stood frozen, powerless to move or speak. "No, my dear. You are not powerless." She smiled and said, "In fact, you are more powerful than you can imagine, and we need your help."

"But how?" I asked, bewildered.

"Go back to sleep," she said. I did.

The next day, I walked around my yard as the birds sang and the sun warmed my face. Yes, the earth was alive, and now I saw beyond the physical to the spiritual life force all around me.

Mother Nature's voice spoke to me once more, reciting these words.

"Feel the power all around, with every sight and smell and sound. Feel the power all around, from sea, and sky, and solid ground. Feel the power all around. Just reach up and bring it round."

I caught my breath, realizing I was anything but powerless. I was part of Nature, and Nature was part of me. I was part of the Team. Count me in. I'm here to help.

Bitter Almonds

Andrea Dejean

She stares out through the kitchen window and up toward the almond tree at the edge of their property. It's not even mid-February and the tree is already blooming. "It's too early," she says to herself, and then vaguely remembers saying the same thing at some time in the past. When exactly? Last year? The year before that?

Walking behind the house, she sees that one of the cherry trees, the later seasonal variety, has begun to bud as well. She can't find the courage to climb the hill to see if the other cherry tree, the supposedly early-blooming variety, is also budding. Last year, they were both covered with cherries. The fruits on the tallest, out-of-reach branches they left to the birds and gathered all they could from the lower branches, but after they had eaten more than their fill, given away baskets of them to friends, and made pots of runny jam, they let the orbs on the late-blooming tree shrivel and dry on their stems, cherry raisins even the birds found unpalatable and left untouched.

As she wanders through her small, sad rose garden, she realizes that although it is not yet March, the month her gardening calendar tells her she should cut back the plants, it's already too late. They have begun to leaf out, feathery bursts sprouting along the sides or at the tips of skinny branches. A guy at the local nursery had told her the best time to cut back the plants was when there were no leaves on them, but the only time there seemed to be no leaves is in the middle of the summer when the parched and sickly plants vainly compete for light and moisture with the neighbors' hulking hedge.

Where were the violets that somehow usually managed to emerge from between the roots of the roses? Native to the area, they were one of the few things that grew unbidden in the poor soil of their yard, but perhaps she had smothered them to death, spreading hopeful handfuls of enriched earth around the recalcitrant roses after dragging the body-heavy bags of "special: rose beds" from her car.

They had stacked logs for the fireplace by the front door but had only burned one fire that year, not because it was cold (it wasn't) but because the evenings were dark and damp and depressing. In late June of the first year they lived in the house, they shut off the heat, cleaned out the chimney, and stacked the logs beneath the broom trees, only to have to haul some back again because they were so chilled in the living room in the evenings their hands were too numb to turn the pages of the books they were reading.

She tamps down the mossy clumps of earth the wild boars have churned up in the yard with their hooves and their snouts, looking for things they never seem to find and so return again dawn after dawn to paw and snort through the barrenness, leaving tracks through the parallel mounds in the potato patch and their rank smell in the laurel and fir along their path. The wild pigs will be back, she knows, drawn by the detritus of meals they throw into the yard, and she wonders how things have gotten to the point where scavenging animals will eat rinds and carcasses of things they normally do not eat and have even learned to coordinate their searching with the meal-time hours of the house's human inhabitants.

In the end, she asks herself, "Does it really matter if the plum tree has hard disks of fungus knifing its trunk, if the hazelnuts that rain down in a strong wind each have a single hole pierced through them? Will it matter when they are gone that the almond tree bursts into bloom in February but then only produces one or two enormous almonds that fall to the ground and turn to stone?"

Blood

P H Zietsman

Iron and salt—a distinct flavor. Blood. My mouth blasphemes at the taste.

His swing, from wide to my right and stealthy but rapid in approach, blackened my vision. I did not see its thunder-like potential, could not anticipate its forceful impact. I spit, still standing, calling home scattered focus. *Nice one.* Grateful fingers clasped the loaf before that blackness. Acres of nothing in my hands now, dripping through hungry fingers. My bread is gone. The truck is gone, and with it, the alms.

The earth gives no more. Its grace, long dead and rotted under our deserted hopes. Merciless, its hunger for us. Its flaming sands suck at our feet, and its blazing breath scorches our skins. She turned tired of the taking and takes of us now—more every day; and swallows us whole into her cold depths—less every day.

The loaf is gone from his thieving fingers, ate. The smile is full of doubt after twice his fill. I understand. The next hunger is already here. His bomb hands wait for a mission. My eyes stare at the dust trail of the truck. I'm lucky; I got water this morning.

Their pesticides killed the soil's soul. Dead earth gives nothing. Our herbicides raped nature's heart. And her poisoned spirit grew toxic vegetation. The rain stopped raining. Her tears dried up like the soil's soul.

The sun stabs holes in my back as I return to the shelter. Rusted metal screams hot insults in my face but gives shade in return. The luxury of a car has become roofs and walls and windows. Shelter. Still. Stagnant. An antithesis of use, life's satirical answer to our wandering ways. *Use your feet, pilgrims.* There are two thousand of us—less every day—at the edge of a malignant patch. Thirst kills most and more daily at our home on the shores of stagnant water. They—the lucky ones—bring a drink on Thursdays, I think. Names for days seem such an indulgent endeavor when each holds mostly the same. The rations are scant and thirsty work. Some die hoping in line. For each three dying, another comes. Numbers are dwindling. Food arrives on any nameless day after a starving length of time. Hunger infests this place.

Thunder-fist walks past my shelter and peers into my eyes. The intensity of his shame shouts into my heart, and I forgive his hungry nature. When food is in short supply, you better adapt and adjust. I don't need much. I lift a hand to wave him on, but his head jerks his sight into not much of a future. Maybe next time, we can share my portion.

There weren't bombs or wars or revolutions. Nothing more than a slow decay of being human. And as our decline into comfort and ease overwhelmed our desire to interact with life, so life slowly died in us. And for us. We ate the foods of our poisoned tree until just a barren wasteland of lethal oasis remained outside of cancerous city limits. Places like this. Slow death camps that offer shelter and a place to expire for the few born into this legacy.

It started as a steady mental collapse. The fear that infected our society, which we attempted to suppress with pharmaceuticals, drown with alcohol, and control by subliminal means, one day caught flame and ignited age-old terrors. By then, we had the means to hide and the spaces to cower within.

Big Pharma stepped up, and where it was a comfortable lie before, it grew claws and a sharp beak—a proper false god. And its right-hand mascot, the media, spread messages for this unnatural savior and its wondrous cures for all things ailing our troubled minds. There were tablets, pills, and capsules. Lozenges and pellets and drops. Injections in the form of inoculations, immunizations, and vaccinations. Booster shots, double jabs, and triple doses. There were quick fixes and deep hits and high pops. The lab-developed diet we craved was part chemical remedy, part food-like substance. Soon, physical degradation followed. And as our health failed, we stayed at home, slept in, lounged in front of TVs that preached pills and advertised shots. *Kill the fear dead—stick it with a needle!* With the chemical murder of fear, that apathy toward life festered. We wished for life to come to us, lift us, save us from ourselves. But life stepped aside as we obeyed artificial death. God became a foreign concept in some bewildered ancestor's feeble mind. We saw a mirror, which showed us ... nothing we wanted to admit. That's when humanity's spirit died. My grandma told these stories, and I listened. I wondered about GMOs and glyphosate and all the ugliness we deemed necessary.

A rumor surprises me the next day. *He's a prophet, and he's coming.* I'm queuing for water. I pay it no heed. There have been government agents and Red Cross regiments and magical gypsy caravans before, all coming to save us. Yet they never pitched, not one tent on our stunted and toxic lawn. Our grave was our home. And vice versa.

I'm sorry I hit you.

Another surprise. I turn around. Itchy fist stares at me. He's sorry. It radiates from him. When you don't consume much and remain aware, sensitivity skyrockets. He's already forgiven.

I accept, I say. All in the past.

I wasn't always this calm. A need to survive drove me to things I'm not proud of. I also drew blood once. Maybe twice. But I've learned life is an acceptance of what comes, time and again. When you trust life, life trusts you as long as you trust yourself to participate.

He says, You can have my bread next time.

I sense the sincerity. It is tempting in the moment, and maybe that's why I decline.

Not necessary, I say.

He says, I'm Jack.

His smile is a joyous song, few of those around a hungry place.

I'm Jill, I say.

An even scarcer commodity suddenly erupts from my flabbergasted lips: laughter.

I'm here for a pail of water but missed the hill, I manage to spew.

Between bursts of hysteria—an old woman in my head—I suck at the dry air. The others stare at us. Best reel it in; insanity is our downfall. But I feel alive, perhaps for the first time since Grandma's stories reminded me I was lucky.

Not all of us died as shadows of a proud race. Some were too poor to afford food and escaped the pricks in search of a meal, flying under the radar. Some got ill from the injections while their minds still worked and decided never again; for them, infertility was the price, or the prize; it depends on your perspective, I guess. And some flat-out resisted such temptations and fought the fear in their own hearts, defiantly surrendering to a higher power. They were ridiculed and ostracized, Grandma said, like a sickness. We lived. To die in the aftermath of greed's tragedy—all that fear stemmed from an idea that enough was out of reach, stolen by the neighbor.

And that nature was out to get us. To die here—thin shadows cast on the dead earth of a once-proud race.

A prophet, they say, Jack says.
I say, More likely a vagrant.
And the laughter teeters on a thin edge.
Jack smiles again and asks, Not a great believer in miracles, then?
Thoughts rumble to life; conversation is laughter's scarce twin in the desolation of us.
I survived humanity's downfall and still walk a poisoned earth, I say. Perhaps I am a damn miracle.

When the concoctions started to abuse us, our minds went to places reserved for holy thought. A hubris developed where everything we didn't understand had to die, and what we could not control, we blasted, broke, and bent into a shape to fit our limited vision. We thought of controlling our destiny and ended up here. For all our assumptions, predictions, and extrapolations, we chose to ignore the massive impact of the unknown. That part of existence we can only wonder at. And as the sun baked hotter, the nights turned colder, and the offset was milder days with higher rainfalls, even some in the deserts. Earth experienced an adaption phase, but we only saw the highs and lows. The rains departed after we sprayed the atmosphere with particles meant to remain particles. Rivers dried up when we thought it best to build dams where rivers should have flowed, cutting water supply from areas that became dead zones growing in number and size. Our beautiful sentiment to feed the needy for profit, a deeply flawed model of mono agriculture, destroyed the micro-organic environment quicker than the pills popped our brain cells. The "cides" finished off the murder of diversity. In water-rich areas, cesspools of muck and mire formed as stagnation occurred, and the fish died from the poisons. In drier places, desertification depleted any chance of arable land. Instead of accepting our flaws to understand them better, tinkering with those parts of ourselves we feared led to fiddling with a divine plan. Grandma said the land died in concert with our minds.

The desert is our home, and every day, we walk out of her. Yet, she's always there. For two months, I've counted nameless days, sixty-three of them. Ten of those were last days, dying days, for one or the other. Yet, here we are, still walking the line. Just like he said, there was always someone, something—and still is. *Maybe he was a prophet.* Last night, it was a stream with sweet water. We drank deep and filled our canisters. There were trees. Oddly shaped and smelling of oil—a rich aroma—we sat under them to rest. Then, we drank again before we continued. We walk at night. The days are for resting—hot, brooding affairs and mostly windy. We hang a tarp on poles for shade. Not much, but some shelter against a vengeful sun.

The prophet—a messenger—I insisted then, knowing it was the same thing; he walked into our sorry camp that afternoon. The day laughter returned. He climbed onto a rust-stained hood, sat cross-legged on its dried metal blood, and waited patiently. The crowd gathered fast. Still, he waited. Perhaps he sensed the stubbornness in the few of us undecided. His silence drew us closer in time. He spat promises of milk and honey like there were infinite tomorrows, and they all lapped it up like puppies. At first.

There is a place, He said. Trees stand there that bear fruit. Soil lies there that yields vegetables. Grass grows there that feeds flock. The waters that flow taste sweet.

His words fell on eager ears, candy to dying children, mouths agape with wonder and eyes ready to fall from our skulls.

He said, People who know live there. They talk to the earth, and they listen. She says nothing, but they hear. If you want to die, die here. They don't take promises; words mean nothing. If you can work, go.

Some heads dropped then, too tired to listen to talk of labor.

There's life, He said, and it asks for life in return. If you want to live, go.

Some got up to leave then, too scared to hope.

He said, Everyone finds a purpose. If you can help, go.

Fewer of us remained for him to paint pictures in our minds.

New ideas birth every day, He continued. If you want to learn, go.

He swayed a hand to the north.

And some were swept aside. Fewer still.

He then said, This earth isn't done with us. Take hope and go.

Instructions followed, and directions, which stars to consult. I closed my eyes and melted into his words. When I opened them, Jack was still there, nodding his head. The following day, we left.

Since we departed the shelter, we come to places much the same. They lie scattered on our path like breadcrumbs, sometimes great distances apart. And then a dying day dawns when our water runs out, and thirst eats the life from us. But miracles happen in the nick of time. Repeatedly, people surprise us on these days; they find us and take us in. They heal us back to walking fitness and send us on our way with food every time. At one such place, an old sister said something I grew into. You're doing it for all of us, she said. Now, as I walk next to my friend, I understand. They have carried us to do what they can't. Passed us along from one shelter to the next and handed us into care.

I've come to know about Jack. His story isn't one of crusades and travels and adventures. It's about survival and living one day at a time, much like my own. The knowing is a deeper thing. A thing he cannot tell but which I feel. Sadness at jumping from one shelter to another, always the outsider, ate at his heart. The unwilling/willingness to fight for a morsel and the shame attached to each bite he swallowed, its bitter taste of desperation. I've come to know this in him, for it is in me. But also asking forgiveness and forgiving itself—I feel that strongest. The good and the bad in us all, I suppose. Our brotherhood is deeper than friendship; it bonds us in heart and mind.

It's been four days since we tasted water. Ours ran out around a bend on a road, now part of our history. Today is a dying day. It stirs in places where places shouldn't exist. Jack stopped talking sometime yesterday. I see his chest rising and falling. Slower and slower. And more shallow each time. Perhaps it's my imagination. Maybe not. We're underneath a large tree, shade at least for part of the day. We've lost the tarp on that road in the past. I've made peace. Our journey was not for nothing. I know myself deeper for its purifying demand; my soul is lighter than my body is lean. And I love Jack. I love someone for the first time since Grandma. Although I'm sad not to complete our mission, the human spirit encourages me. All those people carrying us—there's hope for humanity still. The land has changed much. There's more life—trees and foliage thicker than anywhere I've ever seen. It's just; there's no water. Not near enough anyway, not anymore. Birds wake us in the mornings, which is special; I'm not used to so much life. We've seen some type of animal. A buck or deer or ante-something, Grandma called them. I don't know. Maybe the land heals faster than us.

The birds are singing again, and Jack's still breathing. Maybe today. Perhaps. I lose large parts of the day in blackness. Sometimes, I walk with Grandma again. And we talk of the times before we messed up the plan. When there were rivers and forests, and the sea was full of life. Then I wake to see if Jack's still breathing and remember her most powerful words. Perhaps this was the plan after all, she had said, and we fail to grasp its teaching.

You take that one, we'll carry this one. I hear the words from a vast distance, a strange dream. Water drips on my lips; maybe it's raining, and I'm asleep for such a happening? I feel the subtle bounce of footsteps, but I'm not walking. I'm floating. Then the blackness comes again, and I hope an old woman will come to take my hand.

Wake up. You have to drink something. Those words, coming from another world again. Or maybe another time—a time of life and laughter and joy. Her time. *You need fluids. Wake up.* And I do. My eyelids feel like rusted car doors, but I pry them open. A bleary vision takes its time to clear, and I see people. They've found us again. *Thank the cloudless heavens.* The angel brings water to my lips, and I drink deep. She rips it away.

Slowly there, cowboy, She says. Take it slow. You don't want to spill it all.

A thousand questions form in my mind. But one slays the others about days without names and so forth.

Where's my friend? I ask.

Her face falls—a slight thing, but I notice. And I know.

She says, He didn't last the night. We got him here, but he died this morning.

My small world of talks and laughter and friendship dies with him. But love lives on. Never had I known someone so fully, so much like myself, and so different. He showed me all he was and allowed me the same. An empty space in me, in one of those places, aches and longs for another. Someone to share my joy and pain. Someone like Jack. He's in my blood.

I'm sorry to tell you this, She says.

We've died together more times than I can remember. A hasty mouth blabber.

She hands me a glass of water, saying, Drink slow. There's no rush anymore. You're here.

Here? I ask.

Nuevo Comienzo. You've made it, She says while smiling. I'm Clara, by the way.

My mind plays tricks I don't understand. It conjures questions about what could have been. And it hurts my heart. I should be grateful. I've made it, but I hurt for my friend. She sees and takes my hand. There's silence between us while she holds on, and the pain dissipates.

She smiles again and asks, What's your name?

I'm Pete, I say. My friends call me Jill.

Blue Cassandra

Douglas Arvidson

I

A sail on the horizon. Nearer, nearer. Details form, emerging from the closing distance and the shimmering heat. It's a pretty boat, bright blue and graceful, its sails hauled in tight for sailing close to the wind toward the island. Soon they can see there is no one at the helm; in fact, there seems to be no one on board at all, but the boat is sailing well and true on a steady course. The Watchers all agree: by this evening, it will reach the island.

The Watchers are a small crowd of old people, old teachers mostly. They are gray, decrepit, starving, ill, wretched. They have been surviving here with the twelve remaining students since the last boat left. They have devoted themselves to keeping the children fed and safe, but hope for a rescue is fading. Every week another storm rages over what was once part of the mainland and is now a shrinking island. Every day, the water rises. They spend their days gathered on the flat roof of the school among the sagging, threadbare tents, hanging laundry, and the metallic clutter of the useless ventilation system. Hour after hour, they watch the horizon while muttering among themselves.

"A boat," one says. "Imagine that."

"People," whispers another. "Now imagine that."

"No," says a third, "I don't see anyone on board. But wouldn't you think there would be someone? Someone who knows how to sail and how to navigate?"

"Someone?" says Cassie, the music teacher. She is nearly deaf and usually lost in the scattered tumble of her daydreams. "It's probably being steered by a spirit of some sort. Or AI, maybe. And it's all embedded in the sky and takes its orders from both the sky and the earth, not to mention the stars." She laughs and fingers the large blue topaz crystal that hangs around her neck. She sings out, "I saw it. I saw the blue boat come right out of the sky, right out of that big, big, dirty, dirty cloud. Right out of the middle of it where the lightning bolts flash. And the cloud is growing, growing, growing all across the sky. Just like I said it would. Pretty soon it's going to swallow us up, sure enough. But never mind. No one listens to me."

Everyone assumes the warnings she yammers on about are nonsense because it is agreed she must suffer from dementia, the go-to diagnosis for any old person who wanders around saying strange things. But, in fact, since her high school days, she has been an odd duck, wearing long blue robes and heavy necklaces with oversized blue crystal pendants. Her unruly gray hair is wild, her fingers click and clatter with a dozen rings, and all day, she whispers and hums tuneless songs. She is considered a bit crazy, but everyone at some point has noticed that, in an uncanny way, she is always right.

And she is a good teacher, even a great teacher. To students and parents, she is wonderful: kind, funny, generous, patient, and smart. Often enough, her nonsense makes real sense, and too often, her wild predictions come true, like the one about the expanding, lightning-filled cloud of soot and smog. Just like she said it would, it now blots out the distant city, covers the entire edge of the eastern horizon, and seems to be swelling, expanding, coming closer.

And she was certainly right about the last three storms that had, in quick succession, flooded the first floor of the school, destroyed the electrical equipment used to communicate with the rest of the world, and blasted away most of the playground, leaving only the monkey bars and the basketball hoop. After the storms, the lightning-filled gray-black pall had stretched itself out, moving closer, again exactly as Cassie had predicted. Then, this morning, a handsome blue sailboat had come right out of the middle of it. Everyone agrees with that. It came right out of the middle of the pall of smog and lightning, and Cassie was vindicated. She threw her arms wide and laughed and then turned away, rubbing her crystal pendant and whispering to herself.

Among the Watchers is a woman who is the science and math teacher and a man who is the shop teacher. They are both well past sixty but they make no secret of their December-December love for each other. They do seem to be the perfect couple. The running joke is that their relationship works because even though she is high maintenance, he can fix anything.

At first, their holding hands caused smirking and giggling, but in the end, their relationship was accepted. Everyone realized the obvious: their combined skills were critical to everyone's survival. Even after the storms and the difficulty catching enough fish or growing enough potatoes and carrots, even after everyone was slowly starving and everything had become hopeless, even after the measuring stick they attached to the wall of the shop classroom told them the water was still rising, even after the last boat had sailed away from the island dangerously overloaded with crying children and a few desperate, frightened adults, even after the quick, deadly incident over who would be the last person allowed on board, even after all that, the math and shop teacher had clung to their love and begun designing, building, and fixing things around the school.

Just last week, using magnifying glasses and mirrors from the science lab and rusting tools they had rescued from the sludge of the flooded shop classroom, they had built a contraption they called the sunlight machine. It intensified and aimed beams of sunlight and then, through a system of tubes and tanks and filters and a gurgling pump powered by the sunlight machine itself, it began changing the brackish, muddy rising flood into water that was clear and sweet.

"It's almost pure. Almost," the shop teacher said. "But good enough to drink."

"And a whole lot purer than that acid rain that hisses when it hits the leaves in the vegetable garden," the science teacher added. Then they kissed, and everyone applauded.

But this morning, with the sunrise darker than its usual bloody red and the smell and taste of grit and smog strong in the air, there is real excitement carried on the whispered news of the approaching boat. This excitement rushes up to the roof on the sweet, pure notes of the remaining children who sing every morning in the music room. All the teachers who had managed to sleep in their oppressive, stifling classrooms were now coming up the stairs, and the children came up too, still singing, their voices a lovely, angelic murmur. "A sailboat?" a teacher said. "Who could it be? Perhaps one of the lost ones, finding their way back home to rescue us. They promised they would."

"No, you fool," the cranky, know-it-all reading teacher said with her gravelly voice. "Have you ever seen a boat like this around here? No, never. Look at the shape of the hull, the cut of the sails, look at the rise of the bow. It's an oceangoing boat, for certain."

And they all wondered who in their right mind would come back here anyway after all the sadness and tragedy caused by the struggle to merely survive the storms that were steadily washing more and more of the island away. And in addition to the ever-rising water and the diminishing food supply there was the unbearable heat, the thick humidity, and the gritty, strange-smelling wind. The discomfort, fear, and the constant feeling of doom had put them all in dangerous moods until one day, a teacher's aide, in a flash of anger, shoved the principal too hard, sending her staggering backward. Before she could recover her balance, she had disappeared over the edge of the roof.

It was finished in an instant. The principal, ancient and frail, had fallen two floors right onto the remains of the playground, just missing the monkey bars and the basketball hoop, landing heavily on the tarmac. Without a sound, she died.

Then there was a great howling and crying, and finally, when the shock had subsided, the principal, who was not well-liked in any event, was buried in the schoolyard beneath the flagpole. Cassie, dressed in her flowing blue robes, led the children in singing over the grave. Under the art teacher's half-hearted supervision, a couple of sixth graders built a simple shrine on the spot where she died. It ended up being an unlovely mosaic of broken seashells stuck in gray concrete and topped by a crude angel they painted with the only color they could find: a mud-brown yellow.

After that, a few of the Watchers would pause and dip their heads in respect whenever they passed by the shrine while the person who had done the shoving—a large, gentle woman with a soft voice and a sad, sweet personality—wailed through her endless tears that she did not do it on purpose. It was an accident, she insisted, a misunderstanding. "I just lost it, you know? Who can blame me? Who can blame any of us?" It was agreed, though, that she should leave the island on the next boat if another one ever came. Everyone was now afraid of her.

By then, though, there was no one left who knew how to sail and no life jackets either, so the others were afraid to even set foot in a boat. In fact, none of the cheap, small boats from the sailing club, once filled and sailed away by screaming students and terrified, scolding adults, were ever seen or heard from again.

As for the rising water, it was agreed that certainly, the ocean could not rise forever. It stood to reason. There were only so many Greenland glaciers left to melt, so many Antarctic ice shelves left to slip into the sea. Then the social studies teacher held up a hand and said, "But I remember reading that the melting Greenland glaciers alone will raise the world's oceans twenty feet. And that obviously will be the end of this island and a lot of other islands, too. For goodness sake, when I was a girl, this island was a high and dry peninsula connected to the mainland."

After the killing of the principal, now referred to as "the Incident," even the twelve remaining children had become not just singers but Watchers, too. They had joined the adults in the daily routine of distilling water, growing what little food they could manage, catching crabs, gathering clams and oysters, and hauling in what their nets collected. The social studies teacher, who one summer had traveled around the world, taught everyone what she had learned in Indonesia about making and repairing fishing nets. Now, every day, everyone sat in the breathless heat and foul breeze, working on the nets and watching the water and the sky.

Mostly, they watched the horizon where the water and sky met and formed the growing black cloud and three days ago, a mustard-colored fog appeared that a kitchen worker said must be from the nuclear power plant ten miles down the coast. "There must have been a meltdown," she said. "Haven't I been saying it was bound to happen? And, you know, when the wind changes, all that radioactive stuff will drift right over us and then...." She was stopped by a fourth-grade teacher who snapped at her, "You don't know what you're talking about. Hold your tongue."

After the Incident, everyone was jumpy, on edge, and now they secretly watched each other, too. They watched each other's eyes, sensed the tension in their movements, and listened to the tone of each other's voices. They still watched the water and the mustard-colored sky and especially the expanding black cloud that flashed lightning across the horizon. They kept a close eye on the yardstick that measured the rising water, but they all knew where the real, immediate danger lay: inside each other.

It was too hot for most of them to sleep in the classrooms, but the long nights sleeping on the roof were a torment of crying children, terrified adults yelling out their nightmares, and intense, rainless lightning storms that ripped and thundered across the sky. Days were filled with anxiety, regrets, accusations, and mourning. There were endless, bitter, futile arguments about who was to blame and what should have been done before it was too late. There were no good answers.

Then the sixth-grade teacher, who months ago had run out of her heart pills, collapsed. She had been crying, sobbing about missing her family, her grandchildren, and everyone knew that, like all of them, she was trying to cover up her fear, her heartbreak, her rage. In her last moments, she had looked around at everyone, her face red, the veins in her neck bulging, her lips sputtering, and then her eyes rolled upward and down she went with a gasp and a thud. There was nothing to be done. The diagnoses offered were useless, and the school nurse finally declared that it was no doubt a stroke. She died the next morning and, with much-combined effort, was hauled down the stairs and buried under the flagpole next to the principal. Cassie played a confused tune on the discordant piano.

II

Late the next afternoon, the pretty blue boat was so close that they could read the numbers on her hull but could still only guess at the faint letters in her name. Finally, when at low tide, the boat closed with the shore, came around into the breeze, and dropped her anchor, the science teacher whispered, "Look. You can read it now. The boat's name is *Blue Cassandra*."

Everyone was quiet. *Blue Cassandra*. Yes. The boat's name was *Blue Cassandra*.

"But look," a kindergarten teacher said. "It looks like there's no one on board. The boat is sailing itself."

But then Cassie managed to get on board by paddling out in a half-deflated rubber dingy and struggling up the stern boarding ladder. No sooner had she stepped on deck than the sound of music and children singing began coming from inside *Blue Cassandra*. It was music and singing as beautiful as the music and songs sung by the children in the music room every morning. Everyone was listening and watching Cassie, who was now sitting in the cockpit looking pleased and befuddled, her eyes half open, her lips moving.

"What kind of music is that? Who is that singing?" someone demanded of her. She gazed over at them with her dreamy, half-closed eyes and said, "It comes from the many corners of the earth where there are floating visions, peace, serenity, grateful meditations, and hope. It came from there. I can assure you of that. But for you, it's too late. Too late, too late."

"What do you mean?" someone asked.

"What does too late mean?" Cassie asked.

"Yes. What's too late?"

"Ah," Cassie said, "Ah, ah, ah. So we haven't been paying attention. But listen. Just listen. *Blue Cassandra* speaks."

She was right. The music and singing coming from inside the boat were joined by a voice—a man's or a woman's, they couldn't decide—but it was low, rich, compelling. The voice said, "Children, children, children. Come, please. Come quickly. Swim out and climb on board the boat. We need to set sail. There are places to go, places far and wide, and there are so many more children we need to pick up. And no, no—no adults. Please. Very sorry about that. Too late for adults. Too late."

There were only the twelve children left on the island, young middle schoolers, and without questioning, they obeyed the voice and began walking toward the boat. They were silent as they stepped off the shore into the shallow water and began swimming.

"And where do you suppose you're going?" the nurse said to them. "You don't think you're getting in that boat, do you?"

The children ignored her. Their eyes straight ahead, they kept moving toward the boat. While they were climbing on board, the voice from *Blue Cassandra* said, "No need to worry about the children. No need to worry about them at all. You should certainly be much more worried about yourselves."

Brownian Motion

Cedric Rose

I flick open my father's jackknife and whittle a couple of sticks into spears. We stalk the island, stabbing trash to fill the Hefty bag I carry in my kayak. All kinds of detritus wash up on this strand of mud and pebble drifted around the roots of a flood-stunted sycamore: tires, plastic bags, the door to an ancient Frigidaire. On one side of the island, the river pools deep under a shelf of blue shale. It's a popular swimming hole, a place Dad and I often visited before spring floods washed out a tree submerged there that harbored plenty of fish. On the other side of the island, the river runs wide. Its riffles send a dancing light over our tan skins.

Cassie and I are posted here most afternoons because it's just upstream from Red's River Outfitters, where we've worked summers since sophomore year. Disoriented from drinking alcohol in the murderous heat, the paddlers often miss the sign that instructs RED'S CUSTOMERS: PULL OUT HERE. If they float past the boat ramp, you have to chase them down and drag them in against the current.

This is the summer after high school, our last summer working for Red. Sun-baked, elastic days stretch toward the hazy foothills of adulthood. Cassie will leave soon to study marine biology at a school in Boca Raton. I'd love to move, too, to live by the ocean. But with less-than-spectacular grades and a habit of oversleeping, I haven't even applied. Ohio feels like a great mouth, swallowing me whole.

Three college-age boys beach their canoe on the island to finish their beer. They leap, yodeling from the ledge into the swimming hole. The drunkest, most sunburned of the bunch dumps his cooler of ice melt, empty beer cans, and snack wrappers at the water's edge. I'm over to him in seconds.

"I need you to pick that up," I say, working hard to control my tone.

"Or what? You gonna stab me with that thing?"

I drive my spear into the mud and touch the radio on my vest. "Or I notify the sheriff's department and they're waiting for you when you come off the river."

The sunburned kid moves toward me. His tattooed torso reeks of beer and weed.

"Go on and narc. My dad golfs with the county sheriff."

He prods me in my chest. I step back. He steps forward. Not wanting to run, not wanting to get beat up, I take a half step back. His next footfall twists in the rocks, and down he goes, much to his friends' amusement. As he struggles to regain his footing, a baggie of marijuana flutters from his pocket. I pick it up.

"That's personal property," he says.

"This is evidence." I pocket the pot and scoot my kayak onto the water. Cassie follows. We paddle upstream, above the island, safely out of their reach. The sunburned kid roars threats, lobs a beer can at me. I retrieve it for the Hefty bag. "Pick it up, tree-hugger!" he yells. "And you can clean this up, too." He begins to stomp his cooler. Styrofoam flecks swirl and cling to the water. I radio Red.

"You're going to want to keep an eye on this group coming in. They're wasted."

Red's voice crackles back, "Roger that." But I know he won't do anything. It's called "cabrewing" in southern Ohio. Drinking on the river is illegal, but we don't check coolers when the paddlers board the bus that tows their rented boats upriver. That would involve "liability," Red says, putting air quotes around the word. He knows this stretch of muddy water holds little interest to most people, sober. We look the other way and put up with a certain amount of crap. After the sunburned kid cools off, they return to their canoe, capsizing on their way to the boat ramp. I futilely try to contain the Styrofoam particles. Red radios back. "My office, Troy. Now."

Back at the livery, Cassie clocks out. Red already has a beer open on his desk.

"While I appreciate your conservationist spirit," he says, his bloodhound eyes glazed, "hassling the customers is a definite no-no."

"He shoved me."

"He says you took something of his."

"Yeah? What?"

"I think you know what. I had to refund their money. Do you have any idea who that kid's dad is?"

"This is about more than money."

He sighs. "Today of all days." He slides a notice across the desk. Under the official seal of Ohio EPA, the phrase closed to contract recreation stands out in boldface. "They're closing the river. This time it's fecal coliform and toxic algae. I need you to chain up the boats and lock the shutters tonight. When they give us the all clear, I'll call you. If there's any season left by then."

The news makes me dizzy with worry. Mom's talking about selling the A-frame Dad built on our half-acre of bottomland. She wants an apartment "where we can live like normal people," she says. I get it. Our place on the river is a walk-in memory of Dad. Before he got sick, during summers, which, as a teacher, he had off, we spent entire days on the water. Mom complained he was more like a kid than a grownup when we came home daubed with mud. The river is where I feel him most, the way some people smell their lost one's clothes.

My job keeps Mom from putting our place on the market. But when the EPA closed us down two summers back, I was out of work for a full month.

I hose down life vests, stack boats, bolt shutters, and make sure everything's shut tight. Before I leave, I take one of my sample jars down to the river and fill it with water. I scribble the time, date, and familiar coordinates on its lid. The water sloshes in my satchel as I bike home.

Our place sits in an oxbow where the river curves back on itself. We haven't been flooded out yet, but in recent springs, our driveway has been more and more underwater. Mom isn't home. She works third shift at a retirement home. I take microwaved spaghetti out to the Winnebago, gathering moss beside our A-frame. With its windows slid open, it fills with the river's chatter. I roll a joint from the sunburned kid's weed and pipette a drop of the river water sample onto a microscope slide.

At low magnification, the fluid seethes with zooplankton: shrimp-like copepods, insect larvae, spindly hydra with probing tentacles. I click to higher magnification and refocus until protozoa stand crisp. At highest magnification, I see swarms of rods and spheres. The bacteria count is definitely off the charts.

Cassie bangs on the Winnebago and walks right in.

"I just heard we're closed down," she says. "At least we don't have to wake up early tomorrow."

"Yeah," I say. "But I need the money."

She lights the joint and hits it.

"That kid," she hisses, exhaling, "was in possession of some seriously weapons-grade endo." She nods to the microscope. "Where's this sample from?"

"Red's."

Cassie slides beside me, bringing her aura of coconut oil and patchouli. She peers into the microscope.

"This weed's got me all shaky," she says. "Everything's like, dancing."

I take another look. Sure enough, the bacteria quiver erratically.

"I don't think that's weed," I say. "At high magnification, you can actually see particles being bumped around by water molecules."

She snaps her fingers. "I remember this from class: Brownian motion."

It's getting thick in the Winnebago. We take the joint down to the river.

"When my dad heard Red's closed," she says, "he suggested I leave early for college."

"When?"

"Next week. You'd think he wants to get rid of me." She shrugs. "But I figure I might as well get settled."

The news catches me mid-toke. I start coughing uncontrollably.

"That's like, soon," I wheeze.

All summer, I've known she's leaving. But, like so many things, I've avoided the thought. The coughing gets worse.

"Don't bust a lung." She hands me her water bottle, flavored with her lip balm. She skips a pebble, sending intersecting rings across the inky water. Insects thrum and chatter in the canopy. Mosquitoes steal droplets of our blood into the gathering dusk.

I say, "Let's run the river before you leave. Like we always said. Let's paddle across the sod farm and down to the Ohio River."

"What about the toxic bacteria and stuff?"

"That's why we need to go. I need more samples to get a clearer picture of what's happening to the river."

"I'm in."

South of our suburb lies a vast green grid. These are the production fields of Tri-State Tilth, proclaimed "Our Region's Finest Sod" by billboards up and down the interstate. The river wends across their property. Dad always said the sod farm was a big source of fertilizer and pesticide runoff. The fertilizer feeds algae which poison the water and suck up oxygen. Climate change is making the runoff worse. A massive dead zone is growing in the Gulf, beyond the mouth of the Mississippi, I've read, fed by fertilizer from America's Heartland.

We strap our kayaks to the roof of Cassie's VW. She takes dirt roads through corn and soy to a line of unruly trees that conceals the river's course. Dragging our kayaks and gear, we bushwhack down to a bank of sand freshly churned by egg-laying turtles.

I wade into the water to fill the first of many sample jars. I toss it to Cassie, who labels it and stows it in a hard case. We slip onto the current and drift through the mottled shade of overhanging vegetation. The river darts with schools of fry, its bottom a red shag of slime. A blue heron unfurls, beats low, its wingtips dabbing. We pass the ramp where Red's decommissioned school bus drops paddlers and their rented boats. It's an easy five mile paddle to the livery, and Red's section of river is blissfully quiet today. Cassie waves a last goodbye to the shuttered livery as we pass. We enter scrubby woods, the river edged with broken concrete. A great openness glows through the trees. We pass a wire fence with signs forbidding trespassing and emerge onto the great, green flatness of the sod farm.

Here the river slices into a layer cake of soil and clay. Without roots to hold it back, the earth crumbles into the flow. I take a water sample, note a faint chemical tang. The current is sluggish under a relentless sun. When we rest in the slim wedge of shade offered by the high bank, we get a look across the fields to where the highway runs on a distant ridge.

Irrigation sprinklers throw high, hissing arcs of spray. From up ahead comes the hammer of a two-stroke engine, a mower, I assume, until we reach the source of the sound.

It's a pump mounted in the bed of a white pickup truck backed down a cut in the bank to a gravel landing. Its engine spews exhaust. One hose feeds it from the river. Another runs out into the fields. A bearded man in coveralls smokes against the truck's cab. I pull over and scramble onto the landing.

"What are you doing?" Cassie says, staying in her boat and steadying mine.

"Department of Natural Resources!" I shout over the pump. "What's your permit number?" I'm wearing this thrift-store Boy Scout shirt that looks vaguely, if unconvincingly, official.

"If you're DNR, I'm Santa Claus!" the man shouts back. "And this is private property."

"Navigable waters are public."

"Navigable? This isn't much more than a drainage ditch. Now move on before I report you."

This bubble of rage bursts in me, floods out all thought. I open Dad's knife, and slit his intake hose lengthways like a fish. The pump sucks air and begins to overheat. He jumps to kill it. The abrupt silence leaves a ringing in our ears.

"What the hell, kid? What's your problem?"

"It's illegal to pump from the river without going through the permitting process," I say. "And what else are you spraying up here?"

"I'd say you've about killed the mood for civil conversation," he says. He holds up his phone, trying to get a signal. "Damn this thing."

As my rage lifts, the realization dawns that I will probably now get arrested. Which is not an option for me. We're paycheck to paycheck, Mom and me, and this could break us.

The man yells after us, "You better move quick because I'm reporting this."

"Shitshitshitshitshitshitshit," I murmur with frenzied paddle strokes as we haul hard for the far side of the farm.

"What was that?" Cassie says, grinning. But I don't feel the humor.

"I'm sorry," I say.

"Don't apologize," she says. "That was great."

"That was stupid. Idiotic. What use is starting trouble?"

"Maybe it brings attention to whatever's going on here?" she says.

We reach the far side of the sod field, where the river glides over a low-head dam. We pull off, quickly lower our boats to the pool below, eager to keep moving.

"Aren't you forgetting something?" She hands me a sample jar.

Almost fumbling it, I draw a sample from the spillway. Filthy, beige foam turns on the undertow. The river falls through a rumbling tunnel under the highway. We shoot the narrow channel into a corridor of graffiti-scrawled concrete. Cracked factory walls tower over the water. The loading dock of a roofless warehouse frames open sky. Beyond the buildings, beyond a weed-choked parking lot, there's a main road, traffic. Convenience stores and gas stations cluster around a highway exchange.

"Let's stash our boats and walk out of here," I say. "We'll come back when it's safe."

"You're kidding, right? I'm not leaving my boat."

"I can't stay on the river. You heard him. I'm eighteen now. If I get arrested, it's on my permanent record."

"The planet's on the verge of ecological collapse, and you're worried about a rap sheet? You slashed some farmer's hose. So what? In the grand scheme of things, we're doomed."

"Exactly. So what was I thinking?"

Her face breaks into a grin. "You tell me. You're the one who knifed his equipment. Maybe on some level you did it for survival? Maybe it's better than doing nothing?"

I open my mouth. I close my mouth.

"So take your samples and let's go. You're finishing this. We're finishing this."

And so we float south, onto the last leg of our river before it joins the Ohio. Suburban lawns slope to the water's edge. A man pushes a wheeled hopper, casting blue granules across his close-cropped grass.

At every bridge and water access point we pass, I cringe, worried we'll encounter the cops. I want to be done with this as quickly as possible. But Cassie has other plans.

"Still got that weed?"

"That's not a good idea."

"Since when were you such a prude? We might as well enjoy it. I'm quitting when I get to school."

"Sure you are."

We pull off the water. Cassie rolls a joint. The heavy August sky presses the river into its bed. A small plane climbs above us. I imagine how we look from up there, almost microscopic. How vast the world is, how infinitely twisted. A fish leaps and falls. A car stereo dopplers across the last bridge before the Ohio River. As we smoke, my fear uncoils.

The river is thick, an amber warmth that wraps my calves. Tongues of silt sift through my sandals. I fill one last jar. Our water samples weigh down the case. For the last time, Cassie and I push off. Soon we will reach a seedy marina that looks out from the mouth of our river onto the mile-wide Ohio. We plan to drain our kayaks there, to call Cassie's dad for a ride. And that's where a patrol car will roll to a stop and find us. An officer will get out and put his hat on. He will ask questions about the incident at the sod farm, what we're doing with these jars. When he finds what's left of the weed, he'll ask if that's part of the science experiment too.

But the lure of the Ohio River is too great to end this now. We kayak past the marina, out onto the big river's titanic ebb. Its surface glitters to the frayed green hem of Kentucky. This too is an ocean, I realize, a beginning and an end. Only when the sun begins to fall through a phosphorescent frieze of cloud, and the day's heat begins to break, does Cassie turn to shore. I follow her keel's true course, unswerving on the ever-moving water.

Collateral Damage

Jim Coleman

The name's Barnie Quinn, and everybody just calls me Quinn, which is fine by me because I've never had a good explanation when somebody asks about the unusual spelling of my first name. My older brother always used to tell me I was named after an old barn cat our parents used to have. They denied it, and I'd like to think they weren't that quirky or oddball, but they *are* children of the '60s, so who knows. It's been twenty-some years now since I moved to Florida, just in time to see four hurricanes crisscross the state in the space of six weeks, flattening much of the small neighborhood near Port Charlotte where I was living. I always have to stop and do the math to figure out the "some" part of that number, but it doesn't really matter. There were some close calls after that, then the scenario almost repeated itself years later when two hurricanes hit the same area, again within six weeks of each other. In the aftermaths of all of them, insurance companies scurried away like cockroaches hiding from a bright light, and government assistance was an illusion, with scammers somehow being able to easily make off with millions, while honest, law-abiding residents were forced to wade through endless mazes of red tape for any scrap of assistance. Collateral damage. After holding on for a couple more years, my bank account and I were both about drained from a severe case of rebuilding fatigue, and I had to move in with my parents back up north in Pennsylvania. And let me tell you, if you think it's a difficult adjustment for families when kids move back in after graduating from college, try it when you've been on your own for more than twenty years with parents who have been empty nesters for just as long. I mean, talk about collateral damage. But that's a story for another time.

So here we are, and I think it should be clear by now, except maybe to those living under the largest of rocks, that climate change just might be real. Smothering summer heat, floods, wildfires, tornados in bunches, hurricanes now bordering on the theoretical category 6, winter blizzards that bury entire cities and freeze them in their tracks; it can't all be media sensationalism. What isn't quite clear is who or what is to blame and who or what can do anything about it. Oh, there are a lot of theories, but despite more than half a century of cleaning up industrial emissions, vehicle emissions, livestock emissions (yep, cow farts), and any other emissions that could be imagined, and spending billions on "green" projects, things still seem to be getting worse. And as things have gotten worse, people have become more stressed, unpredictable, and extreme in behavior. Depending on how unpredictable and extreme, that might be where I come in. As Sgt. Friday used to say on the old TV show *Dragnet*, I carry a badge. Well, not really. At least not that kind of a badge. I work as an independent animal control contractor in Westmoreland County, a sprawling mix of farms and small- to mid-size towns and cities in the western part of the state. When the humane society and county shelters are full, which seems to be often these days, I sometimes get called.

On this day, I was on a call that was all too common for animal control and animal rescue organizations: abandoned animals. A farmer had found some on his property. The frequency of these seems to pick up with every downturn of the economy and every disastrous weather event, which sometimes go hand in hand. As people struggle to cope and recover, pets are often among the first expenses to be eliminated. More collateral damage. Some people swallow their pride and ask for help or surrender them to an animal rescue or humane society. Others just walk away. This was apparently one of the latter.

The location for this call was familiar—a small horse boarding and training stable run by a couple of old friends, Bo and Maggie, outside of a town called Ligonier. A few miles farther east and it would have been Somerset County's problem, but such is my luck. Stray animals and drop-offs aren't uncommon around there. It's a very rural area, easy enough for people to dump animals off unseen and rationalize it by imagining they'll find a home on some farm. And sometimes they did. If it was a cat, maybe it would take up vermin control duty in somebody's barn. If it was a dog, more likely someone would foster it until a home could be found or they'd turn it over to a rescue group.

Driving out, I passed through farm country in Unity Township, or at least what used to be farm country. In my youth, by this time of year, the fields would be thick and green with corn crops, each stalk heavy with fat ears of corn. Now, those that were planted were stunted and pale, scorched by more record-breaking summer heat. Others were untended, left to be claimed by weeds and dust ... or worse, irresponsible developers who believe that anything green and leafy should be paved. Climate change? The economy? An aging population and a younger generation uninterested in taking up the fight? Probably a combination of all that, I guess.

Farther along, I drove through the Loyalhanna Gorge, a steep valley carved out of the Chestnut Ridge by the Loyalhanna Creek. Historically prone to high water during severe storms and Spring snowmelt, major flooding was now almost a year-round threat, as evidenced by the once-pristine vacation cottages now abandoned along the water's edge, porches crumbling into the eroded banks. The steep hillsides on either side of the road were riddled with runoff gullies, and remains of past mudslides and rockslides encroached on the shoulders of the highway.

Arriving at the farm, I walked into the barn and saw Bo tending to one of the horses. After the usual small talk, I asked where the stray critters were.

"You're lookin' at 'em," Bo said.

Them? I still didn't see anything. Only the horse Bo was working with, and a couple others ... Hey, wait a minute ...

"The horses??!"

"Yep. We went to bed last night with three in the pasture, and this morning there were two more. One had a note on its halter, said thank you for taking care of them; we no longer can."

"Well, this is a new one for me," I said.

"I figure it was only a matter of time," said Bo. "Pastures are scorched. Hay and grain fields are drying up, or underwater... maybe in flames. If people don't grow some of their own and can't afford the stuff that gets shipped in from Canada or wherever, or if they lose their home or income, well..." he said, motioning toward the horses. "I've heard of this happening in other areas, but this is the first I've seen it here."

"Well, what am I supposed to do with them?" I asked. "I don't have an animal carrier big enough for a horse."

"Oh, don't get your shorts in a bunch. I didn't really expect you to do anything with them. I know some people who know other people, and I'll try and figure something out. I just wanted to report it in case something about them comes across your radar, like if somebody reports them stolen."

"Who steals horses and leaves them in somebody else's pasture?"

"I wouldn't put anything past anybody these days."

We left it that I would file a report and Bo would check with his people who knew people and hope that everything would work out for the best.

Standing there in the doorway of the barn, facing west into the brilliant afternoon sun, it felt like we were standing in front of a fireplace, the heat almost stinging my face. "Another hot one," I thought out loud.

"Ya think so?" Bo was not impressed with my keen powers of observation.

We ran into each other about a month later in the local Walmart. Bo said the owners of the horses had been located. They were actually a nice elderly couple who had fallen on hard times and couldn't care for the horses anymore. They believed they were turning them over to an animal sanctuary and had even been convinced by what they thought was a nice young man to scrape together several hundred dollars out of their savings to pay an "intake and relocation fee" for the horses. Instead, the nice young man drove to the next county and dumped them in the first secluded pasture he saw. Yet another scam cooked up to take advantage of vulnerable people in difficult circumstances. Still more collateral damage. The couple gladly signed ownership of the horses over to Bo and Maggie, who had managed to connect with a couple of local families with horse-crazy kids who had agreed to pay board (and exchange some light child labor) for the horses so their kids could ride. It was a win-win, especially for the animals.

As I left, the change from an air-conditioned store to the outdoors was nearly staggering. Ten o'clock in the morning and it was already in the low 90s. The cooler nighttime air had been displaced by a thick mass of heat and humidity that just a few short years ago wouldn't have arrived until midafternoon, if at all. It was like breathing the air coming out of a clothes dryer. The weather people were again forecasting dangerous storms and possible tornados for later in the day. As I blinked and squinted up into the haze, I couldn't help but think that if we can't change the way things are going, there might not be many more win-wins down the road.

Deluge

Tabitha Bast

There is such wetness at the beginning of the end times, you thought it would be drier, scorched earth, raging wildfires, brimstone, hell opening, a tormenting furnace. But here, in this England still standing, these days could almost be mistaken for the ones before. Still, some latecomers to reality tut about the weather. In the dementia care homes of the wealthy, they say how, oh, it's raining again. In the back-to-backs of the Northern cities, they move the kettle and the teabags to the bedrooms now that the downstairs is sodden. In the penthouses of London, the hoarders reinforce their doors. In the forgotten seaside towns, they sink into heroin and sewage waters.

We don't like what you say about the water. We don't like what you say about us.

You did not like the climate deniers (*nor do we*), though they are mostly in the US of A, which is more of an apocalypse mash-up with the aforementioned fires but also the floods. And the religious vigor. You were pleased to see them die out, old age mostly because that last generation of accumulators is who they were, but some are gone to more modern diseases, and some suitably taken out in that almighty snowstorm that purified all of New Hampshire.

But your arid vitriol is now for us. You call us Climate Collapsers in your latest online spurtings, moved on from

Climate Preppers, but yes, I suppose, in a way, we are both. What are you, though? Disgraced academic, though you deny the charges, but don't they always? There's no smoke without fire. You were once the darling of youth movements across the globe, but tides turn. And if you listened to us, for once, just really listened, you'd know you can't stop a tide.

We prepped. This much is true. That's how to write a bestselling book or two with a generous swing of gracious honesty. I remember when you interviewed me all those years back, when books sold more than they burnt, you took my words but bent them for your meaning. You talked about me on shows with hosts paid even more than you. I was the owner of a chubby house in Suburbia with tins rammed into cupboards like the poor were crammed into what's left of council flats, with my Monica Sjoo prints on my bedroom walls. You mentioned that in Chapter 6. It took me a while to realize you were mocking me for my preparation. Sure, it's a-coming, but this is TOO much was your gist. I had pre-spent my pension on sandbags and emergency flares and hey, who's laughing now?

Same side, you said. You even did some time after blocking a minor road with a few thousand other people. Though half the nation had come out that day, it wasn't just London at a standstill, the demonstrations stretched up to Milton Keynes. Nobody and nothing worked. It was a tide to stop a tide. And stop, you shouted, stop climate change. You were lifted up like a surfboard on a wave by two old-fashioned-looking coppers, one black, one white. Your skirt rode up your thick winter tights; it was unseemly. You should have prepped better. You should have *researched* better. We are not on the same side.

You don't work much these days, the television is not about you. My people have swelled beyond a critical mass. We are a tsunami. The television is about us. They say we are one faction in the nuthouse, that humans cannot adapt to living underwater, whatever the sciences we show them say. They talk about us the way they talk of the mad commies and the right clinging on to President Trump and the crazy African evangelists and the mad Islamic jihadis and all those with irrelevant beliefs.

First they came for the vaccine-hesitant, then they came for us.

I blame you. They arrested my husband on a grimy, overcast morning, 5 a.m., an hour before we should wake. He had his hand rested lightly on my belly that had never birthed a child, but he loved me nonetheless. I woke seconds before they came; perhaps the speed of the quietened approaching cars, or perhaps I just knew. Still, I was shocked when they rammed the door without knocking. Call me old-fashioned, but it was very impolite. And then our room was full of angry men and one woman as if that would make me feel fine, and they seized him, I screamed, and everything changed.

"Everything changed?" said the red-faced, ginger solicitor cross-examining me. He was tall, but they are, aren't they, the boarding school lot? His tie was tight at his throat like a throttle, a hanged man. "Surely everything changed for the SIXTY children drowned? Some barely even born, some just setting out to secondary school and lives ahead of them?"

He was trying to shock the jury with sentiment, of course, and shocked they were. And I explained, even more shockingly had they listened with reason, that there was no life ahead of any of these children unless they adapted to the waters, unless we returned to the source. It is nothing barmy, just evolution in reverse. He called them drowned, we called them salved. They were paving the way for those who would make it.

"It will take a few dead fish to make a new humankind," my husband, the scientist, would tease before they took him. He was an eternal optimist, cheerful with every gruesome phone call from a grieving parent, stoic when there was yet to be a breakthrough. It had to happen.

It already did.

The Sama-Bajau of the Philippines are a marine-based people who have been debased to begging for coins off tourist boats. I saw them with these now bespectacled eyes. The Bajau dive for up to thirteen minutes, to depths of around 200 feet, having increased spleen size. They spend more than half their working week underwater.

Don't trust me, trust Wikipedia.

They looked at me aghast, like I was the one who was mad. Yet me and my husband were the only sane ones in the courtroom. Tall ceilings, cheap floors, a smell of bleach that didn't disguise the continual traipse in and out of the urban deprived. The jury, just a cheap, broken row of miscellaneous items like the worst charity shop in the village.

That changed, didn't it? Only sixty children of followers then, but we grew. As we said, you can't stop the tide. Whatever you did. Your sandbags of articles swallowed up under this wave. Even though he was in prison, all the others thereafter were pinned on him. Hundreds to thousands, some say a million.

After I got six years, and my husband got life though our hands had held nobody under the water, you wrote, as a lively comparison:

"This hysteria is not novel. In July 1518, Frau Troffea began to dance fervently in a Strasbourg street. For a week. Soon, a few dozen others joined in. By August, the "Dancing Plague" had claimed 400 victims, collapsed, died. It was not until September that this outbreak began to subside."

Don't trust you, trust Wikipedia.

When I got out, everyone left in my life asked me how prison was. I'd tell them it smelt of beige food, weed, and menstrual blood. That summed it up and usually shut them up.

If you ask more, you're probably a class above any chance of getting a custodial.

Tides turn. You thought you knew everything about me but, actually, it's me that knows everything about you. I'm out of prison, and I see you. Alarm at 6:55 a.m., bedside light on at 7, curtains open at 8 unless you're away. Visiting your son, or, sometimes, that loyal-despite-it-all friend. Your mum is in one of those wealthy care homes I mentioned. Your son is at university in Norway, hopeful for residency in the top surviving three. You sleep at 10:30 most nights and wake between 1 and 3 a.m. to piss, using minimum light. You have a casual boyfriend you see once a week, but the day varies. He works shifts. He's younger, you disgraced academic, you. You get a delivery once a month from one of the main supermarkets, but you mostly survive off wine and potatoes from the local co-op, even if you have to go in waders depending on the waterlog. You go to that "dry pub in the sky," the joke on dry, on the corner and open 24 hours since they gave up on public health, and it's not half as good as you wrote about in a few advertising pieces, almost like they paid you. I know you visit Dr. Wiseman in person for your HRT prescription on the third Thursday of the month, and you must have some good savings to afford hormones. You go early to avoid the plastic-surgery mothers after the school run. Once upon a time, you went early to avoid the Subutex hordes, but they are gone now, too. The death of our urban fauna.

It never stops raining, does it? Another thing we agree on. You don't use an umbrella. Once upon a clickbait article, "In favour of Hoods, 2025," you described brollies as antisocial and impeached your readers for using decent waterproofs. You were calling upon people to adapt but didn't want to take it to the logical conclusion, the only conclusion. To you, there was a world of difference between telling someone to buy a raincoat and telling someone to teach their children and our grandchildren and, henceforth, to survive underwater.

"YES!" you hissed, when I tried to talk through our differences on the street late October. It was pitch black by 5, the alleyway we met in was empty, even of graffiti, like just everybody had given up. "That difference is LIVES!"

The lives keep going, though, down the no-longer-operational drains, another baby swimmer, come on, girl! She breathes three seconds more, then goes, gives up, a floater. I'm so sorry for her, and her bawling parents, but I keep the faith. Those parents don't. The turncoats speak against us in their trial, and you seize it to try to ride another wave of fame. My husband's bail denied, his face aged, lines like estuaries from his defeated eyes to his down-turning mouth. He spits at the officer who tells him, and I laugh heartily.

Every day, thousands more die from climate change, and you're crying "Stop it!" like a baby while we try to teach the world to transform. Eggs will be broken. You scuttle from your home to your appointments (all in my diary), you weep online that you're afraid of the coming storm. Not the big one, just the one for you. You boast one is coming just for you. Like a purifying snowstorm to New Hampshire, devastate you and everything you are.

I will get you.

The Thursday you next visit Dr. Wiseman, you will check behind your shoulder as you lock your door. You will be wearing wellies and a hood, no umbrella. It will be raining so you won't look too hard. The nearest river to you, had you checked flooding.gov.uk, would say it had burst its banks again. The second nearest river to you was gone, too, and the third was no longer being reported on because it had not gone back to human-accommodating levels for over a year.

Your route takes you past the river, and you will feel alone, but I will be with you. You will even feel alone when we tussle, though my arms will be around you, embracing you, embracing change. Perhaps you will scream "Stop!" again as if this land-living is slimming your vocabulary. When we leave the river, I will come too, baptized forever. If we are lucky, you will know for yourself, we can be roomies, the first. Now that will be something worth writing about.

Because one of us has to change. Us or the waters. There is plenty of propaganda that we can make the planet adapt back, and you are too central to it with your Stop Climate Change. Enough of that. And it's not like we can just make the super-rich stop flying private jets, but once I saw the Bajau dive. They were a young populace. I'm not sure where the older ones were, but the young, they dived deep and long. Two hundred feet and thirteen minutes. Records are made to be broken.

Desert Fish

K. M. Watson (Silver Medal Winner)

Valeria peeked out quietly from behind the creosote bush, watching the old woman carefully step down from the shaded porch of her small, adobe home. Golden light from the early morning sun lit up the desert valley floor. It was Valeria's favorite time of the day. Birds sounded and darted among the scrubby brush, and the creosote smelled like rain when she crushed the stiff leaves. Rain that had seemingly disappeared when needed by the coffee crops on her family's farm in Guatemala. Or came down in dreaded torrents, tearing away hills and flooding valleys.

Slowly, the woman crossed the dirt yard with her pottery pitcher and filled the bird bath with water. She did this every day, at least every day that Valeria had been watching her. The woman might have been the age of Valeria's grandmother, left behind when her family began its long walk north. Her face was creased and brown like the dirt in dry riverbeds. She hunched slightly and moved thoughtfully. After finishing with the bird bath, the woman surveyed the horizon and went inside. Valeria's stomach grumbled. *What will the woman bring this time?*

Sofia knew the girl was there, almost from the beginning. She had been catching her out of the corner of her eye for many days. The girl had been using the hose in the backyard for water and going through the woman's trash for food. Once

Sofia realized this, she began to leave chunks of cheese, slices of ham, and fresh bread on a plate on her porch table each morning. She sometimes included apple slices or an orange.

The girl, she decided, was probably another traveler, a *migrante* coming from the south. Just as some of the woman's distant relatives had journeyed hundreds of years ago from Mexico. Fleeing their lands because of political unrest, they had found a home farming and trading with the indigenous tribes. *But why is this child alone? Did she really come so far on her own?* Out Sofia came with food, as Valeria had hoped. But this time, she sat on one of the chairs near the table. "*Ven,*" she said, motioning with her hand and hoping that the girl understood Spanish.

Valeria froze. *Can I trust this woman? So many angry words have been hurled like rocks at my family since we left our home. Rocks on rocks on rocks.* As the soles of Valeria's shoes became thinner over the miles, she withdrew into herself, like the *tortuga de barro* that lived along the streams in her native country. She stopped speaking to anyone but her parents and younger brother as they traveled by foot, sometimes alone and sometimes with others, over roads and trails, through villages, mountains, and tropical forests. Through deserts, relentlessly hot and parched. Once their supplies, so carefully packed by her mother at the start, began to run low, they scavenged the land for food and water along the way. Often, her family went hungry. Sometimes people they met offered some of what they had. *Perhaps this woman who cares for birds is all right.*

Valeria's stomach grumbled again, and she eyed the plate. Eggs, potatoes, nopales, and tortillas. Fresh, not leftovers pulled from other people's garbage. At home, her family never seemed to have enough to eat, even in good times, when their vegetable garden and coffee plants thrived. The steaming tortillas on the plate, reminders of home, pulled at her indecision.

She stepped to the side of her hiding place several yards away and hesitated, searching the old woman's face for signs of trouble. *Nothing alarming.* The woman didn't look directly at Valeria but stared instead at some of the birds starting to gather in the bushes around the water that she had just poured. She chuckled deep in her throat and pointed at a small bird the color of the desert bobbing up and down on a nearby boulder along the edge of the dusty yard.

"This is a rock wren." Sofia talked to the air, her voice clear and full. "One of my favorites. It is like you, maybe. Determined."

Valeria sat down at the table and began to eat. *Everything is so good, like my mother's and grandmother's cooking.* The corn tortillas melted in her mouth, and the nopales tasted salty and tart. The old woman kept talking about the birds, her voice a soothing, rhythmic sound in the background while the girl's mind wandered. Her memories of home came readily, and she could recall much of the arduous journey north to what her parents hoped was a new and better life. They were sad to leave their family and friends, but the dramatic change in the patterns of the weather made their way of life no longer possible. Valeria's papa could no longer read what was coming in the skies and anticipate whether there would be many coffee beans to harvest. The steady talking behind her thoughts stopped. She looked up. The old woman's eyes were on her.

"Would you like to see my desert fish?"

Valeria nodded yes. In all her time crossing the many deserts in her trek, together with her family and then by herself after they somehow disappeared, she had never seen desert fish. *It is hard to picture fish living in such a desolate place, so different from the forests and streams around home. What they need the most, water, is hard to find.*

This would be the first of many times that Valeria followed Sofia into the dry riverbed near Sofia's home. Each visit to the *pescado de desierto* was similar to the first. Sofia would walk up the sandy bottom, where water rarely traveled except during infrequent and violent cloud bursts. In some places her small feet would sink in the soft sand and in others they would tread across sheets of crust. Sofia would watch for birds and name them in conversation with herself. A red-eyed phainopepla feeding on desert mistletoe, a mockingbird perched on a spindly ocotillo branch, and a family of quails pecking along the ground under desert willows. Valeria had seen many of these during the last weeks of her journey north. After her family was gone, she just kept following the stars the way her father had taught her, foraging on the outskirts of small towns and keeping to herself. In a way, the birds had become her companions as she traveled. What had happened to her family and why she was left with only the birds wasn't clear to her. Somewhere along the way, her family was no longer with her.

Every time the two left Sofia's yard in the morning, the old woman would walk and talk and walk and talk until it was time to climb a small embankment and head to the seep where the fish lived. It was easy to miss: a small pool of water, perhaps the size of a large blanket. Sticky stems of coyote bush hung thickly over the water's edge. Neighboring honey mesquite and arrow weed stood nearby. As she approached the water, Sofia would stop talking. Leaning over the seep to see better, she would move her index finger back and forth above the clear surface, silently pointing, counting, and nodding approval. The silvery blue, knuckle-sized fish, the only ones in the pool, mostly ignored her. It was a ritual that gave Sofia comfort. *The fish don't belong here. But they do.*

As weeks passed, Valeria remained without words. But she learned to see the desert less and less as an adversary. Sofia took her into her home and she helped with new routines, different from those of her family farm. Valeria no longer helped her little brother get dressed or weeded the vegetable garden or picked and sorted burnished red coffee beans from the plants that surrounded their tidy shanty in the forested mountains. The carefully tended coffee plants that had made her father so proud to harvest no longer reliably produced thousands of beans a year from the branches of each small tree. It was as if the droughts that now plagued the remote highland communities sucked the life not only out of the plants but out of those that depended on them for their livelihood.

During the daily walks, Sofia would give new details about the only native fish in the desert. Their ancestors went back thousands and thousands of years, thriving when the land was covered in lakes and streams. Now, the fish survived in scattered remnants of those places throughout the desert. Seeps. Springs. Islands of water percolating to the surface from rains and snowmelt collected deep underground over hundreds of thousands of years.

Sofia's eyes sparkled as she watched two fish circle each other and twist. Their silver scales glinted in the sunlight. "Some people call them pupfish, *cachorrito*, because they are so playful. See? But they are also tough." Sofia smiled gently in admiration. The animated slivers of silver could live under conditions that would kill most other fish. "They can endure the extremes. Hot temperatures. Salt. Rising and falling water levels. These fish are the relatives of the ancient ones that have made it through somehow."

Valeria considered the fish and how such small and seemingly insignificant things could mean so much to Sofia. Perhaps they were her family, like the birds. Valeria had noticed when watching Sofia from a distance that few people had visited her, and no one had come to her doorstep since Valeria had started to sleep on a small cot that she had moved near the back door. Sofia lived far enough away from others that she couldn't see any house lights at night. But animals were with her.

Valeria's thin arms and legs filled out. Her stringy black hair grew lush and shiny. The cuts and scrapes on her face healed, and her skin again became that of a child. Valeria gladly put water in the bird bath and watched for the rock wren at the start of the day. And she looked forward to Sofia's delight in visiting her desert fish.

One day, Sofia was feeling her age in her joints. She didn't talk about birds or the fish on their trek to the pool. Her voice wasn't joyful and full of affection. She was thinking back in time.

"My mother's family has been here for thousands of years, too, like the pupfish," Sofia said in a hushed tone as she willed her legs to push through the sandy river trail. "They were here long before the Spanish and long before the Mexicans and long before the settlers from the east. We lived off of the land and traded with other tribes." She looked to the horizon as if imagining that time described in stories passed along over the generations. "We lost everything." Her voice was low and heavy.

Valeria understood this deep sadness. She held it in her bones, a mourning for her own home far to the south that she had also lost.

That night, the clattering of heavy raindrops on the roof startled Valeria out of her sleep. In the distance she heard a muffled roar. When she opened the front door, a thundering sound filled her ears and shook her chest. The dry riverbed that they had walked so many times was now flooded with crashing waves of water, spilling rapidly down the river's course.

Valeria's eyes widened in horror as she watched, stumbling closer to the source of a rising grief. *No, not again.* The memory that had been deeply buried, that she knew was there but couldn't pry loose, now became overwhelming. Her father, pushing her to the side of a rocky, narrow desert canyon that her family was crossing. Yelling for her to grab onto nearby brush. The sound of rainwater building and crashing rapidly down the canyon. Toward her family. Her mother and brother caught up in the flash flood, sweeping past her father's arms that reached out to grab them. His back as he entered the water hoping to save them. The angry water enveloping all three in its deadly rush. *They are gone in a moment, the people I love the most and who love me.*

A keening joined the storm's chorus. A thin high note and then a deafening wail. Sofia ran from the porch and gathered Valeria into her arms as the girl collapsed in despair. "*Mi familia!*" she screamed over and over, words that had piled up inside her throat, waiting to be released. To fly into the air.

Dislocation

Clare D. Becker

The first time that furniture and boxes drifted in the water rising in the basement, Aida believed the cause was a sump pump failure. Unlikely to happen again. Dante Bartolomeo knew different, but he bought a bigger pump. After they threw out every moldy cushion, box, and book and washed down the walls with bleach, the next venomous rain arrived and water rose to the fourth step of the basement stairs.

She wanted to relocate to mountains west or north, had visions of growing herbs and mushrooms in greenhouses, of moving to a sanctuary, away from the callous sea. Land there will turn to bog after river flooding, he said, but she had contempt for his predictions. Dante worked in coastal transportation with a commute that shortened as water spread inland. He preferred his job to mushroom farming. She argued, gave one deadline, then another, the latest the day after the race.

To Dante, water was a mirror of life. He had been trained by his father and ran his father's last gondola, the *Salvation*. He found it difficult to love a woman who preferred land to water, a woman who wanted to sidestep fate rather than beat it. She said his mind was waterlogged. He blamed the climate. She, his weakness for sentiment.

The morning of the Boston Canals Gondola Race, Bartolomeo's hope is big and he disregards a day of acid heat perfect for pickling.

"If I win, will you stay?" Dante asked her.

"Maybe," Aida said.

In a practice run for the style competition, using the old Aquarium Transit entrance with its orange warning antenna as one axis, Dante turns his boat in an ever-tighter elliptical pattern, is drawn in by the slap/hush against the side of the boat, the vitality of the tide, and insistent draw of its brooding depth. He spirals the boat until diamonds of sun eddying in the water subvert his vision, and he shakes his head to stop his mind from going wooly.

A glass bottle with a scarf of algae around its neck, plink plinks against a barricade. Dante readjusts the oar to stop the boat from careening into it. The visualization: rhythmic, powerful strokes, the oar pivoting through the forcola for speed, turns, balance. The sleek *Salvation* is in good shape. Nico, another water veteran who kept the cooperative going after Dante's father died, has coached him. He is a stubborn leader without personal ambition. He might have to fight his way into a suit for meetings with the Commonwealth Corporation, but he knows how to deploy the crew.

Commuters expect to be moved quickly, and Dante skims close alongside the buildings and turns corners efficiently. To get good tips and repeat customers, he maintains balance as they disembark. He reads the canals, their contours and whims, the roll and swell that pulses around the archipelago of buildings.

In the time before, when they were young, before their son Lorenzo was born, before the multiple, simultaneous breaking points, Dante and Aida could make love under a cover on his gondola. They would let the river rock them, or paddle along an undulating Charles at twilight, sipping wine. Now the sea grazed on land, and the canals and bay swelled and sprawled over the cities. Travel by boat—before it became as common as dirt, a touch of the romantic.

Instead of thinning his ties to home, disaster intensified his need for it. He refused to be one of the domestic migrants. In the attic, he kept his father's old, scarred paddle, the drills and planes, a framed certificate for the Gondozip founder. Inside himself, he kept the rhythm of arm and paddle, the dazzle of light skimming the canals, the camaraderie of the men in the collective, the ceremonial pageants of boats that splashed like birds in spring puddles.

Aida was prepared to tidy up and move on. A woman equally adept at fixing a leaky faucet and comforting Lorenzo in the turmoil of early love and betrayal. Without blinking, she could explain amortization to real estate buyers and to Dante the declining loan-to-value ratio in regard to their own house.

Back in the day, Dante's father laughed when a storm washed the Seaport district with ocean, when they pumped water out of the Aquarium basement, a floor below the glassed-in sea creatures, when they used front-end loaders to move people on the coast. The Seaport, enticingly named—the perfect location for condos and glass-clad offices, the view, the sea, dawn light, pure scenic luxury. A collective unconscious paralleled a few attempts at the reverse engineering of doom. Oil company execs might have planned their mountain or moon retreats. Some paid attention. To the disenfranchised or temporarily-secure, awareness that death will come, that it may come unexpectedly, mattered, just not enough for the others, because humanity cannot imagine its own extinction. The precariousness of lives elsewhere in the world warped their own.

To Aida, the coast was foul, saturated, done. No sump pump could keep up. After flooding receded, ocean salt gnawed at bricks and mortar, leaving them granular dust. The marshes that swirled their way through Boston and surrounding cities reclaimed their independence. Lorenzo needed a solid future, not geographic ebb and flow. She had practical plans, Dante did not.

Dante figures that Aida, as cynical as she could be, would not turn away from the prize money. Winning could be the start of a professional career, with time and money for international competition.

Not his debut race, but this year the pundits granted Dante a chance at the title. The opposition: the world-famous gondolier, Ignaz Alto, three-time winner of the Golden Ferro, with his savvy smile and hair fixed in a meringue-textured quiff, is topping a decade of competing in every world race. Because Dante plies the canals transporting people for a living, he has little time to train. With the Gondozip logo tattooed along one side of his shaved head and a splashing gondola across his back, he wears his identity.

The sun rises, just as it did 2,000 years earlier before the naval battles between Rome and Carthage, now in glorious manifestation of its power over a corrupted earth. Seven in the morning, the air cloying and hot. The canals murmur, the wood pilings that hug the buildings wince. The water, stirred up by last week's storm, laps in rhythm against the concrete barriers. Pieces of the floating wetland system erected after the flood of '29 drift under the surface like derelict underwater glaciers.

At Aida's insistence, he had submitted to counseling. To Dante, Nico, and the others from Gondozip, analyzing anything was a waste of time. With the crew, life was about the moment, squeezing humor out of the lemonade they were perpetually required to make. Instead of talking about childhood trauma, as Dante had feared, the counselor dangled cures. The Buddhist approach—suffering in life is caused by an inability to accept change. Or was it the refusal? Resilience kept a heart beating. Or clutter cleanout: one pile to keep, one to throw, and one to donate. But where do you distribute the parts of who you are? The counselor had given Aida a prescription designed to alleviate climate anxiety. Did Dante want one too?

Talking to Aida feels like chain fraying against a dock loop. Sometimes he wished she'd just leave; sometimes he didn't. He wanted to go back before the time of fracture when life was reassembled ass to front. Even close families could be dismembered.

A traghetti, with three race officials standing in front, maneuvers along the old State House dock. A Commonwealth Corporation deputy greets each official with a handshake and a *USS Constitution* lapel pin. They make an awkward procession down the gently swaying dock and wait under the red-and-white-striped canopy. They sip iced drinks and, like bureaucrats everywhere, blend into the background.

The gold Alphazon banner is strung high above. In the fetid air, it hangs limp. The colored vapor display glows against the backdrop of the morning sky. Names of the top competitors flash in a loop.

Through the drone speakers, you can hear cheers as Ignaz Alto's gondola sweeps up to the dock. The traditional striped blue shirt is so tight you can make out the sculpted musculature beneath it.

Welcome to Boston, a reporter says. *The crowd will favor our hometown gondolier, but it's good to test our mettle against a champion and a genuine Venetian.*

Alto responds with a synthetic laugh. *You can't beat the challenge of the Miami ten-canals competition, but wonderful to be back in Boston.*

Venice has now been designated a vacated city, completely under water.

Unbelievable! Alto says. *We tried everything: raising barriers, building wetlands. But the lagoons morphed into sea, and the roofs of the palazzos ride the tides like floating islands. It is with great sadness that we had to evacuate, that we left behind our beloved Venice.*

Such a sad retreat from the city that meant so much for everyone who follows the sport. Where are you planning to relocate?

Las Vegas, Alto says, *is developing a more extensive, truly exotic, above- and below-ground canal experience. Top-draw effects. I'll be one of the attractions. Like Madame Tussauds, but alive.*

Dante despises the way he talks about abandoning Venice, lost in subterranean oblivion, with twenty words and a shrug. Dante's father loved Canaletto. Prints of his busy canals painted with dreamy Venice blues and greens hung on their walls before Aida replaced them. She preferred things up-to-date and cheerful.

The pre-race style competition begins. Eight men and two women line up. Alto has the flourish, but Dante notices that he's loose on the turns.

The Technical Exhibition Program

Emergency stops

Two-way sideways traverse

Forward and reverse parabolas

Sway and return

Curl and roll

Corkscrew

After every operation, Dante feels his performance is perfect, and nerves rumble under his skin. Suddenly, from the bay, a boat slips around the corner. Two men row fiercely. Nico stands up, raises a fist, and pumps it enthusiastically.

"Nico!" Dante shouts. "You're rocking the boat!" He appreciates the gesture.

At this moment, Dante would like to brag to Aida. In the before, she was never flamboyantly affectionate, but she could be upfront and sweet.

The counselor told him, "You have a skill, and you're a good learner. What about plumbing or operating a ski gondola? Or starting over in a new domain? I have a cousin in Shelburne Falls who raises alpacas." He suggested letting Aida live her dreams. Dante wondered if the counselor was seeing her on the side.

As the gondoliers complete the short program, they shout congratulations to Dante, and he waits until the results appear on the display to respond with a humble wave. Alto 16.7 out of 18. Dante tops the list at 17.5. You can hear a roar from the viewers. Alto keeps at a distance and tries to neutralize a sulky face.

Dante swings away from the boathouse and gives Alto a sympathetic nod. He looks over to the dock, where Aida waves tentatively. Maybe she is pleased or perhaps is mentally spending the million.

By 9, earth and water are cooking. Everyone stands at limp attention to the traditional singing of the Barcarolle. The amateurs wait at the side. They are essential, providing financial support and spreading interest in the sport. One of their boats is bejeweled with rhinestones, reminiscent of the gondolas of wealthy Venetians centuries ago. After the last note of the song, the race chime rings.

Alto blasts off as if burning from his earlier defeat. Dante is not unhappy to slip into third place. Alto plows down Congress Street Canal. Dante plans to hold back a surge, and shifts into a steady pace. Drone cameras cruise above them. As his gondola crosses Fort Point Channel, the water cleaves cleanly.

Water and sky are turning gray, and the smell of brine and seaweed stings. Dante senses an alteration in the current. Something's off. Low tide has passed, high tide not due for hours. He passes the old Children's Museum with the neck and cap of its milk bottle structure, just keeping its head above water.

Speakers carry commentary. *Alto is smoking hot and he's not letting go of the lead. Behind him, there's the wild card, Germany's Ebert Gaspari, followed by Massachusetts's own Dante Bartolome, driving steady and sure.*

Dante sees that Gaspari is beginning to falter. He's tangled up with something, probably debris from wetland construction. The oar is going horizontal and he struggles to free it. The boat begins to rotate and there's a helpless angle to Gaspari's shoulders.

Without hesitating, Dante adjusts his oar to swerve around Gaspari. He refuses to lose time. He thinks this gondolier is so experienced that, although he may not be able to salvage his run, he'll extract himself from danger. Dante steams forward. Alto is out of sight, having already turned into Pier 4 Boulevard Canal.

As Dante turns the corner, like a speed skater, he leans toward the inside curve. A straight-running boat is almost frictionless. Now his boat churns against the water. Dante is used to its many tones. There is a conversation between them.

Water leaps over the boat and sour spray washes against Dante's face. The air moves beyond humid to saturation. Sweat runs from scalp to foot, pools behind his knees.

Suddenly, from behind, sounds pummel the air like a herd of old Harleys. The Salvation begins to sway, but Dante, intent on maintaining balance and pressing forward, resists turning. They're either pirates or joyriders. The Uspeed boats roar up an old expressway ramp, at least half a dozen lunging around the canal. The Baystate Raiders, with their bare chests and flags of multi-colored hair, rev their engines, and zigzag across the water.

Dante bulldozes the oar through the water. The Uspeed boats weave across the canal so fast they skim just above the surface. In a flash, they hit the channel, leaving Dante behind. Their mouths are wide with laughter.

The speakers are abuzz with reports: *Looks like a sortie from the Raiders. The water is choppy, but Bartolomeo is holding his own. Pirates are a fact of life, but this is the first time in our recollection they are so brazen as to try to ambush an official race. Our Boston boy is unflappable.*

As Alto heads back on Seaport Boulevard Canal, Dante accelerates. He understands Alto's desire for glory at the end of his career, but he presses forward. If he wins the prize money, Aida might stay or he could set her and Lorenzo up in a location of her desire. Perhaps he'll meet a new woman, someone refreshing. As he edges closer, the wind drives harder.

Dante sees Alto in the middle of Fort Point Channel. He powers on, hoping to catch up, but uncertain given Alto's big lead. And yet he cuts the distance between them. Alto appears fixed to a point. Dante can see the oar turning vigorously in the forcola, but the boat doesn't move.

A seagull glides above Dante. Others join. Their shrieks blister his ears.

Alto's boat spins within an oval lip, caught inside a whirlpool. At the edge of the swell, a sandbag, an artifact of an old coastline barrier, erupts from the water, then another and another. They plunge down with thunder.

The current and the wind conspire. As the center deepens, the sun turns the rim of the vortex into a prism that colors radiate through. The gondola, its black hull gleaming, rises and recedes. The gulls circle, wailing.

Dante's bewildered. There's the great maelstrom in Nova Scotia, but no one's seen anything like this here. Alto's boat creates a hollow within an elliptical wall. His eyes are seared to a pinpoint of panic.

Sweat on Dante's chest turns cold, nervous. He prefers not to be swallowed up, but Alto needs to be rescued, and Dante drives forward, aiming to break through and run his boat alongside. It's a moment of decision that eclipses the months of uncertainty in his life, but the undeniable force of water is too great. For a moment, Alto's boat lifts. Nature teases the man.

From farther up the channel, Nico rows furiously. Gaspari, free from his own battle, paddles up Seaport Canal, and now there are three boats propelled around the rim of the whirlpool.

Helpless, Alto submerges. The gulls disappear. And then he is gone. The three men in their boats back away.

Dante is the first to slide into home dock. Aida holds him as tight as mother to child. Rescue boats come back empty. Lorenzo is only curious, as if to the young chaos is now natural, has become just part of the scenery.

"You tried to save him," Aida says. She steps away and shakes the worry out.

"On the screen," she says, "it looked like glug-glug, down the plug hole."

He stares at her.

"Poor guy," she adds.

Dante and Nico walk along the dock. "That was something else," Nico says. "How are you feeling?"

"Like a lobster leaping out of the boil," Dante says.

Nico laughs but throws an arm around his shoulder. "They're going to award you the prize money," he says. "No trophy this year, though, due to the circumstances."

After the shock, after the hyper news coverage and photos went viral, the retrieval divers, the investigation and dredging of the canal, after the sea spread its fingers farther inland, farther north, farther south, after gondola services expanded into a now-profitable Metro West, after Dante gave half the winnings to Aida and she left, but Lorenzo stayed—after all that, but for not very much longer, Dante, his son, and Gondozip ruled the Boston canals with great respect.

Don't Ask

Kitty Beer

"I'm Cam, at your service."

Swan looked up to see a tall, lanky young man with a bush of dark hair, a twinkle both humorous and gallant in his warm brown eyes. She couldn't help but smile at his blunt introduction. Sitting on a bench overlooking the frothy ocean, she'd been contemplating her murky future. After a March with alternate sleet and tropical heat, April 2059 so far was a calm interlude. Just now the sun broke through, slanting over the ocean with bright certitude.

"This is a good bench," he said, folding himself awkwardly beside her, nodding out to sea. He looked to be a little older than she was, in his mid-twenties. He turned to her, grinning.

"Are you contemplating the universe?"

"Nothing that grand. I just need a job."

"I come here every day at lunchtime. I work right over there."

They looked behind them in one turn of their shoulders. She liked the sense of his lean muscle. "You mean the *Beacon* office?"

"Yep. Copy editor."

Then they turned back as one to stare out over the bright water, broken here and there with the tops of the old buildings of the old city of Boston, lapped by sparkling waves. Swan was hesitant, but she couldn't resist replying, "That's what I want to do."

"Well, hey. Are you a writer?"

"I try."

And that's how it all started. Cam's uncle was the newspaper's editor-in-chief who had just been jailed for sedition, meaning criticizing Mayor Thurman. Thus, Cam had assumed a little more clout than his position warranted, and he offered to promote her application. She got the job. It didn't matter much that she was primarily and professionally a ballet dancer. All the theaters had been closed for over a year—first for the virus and then (in the name of public health) simply to prevent large, unmonitored gatherings—so performers of all stripes were job hunting. More importantly, during her studies at the Arts Academy, she'd won an essay contest. So the following week found Swan happily ensconced at her very own desk, composing ads.

It was early days yet. Beacon Hill in Boston had become Beacon Island after dramatic tsunamis only a decade ago. The police force had not yet been privatized, and elections were still just postponed—not eliminated. Everybody was used to wild weather swings by then, so strict mitigation was widely accepted and consistently practiced. For example, coastal buildings had no basements, crops resistant to both drought and flooding dominated, strict brownouts prevented frequent fuel failures. It was a happy enough time. They were young, filled with so much hope.

Predictably, after many comradely lunches together on their favorite bench, Cam invited Swan to his apartment for chili. But she was back living at home, and her mother expected an explanation for evening outings. Her father's abrupt departure, even though years earlier and for political rather than personal reasons, had left her mother nervous and suspicious. So, on her way home that day, Swan tried to concoct a reassuring scenario. Too bad she could no longer use the excuse of a rehearsal. Her sister Fin was in the kitchen stirring something on the stove.

"Hey, Swan," she greeted her sister airily, then put on her conspiratorial eyebrows. "Mom's popped over to the store."

Which meant, Give me the naughty news right away! At fifteen she was just discovering the salacious side of biology.

"He wants me to come to his place." Swan tried to sound casual.

"And?" Fin cried when, instead of elaborating, Swan took a big spoonful of the brew and cautiously sipped it.

"I don't know any and. Boy, Fin, this is good. Lentils?"

"Come on."

Fin was dancing up and down. Swan was smirking. They both knew she was teasing her little sister.

"Okay," she conceded. "He wants to make me chili."

"Oh, he really likes you! He has plans."

"Well, I don't know about his plans. I just want to see his place. He's a good friend."

"Yeah, right," Fin mocked.

Mother's footsteps on the outside stairs sent them scurrying to culinary tasks. She hustled in, moaning disapproval as usual.

"You girls stop gossiping and giggling. Honestly, I don't see how you're ever going to learn..."

Swan was working at her desk one Friday in May when a sudden hubbub broke out in the newsroom across the hall. Through the staff crowding around the television, Swan made out the annual Interdependence Day parade emerging onto Town Hall Plaza. A crowd of masked people wearing black armbands started plunging into the marchers, wielding clubs. Various animal costumes stopped, braced, tried to run, and began to fall under heavy blows. Swan searched the screen wildly for her sister, one of many teens participating. She'd helped Fin craft her outfit representing a frog, green shiny headdress with bulging eyes.

Someone cried out, "Where are the police?" but nobody dared answer. It was too well known these days that what was left of the police was in cahoots with the Thurmans, as they called themselves, the muscle of the genial and deadly new mayor, James Oscar Thurman.

The camera panned over the writhing bodies of bears, rabbits, hawks, horses, wolves, butterflies. Then the camera shuddered and the screen went blank. A cheerful reporter explained from a nice, neat news desk that a little trouble at the parade had been swiftly dealt with by the authorities.

Cam brought out his chili in a big red and orange bowl, set it before Swan with a proud flourish. She was sitting a bit awkwardly at his kitchen table, eager but nervous. He had draped the table with a heavy yellow cloth that did not much resemble a tablecloth. It was clear to her that Cam was not used to entertaining, but his effort was endearing. She smiled encouragement, took a sip of her wine.

"Yum," she ventured.

"Yes, well." He nodded satisfaction, sat down. "Grated cheese?"

"That sounds great, if you have it."

Cam dramatically swung a grater through the air, produced a chunk of cheese to scrape onto the steaming chili. "There you go." He raised his glass. "To us."

But after they'd discussed work for a bit, finally, she shook her head.

"Cam, we have to talk about it."

"Let's not argue! Not tonight!"

"No, but are we going to cover it?"

"We did."

"That piece yesterday was a whitewash. You know it."

"Babe, relax." Cam reached for her hand. His long, knobby fingers she so admired when turning pages or tapping keys. His warmth. "How's your sister? Okay now?"

"No. Hey, her arm is broken! I mean, it's not too bad, it's going to heal, but..."

"She'll be fine. That's terrific. I know how worried you were. It was a damn shame. But they just don't want animal-themed stuff anymore. It's subversive. Mayor Thurman says..."

Swan pulled her hand away, swabbed up sauce savagely with a piece of bread. "I don't care what that blowhard says..."

"Look, my uncle's jailed because he talked like that. You've got to be more careful."

"It seems to me," she replied coldly, "the more careful we are, the worse it gets."

At that, Cam surprised her by hanging his head sadly. "You're right. I just want to keep you safe."

Swan dropped her fork and put her arm around his shoulder. "Cam. What are we going to do?"

"Well, your father?"

"What about him? What does he have to do with anything?"

But her aggressive response was delivered in a wail of dismay. She knew very well what he meant. Her father had been made warden for Internal Affairs, an influential role in the Thurman regime. She felt the start of childish tears. Cam, murmuring reassurances, took her gently in his arms. When he swabbed a napkin across her cheeks, she lifted her face to his kisses. The rest of the chili grew cold.

A few mornings later, Swan awoke with grim determination to face the momentous day. Her plan was fully hatched, though she knew it was risky. She'd resolved to try her father.

Swan and Fin saw their father, Jax Bentley, once or twice a year when he made half-hearted attempts at a relationship. They were careful to conceal these meetings from their mother, who would have been distraught at their betrayal. Her daughters were supposed to revile the man who abandoned them as fervently as she did. As for Jax, he cherished a hope that his girls would come to embrace his views.

"We Thurmans," he liked to boast, "are a tough bunch. Don't mess with us. If you've got anything to do with perverts, tree-huggers, or outsiders or the like, steer clear. We aim to clean up this whole island, and then —mainland, watch out! We've got plans for the whole northeast coast, Providence to Portland."

Fin, in the bed next to Swan, was tossing and turning, whimpering from time to time, so her shoulder still hurt. As usual, Mom was hacking her asthma cough in the kitchen. From under the window shade came slices of white-bright sunlight—another burning day revving up, now June, no rain for a month.

At work, she took an early lunch break and headed over to the Plaza. The number seven bus stopped in front of Town Hall, so she didn't have far to walk in the airless heat. She was gratified by her outfit choice: best trousers, white blouse, hair tamed into a twist. She aimed to look professional, like a real reporter. The ruse was tested a few minutes later when a guard asked for her errand.

She replied curtly, "From the *Beacon*."

Angry as she was with her father, she'd not been able to suppress the sweet memories of when she was very small, riding on his shoulders, singing together as he played the guitar, being carried half asleep up to bed. She was only seven when he left, and she was devastated. He did try for a bit to explain—how he was called to fight for James Oscar Thurman, who was saving their world. But to her then, he was swept away like a tornado, no daddy, gone daddy. Mother was a mess and mean about everything from then on, so she was no comfort. Fin was too little to notice much, but their sisterly bond grew ever stronger. Maybe, thought Swan, she was here now on this crazy, dangerous quest for Fin's sake, her precious sister, who was suffering in pain just because she wanted to celebrate frogs. Her father did not get up from his desk when she walked in.

"What did I tell you," he muttered nervously. "Never come here. You embarrass me."

Swan coolly sat herself down, replied, "Relax, Dad. I don't bite."

He opened his mouth to yell but clearly did not want a scene. He was a rotund man with tightly curled red hair, stiff shoulders. She guarded her heart against any dismay at his thinning hair, eye creases.

"Okay, okay," he said. "Is everything all right at home?"

"Fine. I'm here on a professional basis."

"A likely story. What do you want? I'm busy here."

"I just want to talk to the parade organizer about the violence."

"You want what?"

"Fin was hurt. Her arm is broken."

"Hurt? Broken? No, no, nobody was hurt. Come on, now."

Swan was relieved to see he cared. She went in for the kill. "I want to ask about why."

Jax stood up, whizzed around his desk, grabbed her shoulders, shook her. She was glaring at him, but to her horror, tears blurred her vision. He stopped shaking her, his grip softened.

He said, "My little girl, my pal, what happened to you?"

"Father... Dad... What happened to you?"

Jax grew red. "Stop it."

"All I want is an interview with the parade organizer."

"Don't you dare ask me for a damn thing."

"Our Fin is hurting, Dad." She couldn't believe her sobby tone, her humility. But it worked.

He let go of her shoulders, took her hands, and pressed them to his heart. "I'll fix it. Just be careful. Maybe you'll learn something. Maybe we can even recruit you to the cause. That would make your old dad real happy."

He stepped away, motioned to the guard. "Take this young lady over to Price's office. I'll call to tell them she's coming."

As she turned to go, he said to her, "You're a brave girl. Be careful."

"Lieutenant Price is not available," announced the lofty woman who greeted her. "But he asked me to see to you. Have a seat. I am Sergeant Winters. Captain Bartley sent you?"

Swan could tell this was about to become a dismissal. Her flare of hope at her father's gesture had already shriveled to smoldering despair. The waiting room was small and stuffy; benches along the walls were strewn with lolling people who'd clearly been there for ages. The sergeant sat down at the only desk, gestured to a rickety chair. But Swan remained standing, facing the woman with ballet-inspired high elegance. Neck long, shoulders down, back firmly straight.

"Thank you," Swan said. "I have only one question."

"Ask away." Sergeant Winter's reply included a haughty, impatient gesture that somehow implied she was about to die of scorn and boredom.

"Why do you people hate animals?"

The woman stared up at her with shocked disbelief that quickly shrank to slit-eyed suspicion.

"Guard," she barked without taking her glare from Swan.

A uniformed guard appeared at once, saluting at her side. "Yes, ma'am."

"This person is under arrest." To Swan, she said, "You have made a grave mistake, young lady."

"I'm a reporter," Swan protested, in a voice weakened with fear.

"That's just what I mean. You journalists are the worst of the worst. We should string you all up."

"No, no, no," said Henry, again and again.

Swan and Cam were sitting across from him in his office. It was late afternoon, but shafts of heat still sliced through the window blinds. Two fans on either side of them barely managed to push the sweltering air around a little.

"Henry, buddy," Cam insisted. "We've just explained it to you. Don't you get it? This is a brilliant piece, bound to put the *Beacon* on top, boost circulation out of this world. Hey look, Swan wrote it overnight, the very day they arrested her and let her go. It's hot news, what we dream of!"

"No, no!" Henry was getting fed up, hysterical. He had a small mouth emphasized by a bushy blonde mustache, now twisting in fury.

"No!" he shrieked again.

"Henry," said Swan, "I made a lot of the changes you asked for. But I have to tell the truth."

Cam added, "She doesn't say a word that's not pure fact."

Henry sat down, breathing hard. "That's not the damn point. If we print that, they'll close us down. Throw me in the clink just like they did your uncle."

"You're only the stand-in for my uncle, 'til he gets back. They won't blame you, Henry buddy." Cam was trying to be conciliatory. "Look, this is work of prime reporting. We've got a star reporter in the works here."

Cam whipped open his laptop and started reading. "It began with my little sister's love of frogs ... then she was lying in the street twisting in agony, her best friend the penguin splayed unconscious beside her ... the Ministry building is air-conditioned, comfort for the powerful ... The next thing

I knew, I was handcuffed and pushed into a jail cell ... I was let go a few hours later ... Probably assumed I'd learned my lesson.'"

Henry had leaped up halfway through Cam's staccato rendering of her report, pacing in a most melodramatic take on tragedy. Now, suddenly, he stopped, his face cleared, his mustache rose to reveal a dreamy smile. "My wife will love this." He went to the desk, picked up the phone, sang, "My sweet, how would you like to leave right away, tomorrow morning? I knew you would. Yep, the first ferry to Bangor. Get everything ready. Love you too."

"There you are!" Henry was the picture of gleeful triumph. "It's all yours, Cam. You are the new replacement editor-in-chief. I resign."

Now it was Cam's turn to leap up in shock. "You can't..."

Henry's smile was getting wider. "It's perfect. You take over the helm, printing whatever incendiary craziness your uncle will no doubt approve. My wife and I are off to Canada. She has cousins north of Chicoutimi who've been begging us for months to get the hell out of this hellhole here. Who needs this police state we're heading into." He fairly jumped with joy. "And I can say that! I'll be free to say anything I want!"

Swan wanted to tell him he should stay and fight, but she was dumb with amazement, pride, and hope.

That evening, she went home with Cam. They whipped up a makeshift supper, ate ravenously, drank plenty of homemade wine that was iffy but did the trick, made love wildly, laughing and crying at the same time, and fell asleep like stones.

The next day, July 1, 2059, the front page of the *Beacon* carried Swan's article. It was accompanied by good before-and-after photos, the first including a glimpse of Fin in full frog regalia.

Consequences came swiftly. When Swan and Cam got to work that morning, the building was surrounded by police.

Staff members formed an outraged and trembling knot across the street. When Cam headed for the door, trying to bypass the guards, two of them loomed in front of him, shoulder to shoulder, shaking their heads.

"It's closed," Cam reported to Swan.

"What do you mean closed? They can't do that," she babbled. "What does closed mean? What did they say?"

"That's what they said. It's closed. We should've known."

In Times of Change, Root Down to Rise Up

Jessica Marcy

"The stories that tree could tell…" It's a phrase I hear a lot around here. These days it's usually tourists who whisper that in awe as they stare up at my branches, pointing up to the heavens on high. Perhaps that's why they call me an angel. Ms. Angel Oak, that is.

For the past several decades, my branches have been getting heavy, falling to the ground, undulating through the soil, like the nearby waters. They've grown tired with the weight of time. You see, I've seen a lot of things in my time… different people and communities… and a lot of change. But, these days, the changes—rising water, unpredictable weather, and shifting seasons—are coming even quicker. And it's affecting us all: people, plants, animals, even us old live oak trees. Nothing and nobody is spared these days.

But, I ain't going nowhere. Oh, no, child. I'm sticking right here where I'm planted. My home is in the Lowcountry. You see, my roots run deep here on Johns Island. I've been here for a long time, way before you were born, and your parents were born; your grandparents, your great ones, and your great-great ones too. Honestly, I could use a bit of rest…

So, honey, sit down, lean up against my trunk, get comfortable because I've got some tales to tell, stories of not only the land but the people who lived and loved right here around me.

You see, people like to project themselves onto me. They see what they want to see. Some say angels like to rest in my branches, others believe darker spirits like to visit me at night. Some say they can even see the Ankh cross, an ancient Egyptian symbol of life itself, in my very branches. Back in the day, people used to understand that they were standing on holy ground. And they knew that the mighty oak was a sacred tree.

When I was just a sapling, I remember how the Native Cusabo used to gather around me and my elders, circling around us in rituals that marked the shifting seasons and time. Later, British colonialists arrived starting in the 1600s, lured by land and profit. They brought enslaved Africans to cultivate the land and grow rice on the nearby creeks and rivers. Such rice made the plantation owners rich with what became known as Carolina gold. On Sullivans Island, just twenty miles from my roots, over 40 percent of all enslaved Africans arrived on the shores of what would become the United States of America.

In my youth, I remember how such Africans would toil nearby and then take solace around me to eat and pray. They lived in cabins near my roots and would come to me when they needed to lighten their load. They prayed right under my very branches. The plantation days were tough times.

To be honest, I've seen a lot of the worst of humans... violence, slavery, greed, destruction. A few years back, I even had a young white man pay me a visit before going into Emanuel African Methodist Episcopal Church in nearby Charleston. He shot and killed nine churchgoers who lovingly welcomed him into "Mother Emanuel," the oldest black church in the U.S. South. Even the president at the time, Barack Obama, came down to honor them, singing "Amazing Grace" at their funeral and making us all proud.

I swear, I'll never understand humans and the destruction they cause.

"The past isn't dead. It's not even past." I remember hearing those words from William Faulkner spoken by a wise teacher who gathered her students near my roots. I love it when teachers bring their students to learn under my branches. People like to think those things are a thing of the past, but honey, unless you understand them for what they are, they'll continue to circle back just like a nightmare that keeps coming back to haunt you.

In my time, I've heard many things. You know, we trees might not talk like humans, but we've got a lot to share. We communicate through underground mycelial networks, so I'm tapped into a lot of things.

In particular, we oak trees have a special relationship with people. Over the years, I get stories about people from all types of oaks—the council trees, where old men would congregate around after Sunday church to discuss important matters of the week; the meeting trees where people gather for special occasions; the hanging trees where Black people were lynched to invoke fear and send a message of hate.

But, my favorite stories have always come from the oaks that are planted in the sacred cemeteries where Gullah/Geechee people were once buried during the days of slavery. Friends and family would gather under those oaks, praying, singing, and drumming to help their spirits cross over the water on their journey to Heaven. Nothing makes me happier than to hear of people still honoring those African ancestors with gifts—sweet potatoes, butternut squash, honey, sunflowers, money.

"If that tree could speak, what would it say?" That's another question I always get around these parts. You might think I've got the gift of gab right now, but usually, I don't share my tales. I usually just take it all in... like when young lovers slip off to press up against me in the middle of the night. You know, they don't call me Lover's Lane for nothing... But honey, those romantic tales, I keep those all for myself.

I communicate more in energy, a felt sense. You could call me the strong, silent type. And, I'll tell you, I think people these days could use much more of that. The thing that people have forgotten is the reciprocal nature of life. It's not all just what you can get, what you can use. It's about what you can give, how you can listen, what you can do to support others, and not just the human type, but all types. See, humans like to think that they're the center of it all. They forget we're all connected. I have relationships of all types, from the white albino squirrels that race across my branches to the struggling sapling that needs some help. Oh, honey, I feed them all with my acorns and nutrients. Ain't nobody or nothing gonna go hungry with this big old matriarch around.

These days, there are so many people, too many people. So many houses and shopping centers are going in. So many highways are being built. These days, there are so many stories of oaks being uprooted, dug up, so more highways can be built for rich vacationers to get to their golf courses and massive oceanfront houses quicker.

Indeed, the times are a-changing. I had a scientist stop by to pay me a visit recently. He was talking with his colleague about how such development was transforming nearby forests and wetlands and helping to accelerate the forces of climate change. He talked about the warming climate, rain bombs, and rising seas along the South Carolina coast. He was a smart guy, even mentioned how us large oak trees act as natural water pumps and air conditioners. He knew how to respect his elders.

For me, the saddest thing is when I hear stories from the nearby skeleton coastlines where large, dead, gaunt trees line the beaches. Tourists love to take photos of them, but for me, it breaks my heart to imagine my children standing lifeless amidst the ever-rising waves. It scares me to think how the warming temperatures are fueling heavier rains and higher tides. I often wonder to myself, *Do people understand the harm they cause?*

But I'm still here, strong in my roots. Even in the most vicious of hurricanes, when it feels like Momma (the supreme Mother Nature, that is, and don't you forget it) wants to shake me up like an obstinate child, I still hold strong... bending but never breaking.

You see, people these days, they don't understand that we—trees and people, the ancestors and the unborn—are intrinsically connected. Ever notice how the stamp of a person's thumb looks like the rings of a tree?

Time is not some linear thing. Life circles. We're born, die, and are reborn like the resurrection plants that grow on my moss-laden branches after a big hurricane. New life comes after the storms, and even if me and my big ol' trunk might die, I know that my acorns will live on. They'll eventually sprout new life. So, amidst the change, stand proud. Remember the lessons of your ancestors and think about those yet to come. Root down to rise up, that's what I believe.

Landslide

Catherine Chaddic

The old man was watching her, his face all wrinkles and brown spots. His eyes popped out of their sockets, filling up with blood. His face distorted. Waves of loose flesh rolled from his forehead to his chin. She knew what was coming. Desperate to run, she found out she couldn't—no legs. Sweat trickled down her spine. Hypnotized, she stared. Under her feet, the ground released a low growl. She became nauseous as if rolled on a wave. The man opened his mouth wide, too wide, a silent howl of agony. A dark, furry tongue slid out, writhing like a snake, gliding toward her. She thrust her arms forward—no arms. She yelled at the top of her voice...

Hannah sat bolt upright, clutching a handful of moist sheets, her breath loud, heart pounding. She threw her feet off the bed and dropped her head in her hands, not daring to close her eyes. She could still feel the rolling, see the tongue, smell the rot and decay.

The soft shuffle of her mother's footsteps sounded in the hall.

No, Mom, please don't come. But her mother's head was already peeking through the half-opened door, eyes wide with concern.

"You okay, love?"

"Yes, Mom, go back to bed. It's just a dream."

Her mother didn't flinch. "Are you going back to sleep?"

Hannah switched on the reading lamp and glanced at her watch on the bedside table. *Three-thirty, right on schedule. When will this ever end?* "I can't, but I'll be fine. I'll read on the couch for a while."

"I'll make you tea."

The electric light flooded the hall. Hannah listened to the comforting clang of the kettle, the water running in the sink. She dragged herself to the bathroom.

Yikes! I look awful. Hannah supported herself on the rim of the porcelain sink to study the white complexion and hollowed eyes staring back at her. She let the water run until warm before splashing her face. Even a good pat with the towel didn't bring color to her cheeks. *Who is she? Where is the bubbly college kid, anxious to share her ideas on marketing designs?* She threw the towel on the side of the tub, her hands trembling. She slipped on her plush robe, sighing with relief as she wrapped the warm woolen garment tight around her waist.

Hannah picked up her book and snuggled in the corner of the couch, both legs curled under her. She opened the novel but the words made no sense. Her mind was far away. She put the book down and, for the umpteenth time, replayed the events that had turned her life upside down.

It had started so well, only four weeks ago. She could still see the three of them, herself and her parents, sitting at the breakfast table in front of the sunny window.

"Hannah, why don't you go?"

"I have plans for spring break, Dad. I can't cancel the trip to Cancun with my friends."

"Think about it, though," her mom said. "You haven't seen your aunt for years. You would get to see your old home, sleep in your bed, run into friends maybe. It's a beautiful time of year. The apple trees will be blooming. And yes, we would like you to go. I can't take leave from school just now, and your dad is on his way to Chicago. We are concerned about Louis and Justine. There's something wrong. I feel it. He may be sick but she won't say. They avoid our calls, and when we get through, Justine sounds vague."

The idea tempted Hannah. It would be the first time she'd fly internationally on her own, which in itself was exciting. She loved her aunt and missed her. They'd been such good pals, telling each other women's secrets. Then, when Hannah was eleven, her dad packed the family, left Austria, and whisked them off half a world away to San Francisco. She'd cried for days.

"Just two years, pumpkin," Dad had said. "A great opportunity to learn English. Think of it as an experience you'll never forget." But here they still were, ten years later, in a new apartment they loved. Mom had found a good job, and she, Hannah, really enjoyed her school and friends. Mathew got engaged. There was a wedding and whispers of a baby on the way. No one was talking of going back home.

Hannah didn't think long before she agreed to go.

When she stepped off the bus, the scent of forest and freshly cut wood wafted in the air. The trip had seemed interminable. The long flight from San Francisco to Vienna, followed by a train ride that put her to sleep, and the postal bus for the last leg up the mountain.

On the bus, Hannah had come back to life. She jumped off her seat with little squeals of delight as she passed her old school, two small hamlets that shone of happiness with their sunburnt facades and colorful window boxes, and the hotel, which, surprisingly, was closed.

But there was something different and uncomfortable. She couldn't quite put her finger on it. Fewer people, maybe? Several shops out of business, and just now, the bus stopping a mile from its usual turnaround. The four passengers riding with her were putting on coats and gathering their bags.

"Excuse me," Hannah asked the lady closest to her, "why does the bus stop here?"

"This is the new terminal, miss. There's construction farther up. The road was washed away."

Hannah stood on the gravel, frowning. Did her aunt know of this change? The sun had vanished. Night was coming fast.

She surveyed her surroundings. Her face lit up as she noticed her aunt waiting next to a path, holding a horse by its bridle. *Could it be Betsy?*

"Aunt Justine?"

"Hello, my sweet girl. Come here. I didn't recognize you."

"Is this Betsy?"

"Sure is. Twenty-two now, still strong and healthy."

Hannah threw herself in her aunt's arms for a long embrace, then grabbed the horse's head with both hands. "Dear Betsy. Do you remember me?"

"She knows you all right. Listen to her." The horse was nickering softly, brushing Hannah's palm with velvet lips.

"Wow! What's in the wagon? Why all the boxes?"

"Don't worry about that. Hop on." Justine slapped the reins twice. Betsy arched her powerful shoulders and started up the hill.

Hannah forgot all fatigue. The two women regaled each other with news. The more they talked, the more they laughed, especially when broaching the topic of Mathew, Hannah's brother, the charmer forever in trouble.

"How can you get mad at this kid? He must try everything. His youth wants it all," stated Justine.

"I noticed the Alpen Rose was closed," Hannah said, changing the subject. "Shouldn't it be open in April?"

"It closed permanently two years ago. Not enough tourists."

"Really? We had so many when I lived here. The skiing frenzy during Christmas Holiday, the summer walkers. Do you remember the guides singing beer songs at the pub? They were so loud."

"All that has changed. The glacier melted. It reduced by two-thirds since you left. Many slopes have been condemned. Not enough ice to hold them. It's dangerous to walk in many places. Rocks falling, paths crumbling. As for skiing, we haven't had enough snow in the last few years. The telecabin shut down. They built a small ski lift on top of Hof Mayon, y for kids, hardly enough to bring in the tourists."

As they crested the ridge, the magnificent ancestral home came into view. Hannah gasped, taking in the massive structure with its enormous roof, the barn in the back, and the cobbled stone court below with the water trough and stables.

A loud barking greeted their arrival.

"Rollo! Is it Rollo?" Hannah wiggled with excitement.

"It's our Rollo. He was two when you left. He's my baby all right; follows me everywhere."

Hannah jumped off the wagon and ran to her dog.

"Oh, Rollo. It's me. You remember?" She tried to hug the dog, who twisted and leaped, pulling at his chain. Rollo's bark had turned to a whine. He pressed his hind parts against her, covered her face with slobber, front paws on her chest. Hannah felt tears wetting her eyes. "You good, good dog. Did you ever get over me? I love you so much."

"Hannah, go see your uncle. He's in the big room. I'll feed Betsy before we have dinner."

"Can I untie Rollo?"

"Of course. He'll stick to you the whole week, I can see that."

Sick with misery at the idea of leaving her dog after only one week, Hannah entered the kitchen, which shone in the soft electric light. It smelled of floor wax and of the apple pie she could see on the counter. She lifted the lid of a steaming pot of vegetable soup. *Humm, this will be so good.*

She stopped at the door of the great room. The man in front of her, staring at the darkening landscape, looked smaller than she remembered. His hair thin and gray. He always wore shirts of a faded blue color, with the sleeves rolled back above the elbow. A jolt of memories hit her at the sight of his bare forearms.

"Uncle Louis?"

"You shouldn't have come."

Hannah felt like she'd been slapped, her cheeks reddening from the rebuke. She'd expected him to turn around, hug her like he always did, dance a step or two.

"Uncle Louis, it's me. I just traveled a night and a day to see you. Why would you say that?"

Louis turned around slowly and looked at her, mouth stern, eyes devoid of joy. "You shouldn't have come, Hannah," he repeated, his voice serious. "This is not a good time. I told Justine to cancel your trip, but she didn't."

"Why such a bad time?" Hannah felt like stomping her foot.

Louis got up. His familiar smirk lifted a corner of his lips. "You look so pretty, Hannah. Come here, princess; give your grouchy uncle a hug."

Hannah hugged him with a mix of joy and apprehension.

"We received orders to l..." started Louis.

From the kitchen, Justine cut him short. "We'll talk about all this tomorrow. Come and eat now, and then a good night's sleep in your old bed."

Dinner had been so good, tasted full of memories. There was definitely something wrong, but it couldn't be too bad. The house looked beautiful; her uncle and aunt didn't seem sick, though Louis had aged a lot. He was more cheerful during dinner, or at least pretended to be.

It was late and she was bushed. She unlatched the bedroom window, opened it wide, gulping the cold mountain air infused with the scent of pine and lingering sweetness of apple blossoms. The duvet was a nest smelling of laundry soap and sunshine. She snuggled in its softness and fell asleep right away.

Noises invaded the depth of her slumber. Heavy steps stomping on a wooden floor. Wolves howling in the forest. And what kind of beast was screaming in the night? She couldn't see in the dark, though she thought she had opened her eyes, but she could hear. Way down in the valley, a giant howled in pain. The cry started low, a rumble, increasing until it became a crescendo, blaring and insistent, then faded only to resume three seconds later. Over and over, receding then booming. Was someone calling her name?

"Hannah, Hannah, wake up!" Hannah opened her eyes. A rush of adrenaline twisted her gut. Justine was shaking her shoulder, her face distorted by moving shadows as she brandished a flashlight. The howling was real, flooding the room. It filled Hannah with dread.

"What's going on?"

"Put on your clothes, hurry! Shoes, coat! Take your purse... passport!"

"What's going on, Auntie?"

"We must leave! Now! Hurry, Hannah! Hurry! Keep the flashlight! Meet me outside!" Justine was yelling above the insistent blaring of the siren while throwing handfuls of clothes on the bed. Hannah jumped up, hustled into her jeans, flung her feet into the Reeboks without putting on socks. Too rattled by the siren to rationalize, she thought of a fire but didn't detect the stink of smoke.

She stumbled into the dark hall, holding on to the walls to keep from falling down the steps. Outside, dawn was breaking. She made out Justine's feverish hands hitching Betsy to the wagon. She rushed over and grabbed the horse by its halter. Justine gripped the other side. Together they urged Betsy away from the house.

"Where's Louis?" Hannah screamed.

"In the stable, untethering the cows!"

Justine looked back toward the house, dread painted on her face. A floodlight blazed from the valley below, a lone beacon in the eerie landscape, brushing the slope like a windshield wiper.

"We should be safe here," Justine said, holding Betsy to a stop. " Let's wait for Louis."

The barn door stood wide open. A cow peered haltingly, hesitant to step out. Another one pushed past and galloped down the hill, bellowing all the way. Hannah could hear Louis's frustrated screams as he shooed the cattle off the stable. As the last cow cavorted over the threshold, he appeared at the door, holding himself on its frame.

A flash of fur bolted past Hannah, nearly knocking her down. Justine screamed, "No, Rollo, no!" But the German Shepherd didn't hear. He went for his master. Before he could reach the stable, a fissure sliced a vertical rift through the cobblestone yard. In an explosion of pavers and gravel, the ground opened like a gigantic mouth, swallowing the dog, the trough, and the surrounding bushes. A terrifying rumble from deep below stunned them. Louis opened his mouth but no word could be heard. The ground around them shook. Transfixed by the abomination, Hannah stared as the house seemed to take a knee for a better look at the garden. Insidious rivers of melted ice weakening the shear strength of the rich pastures finally unglued them from their rocky foundation. Gulped by the mountain, the house and barn vanished, leaving in their wake a gigantic ravine choking with tree trunks, bouncing boulders, and rivers of mud.

The last thing Hannah saw was the roof of her family's home sailing down the hill, taking with it her uncle and eleven years of her youth. Her knees buckled. Then, all went dark.

The next days had been a blur. She remembered her aunt, erect, holding a wad of cash in her hand, face flooded with tears. A man was leading Betsy away. Betsy followed, head down, for she was a horse, and horses obey.

Hannah and her aunt rode in the back of a jeep all the way to town. They passed army vehicles packed with soldiers. Twice they made way for wide flatbeds moving bulldozers. They sat in an auditorium filled with grieving people. Different speakers talked of relocation, insurance, degrading permafrost, slope instability, denudation... All Hannah wanted was to go home.

Men in uniforms asked her questions, people she didn't know squeezed her arm, patted her shoulder, brought her tea she couldn't drink. A woman gave her a phone and told her to call her parents. She heard herself say, "Mom, come get me."

When her parents arrived, the four of them attended a memorial. Justine sat stern and detached. Locked in her own cloud of grief and anger, Hannah felt lonely in a world she no longer understood.

In the living room of their San Francisco home, Hannah's mother placed a steaming mug in front of her daughter.

"I'll make another appointment with the psychologist as soon as they open. Did you take your pills?"

Hannah emerged from her reverie feeling stronger, more alive than she'd been in the last four weeks. It was time to move on.

"Yes, Mom, and no. No, I don't want another appointment, and yes, I took my pills, but I don't want any more. I'm good. I don't need them."

"Honey, you are not eating. You haven't gone to school for three weeks. You are not *good.*"

"I need time."

"How much time?" Her mother sounded exasperated. "How long will you sit here staring at nothing? If you were fine, you would be back in school."

Hannah put her mug down, stirring the liquid absentmindedly. "Mom... I don't want to go back to school. I'm so sorry, but I can't go back to advertising."

"Hannah, you love it. You were so happy, and you're so good at it."

Hannah thought for a long minute before answering. "Yes, I liked it. It was fun. But it's not me. I changed. Advertising is stupid. Drawing cats that talk, making silly jokes, coaxing people to buy things they don't need. Look at you, Mom. Every morning you come from the mailbox with a handful of glossy ads you don't even look at before you dump them in the trash. Is this what I'll do? For the rest of my life? Create tons of waste people won't even look at?" She stared at the window, witnessing the arrival of dawn. "I know I'm halfway through college. Gosh, it's so bad. You and Dad spent a lot of money. I just can't do it. I must find something else. Something... weather-related-ecology, environment, sustainability—a career that will impact our planet. Even if it's a small part. Even if I can't fix the problem, at least I won't be in denial. I'll be with people who care, those who are trying."

Her mother was watching her intently. Hannah couldn't read her expression.

"Will you help me, Mom?"

Hannah stood and walked to the window. Her mother joined her, put an arm around her. Both women looked out as the first rays of sunshine lifted the dark film over the Bay.

Leave No Trace

Lee Clontz

"Happy birthday, sweet boy," Janey sang. I loved hearing her sing to him. Toby rolled his eyes and smiled a big, toothy grin. Ten is that kind of age: innocent but learning not to be. He had a schmutz of spaghetti sauce in the corner of his mouth that Janey was forever trying to keep clean. He'd already finished his slice of gluten-free cake, and his friends from school had logged off of the birthday video call. Once again, as always, it was just the three of us.

"Thanks, Mom. Thanks, Dad," he said. "Can I go play Poké-mon now?" He held up the game, still half-wrapped in birthday paper. Janey shot me a look.

"There's one more thing for your birthday," I said. His wide blue eyes lit up. "You and I are going camping this weekend!"

"No way!" he yelled, then paused. "But what about the mosquitos?" He looked at his mother, who faked a confident smile.

"Dad has checked everything out, and there's nothing to be afraid of. There's a wall of cooler weather coming in that'll keep the buzzies away. You guys will go up on Saturday, you can sleep in a tent, hike, all kinds of great camping stuff."

"I found your no-allergen, non-meat hot dogs," I said. "We can make them over a campfire. We'll make s'mores. It's been so long since I went camping. Probably since I was a teenager."

He jumped from the table and wrapped his thin arms around my torso. "Thanks, Dad." I hugged him tight.

Saturday morning, and the kid was up and dressed at dawn, even though we weren't planning to leave until midday. He wore what he usually wore on those rare occasions when he could go outside: long sleeves tucked into thin gloves, long pants tucked into his socks. A head net around his neck and a hat with floppy flaps to protect his ears. To look at him made you sweat, but he was used to it.

He kept his distance while I rubbed DEET cream over my exposed face, ears, neck, and hands. He was deathly allergic to the stuff, which is what kept him inside most of the time—almost all the time. Waves of mosquitos had moved northward over the years, and only the vaccine against novel Zika had kept all of us from having to stay inside. He was allergic to the vaccine, too, which we found out the hard way. Six weeks in the hospital and a lifetime in front of a screen.

"I wish I could go with you guys," Janey said. I staged out the gear in the living room. She rubbed her growing belly protectively. We hadn't told Toby yet, just in case. He worried about everything, and protecting him from whatever fear we could was our last gift as parents.

I flipped my phone open and pulled up the forecast. "Weather still looks good," I said, mostly to myself. It was trending warmer than I'd hoped, and the CDC mosquito alert warnings still showed a bright yellow "medium risk" banner. It never showed green anymore. People said they were afraid to make a bad call and have outbreaks that they couldn't control, so we lived in a liminal orange band between quiet fear and overt panic.

I loaded the gear in the back of the car. The garage was sealed, but we kept a bug zapper on at all times. I checked the tray at the bottom and didn't see any carcasses and gave the all-clear. Toby hugged his mother one last time and ran for the car, jubilant. He closed the door, and it hissed like an airlock.

Janey allowed her smile to melt. "Please be careful, both of you." I hugged her tight, rubbed her stomach, and kissed her.

"It's going to be fine," I said. "He needs this. I don't think he's seen the sun in—"

"Weeks, I know."

"And with a heat wave coming up the coast, we'll all be inside next week. Next thing you know, it'll be February and hot again."

She kissed my cheek one more time. "I'll open the garage once you're in the car," she said. "Have a great time." She waved at Toby, and he waved back, already buckled safely.

She waited for me to get into the car, closed the door, and opened the garage. The seal made the sound of rubber-on-rubber, and I turned on the car. It had a full charge and noiselessly reversed out of the garage, sliding through a Velcro slit in the thin netting that surrounded our house. It sealed itself back as we straightened onto our street and departed for the campsite.

Whatever latent doubts I had about the trip evaporated as we left our neighborhood. Toby was ten but had the curiosity of a child much younger. He'd seen so little in his short life, waving at friends through screens and windows, experiencing so much through VR headsets. He laughed at the people walking their dogs under their wide-brimmed hats drooped with weighted netting down to the ground. We even saw a jogger wearing short sleeves and shorts, his legs glistening with insect repellant.

"That's *so cool,*" Toby said, pressed against the glass. "He's not wearing any netting at all!"

"Must be freshly vaccinated," I said. "They say the new shot gives you a few weeks of complete immunity. Have to take advantage while you can."

"Yeah," he said. His unasked question hung in the air, but he knew the answer. Barring an unforeseen breakthrough, precaution would always be his only defense against n-Zika.

The car hummed outside of our neighborhood, and we merged onto the highway. Autotrucks cruised past us in the dedicated lane for autonomous vehicles. I kept the car in the last remaining manual lane as the electric motors pulled us quickly to speed. Even though we didn't *need* to drive anymore, I liked the feeling of being in control.

An insect impacted the windshield in a small spray of clear liquid, and Toby jumped a bit. "What's that one?" he asked.

"Looks like some kind of water strider," I said. "Nothing to fear." The whole society had become forensic entomologists, able to identify safe bugs from mosquitos by the shape of individual body parts. Toby reflexively treated them all as potential hazards. The car's navigation system told us that we'd arrive in less than two hours. Cooling air blew on us through filtered screens.

"Nothing to fear," he said out loud and stared out the window as the world flew by in streaks of browns and grays. He rolled up his sleeves a little to show me he was brave.

The road began to ascend as we put more distance from home, and we crested the "green line," where trees still looked the way I remembered them when I was younger. Everything at sea level was so warm and humid that many varieties had been slowly dying out and replaced with more tropical varieties, but above the green line, we started to see fir and oak, trees that Toby had only seen in VR.

"Wow, look how big that one is," he said over and over. As we climbed higher, the temperature was dropping, finally down into the 80s at midday. A little warmer than I'd promised. The weather was so unpredictable anymore, though you could rarely go wrong guessing hot.

A sign that read *Uwharrie National Forest* in a friendly typeface told us where to turn onto a small gravel road, and I guided the car under the tree canopy that towered above us. The ranger station was ahead, covered in netting, and I pulled the car through a slit that sealed up behind me. An impressively sturdy woman dressed in ranger fatigues and a netted beekeeper-style hat came out of a small shack with a clipboard.

I cracked the window just enough to be respectful. I could hear Toby tense up in his seat as the fresh air entered the car. "Hi, there, ma'am," I said, "we're here for a reserved campsite. Last name of Tyler."

"I've got you down for the night, up at Arrowhead," she said. "Want to be next to the lake?"

Toby grinned and nodded vigorously. The ranger smiled back. "He looks excited," she said.

"Our first time," I said through the thin gap in the window. "What's the weather looking like?"

Every adult knew what that question meant. "It's a little warmer than the forecast, but it should be okay if you're vaccinated and you have good nets. We're not expecting mosquitos, but ..." She shrugged. "You never can tell these days."

I silently begged Toby not to tell her about his lack of vaccination. People judged, and they didn't understand, and I didn't know if she'd turn us away. He didn't respond, though, and I knew then that he was now old enough to lie by omission, a useful tactic for adulthood. "We've got good nets and a couple of Thermacells to keep any buggers away. It's his tenth birthday."

The ranger exaggerated her response to draw out a smile from Toby. "Well, then, you didn't tell me that you had a young *man* in the car. That's a different story. I'll put you in campsite 32, right on the lakefront. Should be beautiful as long as the weather down east stays put. If you hear the alarm, just seal up in your car and hunker down until it passes."

"Does that, uh, happen often?" I asked.

"It happens," she said. "Some of the mosquito breeds are getting hardier, so they stray up this way sometimes, regardless of the weather. We've got sensors for them, so just keep an ear open and the car unlocked, and y'all'll be fine."

We continued on the small dirt road, and the trees gave way to a wide expanse of dark blue water that extended the horizon. Small islands dotted the lake, exposed to lowered water levels that felt permanent. We found our campsite with the aid of a wooden sign with an engraved *32* on an elevated post. As the ranger had promised, there were bunches of fumigated wood stacked for us, with hooks hanging from the trees for mosquito netting.

"I know you're excited, but wait for me," I said to Toby as I quickly exited the car. I pulled the rolls of netting from the back of the car and put the suspended hooks through the grommets. I pulled a sleeve of netting to the car and magnetically attached it around Toby's door, creating a protective corridor.

I nodded at his bright, small face, and he gingerly opened the door. The freshness of the air stopped him for a moment. The loamy scent of the lake mixed with the warm breeze and the sound of the rustling trees in a way that immediately intoxicated him. He threw open the car door the rest of the way and ran into the covered campsite, staring at the water through the net.

"It's so beautiful!" he said, and it was.

We spent the rest of the afternoon setting up our small tent and building our campfire alongside. I showed him the skills that I'd learned as a child, how to kindle a flame and build it up. "If you throw the logs on too early, it'll never catch," I said. "You need to let it build up first."

"So *cool*," he said. I let him strike the match himself, and it was like he'd been granted the keys to a car. He singed his fingertip but pretended he didn't, and I let him learn to let hurt pass. Maybe I was teaching him too late, but I hoped not.

We only left the safety of the netting twice and briefly, once to walk down to the water to look for fish and once to pee. I worried for a moment that the child might spring away like an excited puppy, but he stayed close to my side. We kept the Thermacell humming, emitting a chemical scent that would hopefully keep stray mosquitos at bay.

The sun began to set through imposing clouds to the east, but the evening stayed warm. This was just the way it was now. Winter was warm, spring and fall were hot, summer was unbearable. Regardless of the heat, we sat close to the fire, and he made his gluten-free hot dog stabbed through with a stick. He guided a curious ant off of the stick with his finger, and I marveled that he was unafraid, even delighted. He held the creature aloft on his small finger and we sent a picture to his mother, who responded with a shocked emoji and a kissy-face.

Night fell, and the winds out of the east grew stronger. We huddled in the tent while the trees rustled around us. I had no idea how well our tent would repel water, but the stakes in the dry ground held up against the wind. I felt something heavy brush against the tent in the wind in the darkness—the netting, I suspected. We stayed in our sleeping bags, awake together in the dark, feeling the power of the wind and the trees around us. We couldn't see anything, which was probably for the best, but Toby narrated the goings-on with the intensity of his imagination. "Maybe there are bears outside," he said, even though bears hadn't been in this part of the country for years. "Maybe a moose or a camel."

"Maybe it's Yogi," I said into his ear. "Okay, Boo-Boo!" He giggled and snuggled close to me, and we both tried to sleep.

It was still mostly dark when a shrill shriek pierced the waning night. I snapped to attention with a laser focus and Toby woke right after. "What's that?" he asked, and I knew there was only one thing it could be.

"We need to go," I said.

The overnight wind had brought with it a sickening wave of humidity, and the early morning was already hotter than the previous day. I checked the weather app on my phone for the region and saw a red warning from the CDC: "nZika mosquito warning! Seek shelter immediately." The alert had been buzzing for a half-hour but I'd slept through it amid the sounds of the night.

I mumbled a profanity under my breath. "Dad, language!" Toby said, giggling.

"Sorry, buddy, we need to quickly run to the car."

"You said the s-word!" he said, laughing hysterically.

"I did, and I'm a very bad dad," I said. "C'mon, pal, we need to get to the car."

I carefully unzipped the tent and peeked out to find that the netting was knotted and askew. The wind had blown two of the grommeted connections loose and the path to the car was completely uncovered. It was only twelve feet away. "We're going to make a run for it, okay?"

"What's that sound, Dad?" he said. For a moment I assumed he meant the alarm, but he knew that sound well. There was a different sound, a low thrum, familiar and ominous. I said the s-word again, but this time he didn't laugh.

"Let's go, now!" I picked him up and wrapped him in a sleeping bag and pulled the tent's zipper wide.

I could see them in the morning sun, covering the water like a dark mist. The cloud darted in this direction and that, seeking heat and blood and hosts. We ran from the opening of the tent for the car, and the sound of the swarm grew ever louder. I reached the car and pulled the handle, but the door didn't budge. I glanced back at the tent where I knew at a moment my phone and my keys were stored and saw the dark mass of insects surrounding where we had been, attracted by us.

"Don't be afraid, buddy," I said. "Don't be afraid." I placed him on the ground and zipped the sleeping bag around his head, encasing him in the thick cushioned fabric. I hoped it would be enough.

I ran back toward the tent and was immediately beset by the swarm. They probed for a DEET-free patch of skin with an almost emergent intelligence, looking for somewhere I'd missed. I closed my eyes and reached into the tent, yanking out the remaining sleeping bag and the canister of DEET. I pulled the sleeping bag over my head and quickly fumigated the inside. I blindly fished for my keys and phone, finding only the former, and ran back to where Toby lay next to my car.

I couldn't chance opening the door because of the intensity of the swarm, so I laid on top of him, safely zipped, another barrier against the swarm. The insect repellant fumes were nauseating and intense in the damp, enclosed body humidity of the sleeping bag, and I swatted at the few remaining mosquitos trapped inside with me. I laid across the child, me in my sleeping bag and he in his, covering his body.

"Can you breathe?" I asked. "Did you get bitten?"

"Yeah, I can," he said in a muffled voice. "And no, I don't think I did."

We lay there, huddled close, separate but together, while the thick swarm probed at our bags for an egress before finally dissipating. We waited a long time before moving and a longer time still before we risked opening our bags. I unzipped mine just enough to reach out a hand and moved it to his. I unzipped the bag an inch or so and put my hand inside, abutting the zippers together to protect us. He held my sweaty hand tight, saying nothing, and we waited for a long while before emerging into the world.

Lookout Point

Benedict Joseph Amato

In practiced unison, they woke several minutes before the alarm. It was dark and still and a long way from light. She silently slipped out of bed and headed to the bathroom. He rose slowly and moved into the chilly kitchen, switching the coffee maker and oven on. He then made his way to his half bath, right outside the office.

Long Island juts into the Atlantic Ocean, over 120 miles east of New York City. It ends at a hamlet named Montauk Point. Beyond its lighthouse is the Atlantic Ocean. They lived on the north side of the Point, overlooking Fort Pond Bay, a wide harbor with three protected sides and deep water. The fourth side was a mile-wide inlet for the North Atlantic tides to flood into twice daily. This harbor is known for attracting squalls, thunderstorms, and an occasional massive hurricane. No ship could anchor there for long.

As usual, at twenty minutes before dawn, he was at his keyboard ready to hit restart. He took a gulp of just-brewed coffee but it already felt stale. The last few weeks he'd been sleepwalking through his days, diligent but emotionless. At this point, he didn't really care. He didn't even wonder if she still did. He looked out the office window that would soon show the shoreline. Even though it was the deepest of black, he could see the cold.

He put on his headset and hit return just as a red glow appeared on the horizon. The monitors on his desk came alive, and across the bay, dozens of underwater buoys began their daily scans. The array sent data to his hard drives and the cloud to be shared with the other observation posts from Maine to Key West. He sat in the dark and listened to the Atlantic Ocean waking up.

She silently slipped into the kitchen. He made sure everything was recording and joined her. They moved through their morning routine like a Russian figure-skating pair. They were precise and practiced but rigid, devoid of any expression on their face. She glided from the pantry to the refrigerator, pivoting sharply to stop at a small kitchen island. His bare feet slid from the cabinet to the counter, with silverware, plates, jam, and napkins. The oven chirped when it reached 400, just as she poured the batter into the pan. The corn muffins went in and she disappeared back into the bedroom.

He returned to his terminal, put the headset on, and called up the morning's data. The three monitors each had a bar graph, rows of changing numbers, and five small boxes along the bottom of each screen. These displayed different shades of color, from fiery red to the deepest of black. His face darkened as he looked from left to right. The project was to listen to the ocean, using sound to record its pulse. For the last three years, temperature, currents, tides, carbon dioxide, oxygen, solar energy, and the metabolic rates for dozens of species were charted and analyzed. They were taking an ultrasound on the Atlantic. The patient was sick.

The warm smell from the kitchen stirred him to take the headset off. He looked out the window to the shore, dock, and boat. Most days the boat stayed idle, but at the start of the project it was essential. And amazing. They motored out daily to place their sensors. Every tenth of a mile just off the barren shore, they added more to the array. They would dive into the cold water of the bay, twenty feet down, and anchor the listening devices. Then they would resurface to the blistering East End heat and move the boat to its next designation. The rinse and repeat of the salt water and sweat gave them the best tans of their lives. It also was the best few weeks they would ever have together. Afternoons, they would drift off the cliffs that lined the western half of the bay. Protected from the prevailing wind, they would lie on the deck and enjoy lunch, wine, the sunshine, and each other.

That part of them died when the project went live. Instead of being researchers on a mission, they became bystanders to an unfolding horror. The graphs on their monitors were steep and, over time, became dramatically worse. The colors of the status boxes began dark and deepened daily. Within a year, the answers to all of the questions were too obvious to ignore. No matter what they learned about the Atlantic, nothing could make it better. They wanted to record the heartbeat of the planet. Instead, they had the soundtrack to its demise.

Wildfires went global, darkening entire continents. The skies were burnt orange, and each breath brought coughing and burning eyes. Months without sunshine starved the ocean's algae, followed by massive dead zones dotting the Atlantic, including Fort Pond. You had to mask up just to go out to the dock. Between the stench of the rotting fish and the acidic air, it became the norm to have tears in your eyes. At least it was for them.

The tipping point was the breakup of the Arctic glaciers. Greenland melted away, its fresh water diluting the salty, dense North Atlantic. The Gulf Stream slowed, paused, and died. The stagnate ocean superheated the mid-Atlantic states. Afternoon thunderstorms battered every coastal city. Tornadoes tore through New England, making commerce along the Northeast Corridor treacherous, unpredictable, and often deadly. Half the nation went into pandemic mode with mass isolation and scarcities.

Temperatures immediately dropped by ten degrees across Europe, with global ramifications. Spring and fall became nonexistent, reduced to a boundary between the swelter of summer and a winter of bone-chilling cold. Daily, everyone's skies and lives darkened, either from smoke or massive sudden storms that would drop feet of stinging rain or very gray snow. The media hyped it as a new Ice Age, and their headlines weren't wrong. Life went into hibernation with no spring in sight.

He felt a cold breeze as she rushed by the office door. Breakfast came out of the oven, and then he heard something drop on the counter. It sounded like a coin, spun about a few times and then landed flat. Moments later came the sound of her car leaving the gravel driveway.

He looked out the window at the red morning sky.

Later, he saw her ring.

The muffins were tasteless and dry.

My Dearest Daughter

C. B. Buzz

I looked at the picture on the thin, worn paper, running my fingers over the different shades of green. It was a news clipping Dad had saved. From before. "The Colors of Nature," the headline. It was beautiful, vibrant, if now fragile from the constant wear of my fingertips. I had stared at that image for hours, memorizing every detail of the trees and sweeping meadows of wildflowers ... It was breathtaking, that image. It made me happy. But that is all that little scrap of paper was. An image ... I'd never seen trees because they were all gone, following in the footsteps of the flowers and bushes, disappearing in a flash of fire fifty years ago and more.

When I get Dad going, he rambles on about the O2 decline that followed after years of fires and the carbonization of the air. I don't really understand the technical bits, just that it's harder to breathe now than it was when my dad was my age. That doesn't stop him from trying to teach me, though. Dad is the scientist. Me? I'm just a digger. And I'm fine being a digger. I'm good at it. Dad has always said I have the nose of a mole. I guess? I've never seen one of those either, but between me and Dad ... I find the best buried treasures.

I tucked the picture back into its special inner pocket in my jacket and stowed my water after one last pull. Gloves back on, I took up my pickax. The rhythmic strike of my tool against the packed dirt and debris thudded dully in the narrow space as I resumed my digging. I know I said I didn't mind being a digger ... But some days, I just wanted to stay home and read or play cards with Dad. I hated that we had to dig so much ... But that's how we stayed alive. We dug into the collapsed infrastructure of the old world, gathering any broken but usable items and, most importantly, scrub cans. Those little cans were the shinies in the mine and meant we'd be able to breathe when the cotwo descended.

All the survivors around here are diggers, though I hadn't seen any for some time. Neighbors didn't check in on each other unless it was to see if they were dead so they could scavenge their corpses, so it wasn't that unusual.

Other places in the world? I couldn't tell you. Sometimes we heard rumors, the kind that gave us hope. Maybe we wouldn't always have to live like this. Maybe it could get better ... Maybe we could reach the new settlements to the east, the ones with domes, clean air. *Plants* ...

The sound of rusted metal beams groaning above me brought me back to Earth, to my body. My tunnel. *Crap* ... I'd been daydreaming again. Dad was always warning me to keep my head out of the clouds ... I looked up, surveying the rusted beam that ran the length of the ceiling. I was following it deeper into the building, using it and all the cross members that stretched out from it as a support. They were like the ribs of some great beast, and I was carving it up for dinner. Only there wasn't any meat inside, just dirt, broken equipment.

I knelt silently, keeping my breath steady as I listened to the mountain of scree above me. I was at least ten meters down. The thought that a huge mountain of dirt sat between me and the sky had never bothered me. Nor the fact that one wrong stab of my ax would spell out my tomb. Fear leads to panic, and panic could mean death. Fear was a killer not welcome in my tunnels. Today though ... It crept in when I wasn't looking ...

As I made ready to continue digging, the shine of something promising caught my eye. I scraped away the dirt around it, sitting back on my heels with a gasp. Wedged between an upright support and a mass of shattered concrete, a large crate with silver cans inside stared out at me. It was scrub ... A *whole pack* of scrub. Giddy with excitement, I found a place to wedge in my pickax and torqued on the handle. Chunks of concrete fell away from the wall. I scooped them to the side of the tunnel where an esker of dirt and debris was starting to pile up. I'd have to take a break soon and start clearing out my progress before I went much deeper.

But first the scrub ...

With the light finally in sight, I surged out of the mouth of my tunnel, sprawling across the ground as I gasped in lungfuls of air. Tears stung my cheeks. I'd almost died, almost been buried alive. The box of scrub ... I tried to get it out, and I'd almost died. How ironic, the thing that kept me alive out here had almost killed me ...

"HEY!" I heard the shout from across the pit and felt a fresh wave of tears flood my cheeks.

"Daaad!" I wailed, suddenly in need of comfort, in need of protective arms wrapping themselves around me. I struggled to my knees, gasping for air but still feeling empty. Dad was running across the pit.

"Are you okay?"

"No ..." I sobbed again, running through the events in my head. I'd gotten out the scrub, went for it, but then I felt the rush of dirt as it fell over me, the pressure immense as it started to pile up on my body. Then the frantic panic squeezing my chest as I tried to escape ... Every wrong move I'd made was playing on a loop.

"What happened?" Dad skidded on his knees the last few feet, pulling me into one of his bear hugs.

"A whole box, Dad ... A whole box. But the tunnel ...! I almost didn't make it out ..." Tears blurred my vision.

"But you did! You did ... You made it out. It's okay, it's okay ..." Dad kissed the top of my head, started rocking me back and forth, "Say woebell ..."

"Dad! I'm not three years old!" I laughed, suddenly feeling better.

"Please ... I still say it when I stub my toe. It works!" He pushed me away, smiling down at me.

"Yeah ... Maybe it does ..." I smiled back as I took a deep breath. I did feel better ... Maybe it was just him holding me, rooting me back to the plane of the living. I took another deep, shuddering breath and just let myself ... Be ... For a moment.

"It's still down there ..." I whispered.

"Leave it. It's not worth the risk," Dad shot back like he was ready for me to say it.

I smiled against his coat, not even minding the harsh chemical scent that had built up on it. I was about to tell him we needed to clean our gear before we went out again when I heard it, the shrill sound of the siren, the one on Dad's shoulder strap that said, *Hey, better have a mask cause you're about to be out of oh two.*

"Cotwo storm ..." Dad murmured against my dirty hair. "Get your mask on."

I pulled the mask out of my bag, placing it over my face as I checked the seal and tightened the straps. We shouldn't have been out this long ... But it seemed both Dad and I had gotten caught up in what we were doing, forgetting the threat. I pulled a scrub can out of my bag, frowning at the yellowing indicator on the bottom, and clipped it into the mask's receptacle. I went for my spare when I remembered. I hadn't brought one ... There were so few cans of scrub left at home ... I'd thought we would be well on our way home by now, that I had enough left in the last can I'd used ...

I pulled my tools together, shouldering my pack as Dad jogged back for his gear.

I have to tell him ...

I could already hear his voice, low and rumbling, as he admonished me for not bringing another.

"I'm in the yellow and ... I forgot a spare." It's a half-lie.

He looks at me for a moment. Then ...

"Time to go."

But I hold his dark brown eyes with mine. Dad's are tight behind the circular windows of his mask. He looks worried? Me too. We stand there a moment, wasting our scrubs, 'til the urgency to move returns. Before I manage to turn and pull him with me, Dad's eyes change. They lose the tightness and brighten; I can see his smile in them. He rummages in the sack on his side and pulls out a can of scrub. Hands it to me. His spare.

I take it, brow furrowing.

"You'll need this if you run out." My voice is quiet, muffled, and rubbery behind the mask. It's enough to get my point across.

Dad just looks at me and shakes his head. He pulls the satchel slung across his back around to his front and opens the top, rummaging inside it. He pulls up a can of scrub. It's battered and looks like it's seen better days, but it's a can. Relief instantly floods through me. He brought a spare. *Two* spares ...

Dad always says to be prepared for any eventuality. I do my best to remember, but at the same time ... I struggle with the reality of our situation. Scrub cans are hard to find, let alone the supplies to make them. That can today was the luckiest I'd gotten in months ... I could have brought a spare today, lived to make it home if Dad hadn't been here to back me up. But what happened then? With our supply dwindling? Did we just die when we ran out?

Unsettled, I pocketed the can Dad gave me, determined to redline the one connected to my mask before I switched. It was a dangerous move but I wasn't about to waste more scrub than I needed to. Plus, I had experience with hypoxia. I could manage. I hugged Dad then, squeezing my arms tight around his bulky coat. I couldn't feel his warmth like I usually could, but that didn't matter. A hug was a hug. I pulled away and grabbed him by the arm, leading him to the edge of the refuse crater and the ladder out of the pit.

I tried to walk at a measured pace, that place where maximum speed met minimal oxygen. It wasn't long before my feet began to eat up the ground between us and home, Dad's too, as he kept pace next to me. I made sure to check my can regularly, taking a deep breath and holding it as I unclipped it to check the status through the window on the bottom. When it hit red, I kept walking 'til the toes of my feet started to catch on rocks that weren't there. With numbing fingers, I swapped cans and suppressed the desire to gasp in huge lungfuls of air as oxygen graced my blood.

I didn't notice at first when Dad stumbled, fell to the ground. I didn't see his knees scrape across the rubble as his legs collapsed, hands outstretched to catch the brunt of the fall. Didn't see him shoulder into the dirt. It took me longer than it should have to notice he wasn't next to me anymore.

"Dad?" I spun on my heel when I caught sight of him, nearly falling over my own feet as I hastened to his side, his breathing labored.

"Dad, what's wrong?" I ask him, pebbles stabbing at my knees as I slid to his side and helped him to his back.

What's wrong?

I check his mask, confirming a good seal. Dad's curly black beard always got in the way but it didn't look like it was causing a problem. I cinched the straps anyways and twisted the can on his mask, making sure it was sealed tight. It was. But then I noticed the red in the window on the end of the canister, just like mine, the one that shows you via chemical saturation how much scrub is left.

His is bright red.

"*Dad!*"I pulled the shoulder bag out from under his body and found inside the can he'd shown me earlier, "Deep breath!" I shouted as I counted to three and unscrewed the empty one from his mask before replacing it with the fresh scrub.

"It's in ... Breathe, Dad, breathe!" I pulled his face over to look at me. Glassy eyes stared back.

"I know you ..."

"Of course you do, Dad. Just breathe. Breathe."

"Breathe ... Okay. I'll breathe. I'm ... I'm breathing." He still didn't sound right ...

"Dad -"

"She's pretty, isn't she?"

"Who?"

"Our daughter. I bet you she grows up lookin' like you."

"Dad, what are you saying?" I shook him, like that would help. "There must be a leak in your mask!" I checked his gear again. But everything was sealed, even the can, the little window showing a neutral off-white color.

"Blue ... Blue square ... Blue squares under the bed. The blues go to the circles ..."

"Dad, look at me!" I cried, shaking him again. He did, but his eyes weren't focusing on me. He was looking straight through me.

"Love you ...! Love you ... Bee, there ... Climbing a tree ..."

I staggered back to the house, alone, following the bright blue ribbons whipping about in the dusty wind. The empty can and its faulty indicator clutched tight in my fist ...

The cotwo storm passed a day later. I'd gone through another can of scrub as I lay there, barely moving, barely breathing. *Numb.* I'd used the techniques Dad had taught me to lower my heart rate. When the cotwo meter quietly chirping away under a pile of clothes finally went quiet, I pulled off my mask and pulled myself out of bed.

My gear went on slowly, arms and legs dead with fatigue and weighed down with loss. I had to go back and take care of Dad. I couldn't just leave him there. But also ... I needed his gear. The survival instinct kicking in made me sick to my stomach. If I'd bothered to eat anything, I'd have thrown up.

I grabbed the meter, stuck its Velcro case to my chest, and stuffed my mask in a bag. It had a few hours left on the can and I doubted I'd need more than that. As I opened the door, inhaling the cocktail of chemicals in the air and the remnants of the cotwo storm, I stopped, reconsidering. Dad died because of this. Because of me ... I walked back into the house, pulled open the supply cupboard, and opened the scrub can box.

"I hate you ..." I whispered to them.

But the lifeless hunks of metal didn't say anything back. They sat there, mocking me, lips curling with their indifference to my existence. Maybe they were talking ... whispering to me the silent truth ... "Use me. Or not. You are still going to die. Just like him ..."

Tears burnt across my cheeks as I took one of the remaining five scrub cans inside. I shut the box, covered their faces, put them away. I couldn't look anymore at their accusing stares.

I'd taken the essentials back to the house first in case a cotwo spike hit. I was lucky, though, and easily recovered

Dad's supplies. It'd taken the better part of the day to bury him in a nearby mound of debris. It wasn't his favorite spot, just convenient. The macabre conversations we'd had late at night had come back to me as I dragged his corpse away. "Don't expend energy on me if I die. I won't for you."

I'd buried him anyways, then gone home, wrapped myself in his coat, and wept.

The next day, I washed it. But as I emptied the pockets I found a letter hidden inside.

I found myself on my knees, looking at a box I'd found under Dad's bed with a square blue note stuck to the top.

-For my daughter,
Love Dad-

I opened the box.

Scrub cans ...

My Dearest Daughter,

I love you. You are my everything.

If you are reading this, you're either snooping in my things again ... Or I am dead. I dare say it is the latter ... I am sorry that I had to leave you ... I wish it could have been different, that I could have been there for you longer.

The point of this letter is to tell you ... that is, in case something happens to me before I have time to ... My daughter, I would do anything for you and have. As much as I can, though even that may not be enough. I lied to you. And for that I am sorry. But I wanted you to live and I believed this was the best way to make that happen.

The diggers are gone. We are all that is left. The others are either dead or moved on. Cotwo storms have gotten worse; I'm sure you've noticed. Cans are in short supply as is food. We have had to take even more risks to survive these past months, digging deeper than is safe. We can't stay here forever.

Still, even with the extra box of cans I've been saving, even with the survival tent and food stores I've been hoarding ... We can't go together. It won't be enough. So I've taken steps to ensure your survival, steps to take myself out of the equation. I had planned to tell you myself, hold you one last time, kiss the top of your head and tell you it's going to be ok. But it seems best laid plans ... I know it's going to be tough for you without my constant nagging ... But I know you'll be ok.

Now go to the domes. And, be adequate.

I love you,

Dad

Noah's Great Rainbow

A. A. Rubin (Gold Medal Winner)

Before I start, I think about the soot, the soot which saved our lives, the soot which stole our souls. I sit and contemplate the dusky particles we shot into the atmosphere to deflect the sun's light and cool the planet by obfuscating the sky.

Temperatures are no longer rising. The ice caps have stopped melting. But humanity has ceased to dream. How can we strive for the stars when we cannot see them? What does it mean to reach for the sky when the heavens are so close and so gray? How does a generation born in eternal twilight strive for a new dawn?

They called it geoengineering: dimming the sun with stratospheric aerosol injection.It was originally supposed to be a gas injected into the atmosphere to reflect a portion of the sun's rays back into space, but over time it became particles, particles to mimic a volcano's eruption, ever bigger and ever darker with each test, as we raced against time—against the burning earth and the rising seas—to save ourselves from the coming Armageddon. Colloquially, however, it came to be known as "the soot," as we joked that the only way we could stop the effects of our pollution was to further sully the sky.

The soot was supposed to be temporary, a stopgap until we could slow our carbon emissions, but once our immediate existential crisis was averted, we lost focus, and the soot remained, a constant reminder of our failure to change, generation after generation.

Our ancestors used to escape to the outdoors. They ran to climb mountains and looked toward the horizon for inspiration, but all that's on our horizon is dull and gray. Dawn's rose-red fingers have been gloved in soot, and there are no more sunsets to ride off into, which must be why we have so few contemporary heroes. Now we stay inside, avoiding our bleak sky and our bleaker future.

We try to fool ourselves, but our attempts are flawed. We experience the outdoors by looking at paintings in old museums. We imagine the cobalt blues of Monet's French countryside, the pale blues of Frieda Kahlo's Mexico, or the ultramarine firmament above the Raphael's virgin mother are our own, but we cannot commit to the escape, for we, like the canvases, are trapped in our frame. Conscious of our boundaries, we resign ourselves to a world created by our own mistakes.

Unable to look forward, we seek answers in the past. We return to the old masters, those who strove for—and who achieved—greatness in a time that seems so long ago. It is a useless nostalgia, but it keeps me employed.

I am a painter. I have some talent, but it is more for mimicry than for originality. Luckily, mimesis is in style these days. Our contemporary masters starve. Their art is too depressing.

The town has commissioned me to emulate Michelangelo, to fresco the ceiling of the communal hall, to depict the heavens we once knew, the skies of our ancestors that lifted us up, that gave us hope. Though my work may not have the infinite grandeur of unsullied nature, I imagine vainly that, perhaps, it will inspire us to strive once again.

As I climb the scaffolding, I imagine I am ascending to heaven on Jacob's ladder. God is dead—or at least indifferent to our plight—but in his absence, are we not gods? Did we not first doom our planet and then save it from that destruction with a plan of our own design? If we are limited, it is only by our own lack of vision. *The fault, dear Brutus, is not in the stars but in ourselves that we are underlings.* Why must we *peep about to find ourselves dishonorable graves?*

I ascend the rungs, thinking about my models. I scan my memory and my education, reviewing Rembrandt, El Greco, Van Gogh, Rivera, and Matisse. What colors most inspire? What forms speak to the soul?

I reach my platform and mix my hues on my palette. The swirling shades compose my materials out of chaos. I take a deep breath and begin to create. I drag my brush across the white plaster, a first azure stroke, and begin painting a sky I've never known.

I mix the white with the blue, one color on each side of my brush, pulling the pigment across the ceiling to create the illusion of motion, the illusion of windswept clouds on a crisp autumn day.

Ah! Those halcyon days before the long summer, those days of chill and breeze, those days of changing seasons, those days of different habitable zones, different climates, both tropic and temperate, across the face of the globe, those days before our scientists homogenized the atmosphere with the soot, dulling the variance between both regions and seasons, to make it easier to regulate our precious remaining ice caps.

The heat is getting to me, not only in the figurative sense but in the literal as well. Hanging from ladders and scaffolding, stretching my arm to its limit with every brush stroke to create the illusion of motion strains my muscles, and the stuffy air in this poorly ventilated old stone dome doesn't help. I wipe the sweat, by which I earn my daily bread, from my brow with my sleeve and descend back down to the floor. I open the door, hoping to conjure that breeze from my memory, hoping for respite for my aching muscles and for my tortured mind, but the breeze these days blows harshly, hot and dirty, with the occasional stray piece of that damned soot strafing the eyes and the heart like a rebellious, fluttering angel fallen from heaven, descending down on dark wings.

I lie on my back, gazing up at my creation. I consider the totality of the piece, the depth and distance, the verisimilitude, the verity. It is some of my best work, but I must admit it falls short of my purpose. In my effort to reach for the sublime, I have become a Romantic. My skies have too much Casper David Friedrich in them, too much gray mixed in with the blue, too much danger, too much of the hint of storm creeping in from the edges of the composition. The power of the divine is there, which may have been effective in his time, but that power is neutered now, neutered by our own actions, actions which brought the end times down upon us in fires and flood, then saved us from annihilation at the last possible moment. Are we not masters of the Earth? Is this not the Earth which we deserve?

No! The Romantic spirit is gone. Everyone now knows the power of nature. The mystery is gone and with it, the magic.

Still, I cannot start over. Resources are scarce, the land has not recovered from the floods and the fires, and paint is considered a luxury item. My ceiling is large, and neither myself nor the municipality can afford the supplies for me to begin again.

As I lie on my back, my mind wanders. I think of the soot, and I think of the sky. I see my freshly painted white clouds darken and swell with foreboding rain. I close my eyes to clear my head and to meditate on how to save my composition, but still my mind wanders. I see the papers with their columns written by the scientists which warned us of the coming Armageddon, columns which prophesized Cassandra's utterances to an unbelieving public.

I try to clear my mind again and bring it back to my present predicament. If I can't move beyond the past myself, then how can I expect that of my audience? I think about my clouds, swelling with rain. I think about my remaining paint, my references, my education, but before I can seriously contemplate the issue at hand, my mind, perhaps influenced by the paint fumes, drifts into another daydream.

I see the first drops of rain fall from my newly painted clouds and imagine that I'm Noah building his ark. I collect the animals, two by two, and shut myself in from the world. After 40 days and 40 nights, I open a window and send out the dove, but instead of soaring through the unsullied sky of renewed creation, the bird of peace chokes on the soot and falls down dead into the water that still covers the coasts not only of our shrunken continent but on all the others as well.

The image of the soot breaks my reverie, and I return to a reality where the waters of destruction did not fall from heaven but rose from the sea with the melting ice caps, a reality where the hellfire was not reserved for the afterlife, but, instead, scourged us for our sins of hubris and incompetence in this life, burning wildfires across our forests from California to Australia to the Amazon, visiting the punishment on our children and our children's children in this world, not the next, for generations to come.

We did not need gods to destroy us. We did it ourselves. But we saved ourselves with the soot, too, though we seem to have forgotten that fact. With renewed purpose—and with Noah still on my mind—I climb my ladder, my stairway to heaven, ready to show the world a sign to help it remember.

I dip my brush in the paint and draw a fiery red arc across the sky in the parting between the clouds. I texture the red like those flames which burned our forests, integrating the reminiscence of our greatest crisis into my vision of hope.

Next, I mix red and yellow, searching for the perfect shade of orange, the orange of chimeric sunsets which I've only seen in photographs, sunsets whose brilliance belied the pollution which fueled them. I streak paint subtly, blending tints and hues, and draw some of the red flames from the arc above it down into the orange to enhance the parallel.

Luckily, I have reserved some pure yellow for the next arc, which depicts the yellow of the sun at midday, our closest star which beat down on the people of Earth ever more brightly and ever more intensely until we obfuscated its heat and its glow with the soot we sent up into the sky. The sun, which for generations was a sign of life and hope, our source of energy and life, which, through our greed and carelessness, heated our atmosphere and boiled our oceans like Dante's rill, melting the ice caps and flooding the coasts, sending the remnants of humanity inland and toward higher ground. How fitting, then, that I paint its arc above the green one, the green of tide and sea, the green of typhoon and flood, the green paint swirling like Charybdis, drawing us down, inevitably, toward our doom.

The floodwaters settled, reflecting the still blue sky, similar but darker, sullied by the earth which it dredged up from the earth, foreshadowing the soot, foreboding the gray. I dull my blue paint slightly, tinting it a shade darker to differentiate it from the azure of my sky, and trace the next semicircle across my domed plane.

Truthfully, though, that sky was seldom seen in the years after the great floods. The temperatures in the day were oppressive, and humanity became nocturnal out of necessity, contrary to its nature, living in the relative cool of the dark while learning to sleep through the sun-drenched heat.

At the midnight hour, our scientists worked tirelessly to avert our destruction, and they launched the fateful rocket at the witching hour into the indigo sky, complete with a strange brew of dust and chemicals designed to reflect the sun's rays back into the blackness of space, cooling the atmosphere and ensuring our survival. I speckle the indigo arc with white stars, pinpricks of light, ubiquitous then, but which no longer pierce the firmament since that fateful day.

On that night, the sky blazed purple briefly, exploding out from the rocket as it reached its apex, filling the heavens with a brilliant light that belied the coming darkness, a light of ancient royalty and riches, a violet light of creation with which we remade our world.

I descend the ladder and take in what I have painted. I hope that, like Noah's rainbow, it will become a sign of a new covenant, not a covenant between god and humanity, but between humanity and itself, a sign, like the one in the Biblical story, *that we will see and that we will remember,* a promise to never bring our world to the brink of destruction—through fire or through flood—nor through any other human-made means, ever again.

The soot and fog may have dulled the sky, but why should it sully our souls? Sure, we are bounded by the earth, but was this not always the case? We've never traveled beyond our own moon, never established colonies either there or on Mars.

Maybe we can no longer dream of paradise beyond the heavens, but we can still work on transforming our own planet into the utopia we seek. After all, before we cooled our earth, we had to cool our temperaments. Already in the first decades of the century countries shared their scientific knowledge. The research into geoengineering occurred throughout the world. The launch took place under United Nations colors.

For a brief moment, the critical exigency of our situation brought us together. For a brief time, we were united, one people, one species working to avert disaster. In that brief moment, we achieved greatness. That moment, however, did not last. Without the threat of disaster, we retreated back to our now-smaller corners of the world and went on living our lives, our heads hanging with sorrow and regret.

Hours later, the people come in. I have covered my work with a tarp, hiding it before my big reveal so that everyone in the community will see it at once. I climb my ladder once again, not of necessity this time, but so as to gain a vantage point from which I can observe the public's reaction to my piece.

I give the signal, and someone pulls the rope. I watch the people's upraised eyes, hoping they really are windows to the soul. The smiles light the room with a pre-soot sparkle, showing me that their hearts, indeed, *leap up when they behold a rainbow in the sky.*

I delight in my success, but only briefly. Though my work has inspired, others must figure out what to do with that spark of inspiration. The journey back toward hope and progress will be long, and others, both within our small community and beyond, must fan the flames of our ambition once again. Still, it is something, and that is better than what we had before.

Planet Suite

Martin Phillips

I

Lat. 48°12'59"N Long. 4°04'10"W

Dominic Kermoal was the fourth generation of his family to bake patisserie in the little shop on the quay at Port Launay. Kouign-Amman was the Kermoal specialty, a type of Breton cake once memorably described by the *New York Times* as "the fattiest pastry in all Europe." Every morning at five o'clock, Dominic got up, put on his heavy canvas apron, and began layering butter and sugar into the bread dough, which he then fashioned into round cakes with a diameter of 20 centimeters. When the oven was up to temperature, he'd slowly bake them until the sugar caramelized and the butter expanded the mix into sticky layers. Only once the signature delicacy was finished did he turn to the less demanding fare: the croissant, the pain au raisin, the Far Breton, the supporting cast to the main event in the display cabinet out front. Prominently placed on the wall behind the counter was the certificate confirming that in 2013, Patisserie Kermoal had created the best Kouign-amman in Brittany.

For Dominic, there was something elemental about his daily ritual. In the quiet early morning, as his fingers worked the mix on his wooden board, he sometimes imagined his great-grandfather doing precisely the same thing. As each batch was baked, he'd carry the finished pastries out and arrange them in the glass-fronted cabinet, every row in perfect symmetry as befitted works of art. If the mist had risen from the river, he'd gaze out at the huge oak tree on the opposite bank of the River Aulne, hoping to catch sight of the heron blundering out of its nest of twigs and descending to stand motionless in the shallows, waiting for its prey.

His was one of the few trades which had remained unchanged for 150 years. The rhythms and rituals of the farms which worked the soil of the hills along the valley were still governed by the seasons and mostly worked by the same families who had owned their land for centuries. But the Hichers, the Roperts, and the other farmers had long since replaced their horse plows and threshers with tractors and an ever more advanced array of sprayers, spreaders, and drills. Harvest, once the center of the commune's annual cycle, involving everyone, including the children, was now rushed through in a day or two by gargantuan combine harvesters.

Like farming methods, Port Launay had changed almost beyond recognition since Patisserie Kermoal first opened its doors in 1872. A straggle of thirty houses nestled between the River Aulne and the fifty-meter cliff, which was so close to the backs of the houses that they had no courtyard or garden. Strategically placed in the tidal reach, where the Aulne doubled as the Nantes-Brest canal, the little town was the main hub for the distribution of sand dug from local quarries. This trade survived until the 1930s. Barges, laden with their cargo, lumbered into berths. Huge heaps of sand, high enough to block the view of the river from the houses, awaited despatch as a crop growing agent to the farms or for use in construction. Lorries thronged the cobbled quayside.

Dominic's father, Loïc, lived through the darkest days: the Nazi occupation. A section of cobbles just outside the shop was left uncovered when the quay was tarmacked in the '60s. It was the spot where three resistance fighters had been executed by the Germans, in full view of the townsfolk. The war killed the sand trade, too. The population, which had been

1,200 in 1872, had dwindled to little more than 400 by the time of the liberation in August 1944.

These days, Patisserie Kermoal was the only remaining shop on the quay. As old people died and young people left for jobs and more exciting life in the cities, houses along the waterfront stayed empty and decaying.

Floods in Port Launay were, quite literally, once-in-a-generation events. Every thirty or forty years, the Aulne would gradually rise, creep slowly across the road, and flow into the houses of those who hadn't adequately sandbagged their doors. People mopped up, dried their furniture, and life returned to normal. But three inundations in six years was something altogether different. The insurance covered the replacement of all Dominic's equipment and the redecoration after the first time it happened, though to get proper cover back in place, his premium more than doubled. They paid out again for flood number two—but after that, his insurers wouldn't offer him a policy. From then on, every time a hard rain fell, his chest tightened and a dull ache throbbed in his temple.

The final storm blew in overnight on Monday. The meteo issued warnings, so Dominic sandbagged the shop door to a height of half a meter. By dawn, the sandbags were just managing to keep the river at bay. The final breach of Patisserie Kermoal's flimsy defence came at 0950. And then the levels rose so quickly that there was nothing to do but retreat into the apartment over the shop and watch out of the window as the river flowed in below. At its height, the level topped out more than a meter above the previous record. The shop was filled to the ceiling and the muddy slop had started to climb the stairs.

It was midmorning on Tuesday before the water finally receded and Dominic was able to survey the damage. The main display cabinet had been swept outside, smashing through the plate glass window and ending up beached in the middle of the road. Out the back, both fridges were upended. One had toppled onto its back and was now a trough filled with watery mud. All flat surfaces—not just the floor but every shelf—were slathered with a layer of silt two or three centimeters deep.

As he stood in the sludge, Dominic knew this was the end. With no insurance, he would never afford the cost of setting up again. A century and a half of baking the croissant, the pain au raisin, the Far Breton, and the best Kouign-amman in the whole of Brittany was over.

II

Lat. 41°49'36"N Long. 122°0'19"W

Patti stood in the center of the living room floor. She stared at the fireplace that Hank had built himself from rocks carried up from the river. He'd crafted them with his stone chisel and hammer to produce sturdy, irregular-shaped blocks of sandstone. The chimney stack above it was built from ordinary red house brick. Both the sandstone and the house bricks were now blackened by the intense heat and smoke of the fire.

The town clung to the foot of the mountain, looking down onto Rock Chute Creek, close to the border with Oregon. It was much like any other small-town American settlement: Main Street with a drug store, general store, bank, diner, schoolhouse, gas station, church. The town sign, just as you turned off Route 69, claimed an optimistic Population 564. Everyone agreed it was less than that. Jobs on the railroad had gone, and the sawmill closed. Like most of the folk who were left, Patti and Hank Roberts had both been born here and had roots too deep to pull up. They'd known their neighbors, Chuck and Julie Keble, since they all went to school together. Marvin McKinley's great-grandpa was a founding father of the town. The old boy had cleared a space in the forest, set up home and a logging business. Marvin always said the place should be called McKinleytown, only half joking. But now all their kids had moved away; a few to Eureka or Reno, but most to San Francisco. A regular topic of neighborly chat on the Keble's porch of an evening was whether the town was dying.

Summers were always hot, but never as hot as the one that started it all. When the temperature topped 119°F for the third day in a row, Hank told those on the porch that night that they were making history.

"Warmest place in the country three days in a row!"

Everything was tinder dry. Though they never proved it, most of the townsfolk thought it was a spark from a train that set off the brushwood down by the railroad. Certainly, Patti first spotted it near the tracks by the bridge over the freeway. She was driving back from the big Walmart down the valley. As she rounded the final bend and the town appeared, she saw the thick column of black smoke.

By the time she reached the underpass beyond the gas station, the sun was already being filtered through a blanket of smoke. As she neared home, she met Hank running toward her. He leaped straight into the cab, shouting, "Go! Back over the river!" She wrenched the truck through a U-turn, tires spraying loose gravel, and headed at speed back to the creek, over the bridge and pulled up on the far bank. They got out and gazed at the roiling smoke and flames which now engulfed the whole town. They put their arms around each other and stood in silence.

The day after it was all over, the press and TV turned up to eavesdrop on the disaster. "Seems weird," Chuck told one of the American network crews, "but it was the sight of that great old sequoia tree slowly keeling over and crashing into a heap of sparks that set me weeping. That tree had stood in the center of town since the McKinleys set things up. It going down sorta seemed like a symbol for the whole darn disaster."

"It spread so fast it was all any of us could do to get across the river to be safe," Julie chipped in. "The howl of the wind is what really spooked me. Normal times, flames from fires go upwards. These ones was horizontal. The whole town was a blizzard of smoke and embers. When it really got going, it was like the whole place was exploding. Every aerosol can in every home was blowing. Then it was the compressors in the fridges. The really big bangs were the bottled gas cylinders. You could see great chunks of metal flying about. Armageddon."

After a few days, the news people lost interest. Even before the embers had fully cooled, they'd moved on to other disasters and scandals.

"It ain't easy," Hank told the one crew who did turn up a month later to see how they were all coping. "We're left here just sitting in our motel room moping. On our porch of an evening we'd often talk about whether this place was dying. I guess it really has now."

The camera operator framed one final shot for the end of their package. He stood Patti in the middle of her living room floor, looking at Hank's fireplace. Starting in close, he slowly pulled out to reveal the twisted, blackened metal and ash, which were the sole remains of their home.

III

Lat. 15°7'0"N Long. 3°29'40"W

A solitary figure dressed in a long brown canvas robe stood just outside the settlement. A gentle gust of wind disturbed the sand in front of him. It spiraled briefly into the air and then settled. Sand had drifted into waist-deep piles along the left-hand side of the little road that led into the village. The mudbrick walls of the houses had mostly shed their daubed mud render, revealing the block work beneath. The walls and the sand were identical in color: a baked beige. The pale blue paint of the shutters and the wooden doors, some jammed open by the drifts, offered the only contrasting hue. Keida Kater picked his way through the sand, occasionally peering into one of the deserted homes of the village he'd been born in sixty-two years before. He made the pilgrimage to the site once a year on the anniversary of the final migration.

The problems in Keida's region of northern Mali had started with the droughts of the 1970s. For centuries, the river had flowed strongly, and the great lake was so deep in the center that his mother had warned him not to venture far from the shore. But then the rains stopped. The river slowed. Now, it wasn't the lake that held the danger. "The Sahara is coming to swallow us up," his father had told him.

The encroachment was slow. At first, as the lake shrank, the villagers were pleased with the new fertile silt round the edges in which they grew crops of millet and onions. But in the '80s, more droughts pushed nomadic herders south to graze their animals close to the village. The vegetation cover dwindled and the soil was trampled. The wind stripped the surface, blowing the sand into great dunes. They tried making fences to stop the Sahara's march, but the dunes soon swallowed them. By Keida's fiftieth birthday, there was no lake and the riverbed was dry all year around. But it was when the well finally dried up that they knew it was over.

Keida slumped down with his back against the wall of a house close to the center of the village and began to mine his memories of how things used to be.

Around its edges, four huge baobab trees watched over the settlement. Lassine Koné, the village elder, said the large one on the eastern side was 2,000 years old. Standing nearly 100 feet tall, the baobab trees were sacred and magical. Most days between October and June, the villagers harvested the leaves, boiled and ate them. They pulped the tree's edible fruit, monkey bread, and munched it raw, preserved it in jam, or roasted and ground it to make a coffee-like substance. The bark was stripped and pounded, the fibers making everything from twine, mats, and baskets to paper and cloth. Like so many settlements across the Sahel, the baobab tree was their Tree of Life.

One of Keida's earliest memories was Lassine Koné's funeral. Keida was seven. The old man's body was wrapped in a shroud and laid on the ritual stage beside the well, ready for the journey to the spirit world. Masks and costumes were taken from storage and given to the women of the village to check and repair, ready for the celebration. The traditional headdress of his village was a long black fabric hood decorated with kauri shells, some braided into tassels while others were sewn into two skull-like eyeholes. A billowing skirt of baobab twine, dyed turquoise, pink and gray, formed each dancer's plumage. The performers emerged from their houses to process through the village when summoned by the drumbeat. Hopping, swaying, and stamping their feet to the rhythm laid down by the djembes, they chanted their incantation, leading the soul of the departed to its final resting place.

Twice in his life, Keida had been granted the privilege of dancing, an honor bestowed by the headman on those exhibiting exemplary moral values. It remained Keida's highest social achievement.

As he turned to go, a single sandgrouse fluttered down onto the rim of the well. Its head twitched and dipped, but sensing no water, it quickly flitted on its way.

The engine of the hired Landcruiser roared with effort as Keida drove it along the loose sand track on the way back to his dwelling in Sanga. The one which he would never call home. "Life is a lot easier," people said. These were the people who liked the fact that they could buy everything from toilet paper to cornflakes, Castel beer to Lipton's tea bags from Koussayer et Fils: Alimentation Moderne. No more hauling buckets of water from the well now that Mohammed Koussayer could sell you 5-liter bottles of eau minérale naturelle. A truck collected the produce they grew on their cultivated strips at the edge of town, paid them a fair price, and took it into the bigger market at Mopti. And best of all, Sanga was a tourist gateway to the great escarpment of Bandiagara. Carved figurines and masks, woven bags and traditional fabric, which back in the village would have been sold cheaply to unscrupulous traders from Bamako, now fetched five times the price in direct sales to the wealthy Europeans passing through to tick off "tribal dances of the Dogon" from their list of things to see before they died.

"Life is good, Keida Kater!" his friend Boubakar would chide him when he began one of his many morose lamentations about the days before the desert swallowed their village.

"My spirit doesn't agree, Boubakar Guindo," he'd reply, as he tamped tobacco into his pipe.

At least no one had suggested that they reenact the funeral dance to amuse the tourists. Keida was proud that his people had only ever enacted the ceremony for its sacred function—to honor the dead. And he would always have an unspoiled memory of the final time he had seen the black hoods with the kauri shells and the billowing layers of turquoise, pink, and gray vibrating to the beat of the djembe. On the day before all the families of the village packed their lives into the fleet of lorries sent out from Sanga to take them away, the ceremonial dance was performed. The souls of all the generations who'd come before were finally laid to rest. The next day, the trucks sped off toward the town, kicking up clouds of the sand that had killed Keida Kater's home. The same sand that had engulfed many, many more villages across the length and breadth of the Sahel, from Senegal in the west to Somalia in the east. The Saharan sand was slowly strangling the life from the land.

PLaNT Man

Maura Morgan

I watched the trees sway, the lightning flash, and the rain pelt the segmented picture window of my mountain home. My mutt Rex lay on the couch, snuggled tightly beside me, quivering with every rumble of thunder. No whispered words could convince him we were cozy and safe from the storm outside. It comforted me, though, knowing my home, impeccably built by fine craftsmen into a cliff face in the mountains outside of Seattle, would survive this onslaught of anger from Mother Nature, a five-day storm covering Vancouver to Sacramento, with a forecast of up to thirty inches of rain bearing down on the region.

I'd begun watching the storm on HD radar two weeks ago as it formed and came in from the Pacific. I notified the Department of the Navy and received clearance to deploy PLaNT, *Precipitation Lessening and Neutralization Technology*, a cloud-seeding program I'd worked on for ten years since 2026. Three days ago, I authorized the seeding jets to fly, knowing there'd be no going back once I did. The program had never been broadly deployed, so what would happen was unknown.

I finished my tea, laced together my fingers, and stretched my arms palms out until my knuckles cracked. Then I flipped up the screen of my laptop and opened multiple browser windows to news sites, witnessing firsthand the chaos unfolding as the storm raged and tracking the deployment of the cloud seeds. I was uniquely qualified to interpret these events because, as their orchestrator, I knew what was happening and could evaluate it all scientifically. The seeding technology worked perfectly in all models and closed tests. I owed it all to Maya, who, in her wisdom, dumped me without fanfare after I received my sixth advanced degree. If she hadn't broken up with me, I might never have found the diligence, commitment, or fortitude to work on my climate control projects.

Maya, with her long, ebony hair and deep brown eyes, whom I'd loved since high school. The more I got to know her, the more I learned just how smart she was, though not in the same way as me. She was literary and philosophically astute, and I was convinced she'd be president one day because she could solve problems like no one else.

I was a geek then: gullible, impetuous, and impressionable. In the spring of our junior year, she sat with me at lunch on a dare from her friends, and we talked. By the end of lunch, I'd found my footing and asked her on a date. In proper geek mode, I suggested a superhero movie, and Maya agreed.

At the movie's climax, when the supervillain had collected all the necessary magical stones, he snapped his fingers and turned half of all living creatures in the universe to dust. Everyone in the theater gasped and an uneasy silence followed, even between Maya and me. It followed the two of us to Applebee's, where we slowly eased into a conversation about the movie, a conversation that soon became a lively discussion, which became the tone for our relationship for the next eight years. She was adamant the supervillain was wrong in every way. I was not so convinced. I thought he was a sympathetic, misguided character because he honestly thought he was facilitating what the universe required: a correction. He'd tried to convince others of the necessity of what he was doing, and when he was ignored, he believed he was chosen to balance the universe by randomly eliminating half its inhabitants. As a budding climatologist, biologist, and chemist, I viewed his actions with less condemnation. Maya vehemently disagreed: who was he to dictate the best course of action to correct the universe? I adjusted my pronouncement and softened my stance. His actions were despicable because he didn't include himself or his minions in the equation—logic dictated this assumption; otherwise, who'd fight for this villain only to vanish upon victory? It wasn't totally random. That's what made him a villain.

I received my second PhD in 2026 and dived into finding solutions for the climate crisis.

Maya's breakup with me wasn't totally unexpected. I was fighting climate change through science; she was battling it through action, persuading people to change their ways. Both of us were failing, which battered our relationship. In the middle of our campaigns, she dropped a bomb on me: she wanted a child, maybe children. I balked, and we fought. Climate change alarms echoed loud and clear worldwide and led me to a higher calling than fatherhood. Children? No. I was called, metaphorically, to marry Mother Nature. I wanted to be part of the solution to climate change, not part of the problem.

We parted as friends—both of us knew it was best. I still loved her and would do anything for her, but I was determined to stay out of her marriage even though her husband, Max, understood our past and didn't mind her keeping in touch with me. I fully immersed myself in work and retreated to the mountains, working from home. She stayed in the suburbs of Seattle, in a house on Lake Washington, and continued her climate advocacy.

We shared a goal, and little successes demanded we keep in touch.

She called me when Max was out of town on business, which was frequent as of late. I was her only family in the area, and she was mine. Though Maya had many friends, she told me nothing was better than a lover turned brother. I was truly happy for her when she called me with the news she was going to be a mother.

A glance at the calendar reminded me she was due very soon. I bit my thumb. I knew when I planned this event I might lose people I cared about, but I kept telling myself the pain of loss would come sooner or later for everyone. I had to be willing to accept whatever the outcome with friends, neighbors, coworkers, and myself. As I watched the mass of green on the radar move over Seattle proper, my resolve slipped. Maya's baby hadn't even begun to live yet and held no responsibility for how the world was. How could I possibly condemn the child? And for Maya's baby to survive, Maya had to live. This storm and the baby's arrival were colliding, something I could never have anticipated. I called to warn Maya, hoping I wasn't too late.

I tapped my foot on the cotton rug while waiting for her to answer; with each ring, I urged her to pick up, hoping she hadn't fallen victim to my ruthlessness. The call finally connected, and I wasted no time.

"How are you feeling? And Max? Is everything okay?" I asked, trying to ease my way into this delicate conversation. "How's the baby?"

"I'm fine, Nate. Watching the storm, hoping Max gets home soon—the baby's fine. She's not due for another week, and I hope she waits that long. What's up with you? You sound agitated."

Her voice echoed casual and relaxed.

"Max isn't there?" My heart wrenched. How could he leave town so close to Maya's delivery date?

"On his way, last I heard. Driving back from Sacramento. Had some important meetings with industry leaders about their companies' effect on the atmosphere. Talked to him this morning, and he said he'd just left, and it might take him longer than the normal twelve hours. Like here, the storm was raging in California. He said cars were strewn all over the road, and EMS were everywhere. When he stopped for breakfast, the restaurant was crazy with people sleeping in the booths and on the floors, and he didn't quite understand why that was. I told him I'd read something, that it was happening because of the storm. From my sources, they think there's a rogue virus in the water."

My heart thrummed in my throat. My hands grew cold, and I flexed them to encourage the blood flow.

"Yes, yes, there is. And it's very, very dangerous. That's what I was calling you about." I jumped up from the couch. Rex stirred at my sudden movement, and his eyes followed me back and forth as I paced in front of the window. "Listen, Maya, listen to what I tell you. Have you drunk any public water or had a shower in the past few days?"

"No," she said. "We don't use the shower in storms like this—the septic system overflows. And our water purifier's been full."

"Have you been outside?"

"No."

I gave her instructions: stay inside, turn off the water purifier so no additional water enters the system, drink only bottled or already purified water, stay away from the public water system for five days. Wash only with boiled water. No showers. Do not let any water from this storm touch you in any way.

"Nate, you're scaring me. What do you know?"

She knew, in generic terms, of my work with cloud seeding to reduce the potency of storms. What she didn't realize was the secondary purpose of my work.

When I finished school, I applied for grants to reduce climate change. Thanks to austere, climate change deniers in charge of the government, all initiations to minimize the damage were abandoned, and the world suffered for it. Drill,

drill, drill. Frack, frack, frack. I was forced to seek out private, like-minded investors and became part of the CCAC—the Climate Control Advocacy Council. Meanwhile, the earth's temperature rose by 1.5°C.

Darwin's natural selection wasn't working anymore; we'd become too civilized to have any such thoughts about one's death being for the benefit of all. Without major wars or plagues, our own worst enemy was ourselves. Climate change catastrophes, like droughts and floods, were tipping the balance, but only slightly. While most scientists searched for workarounds for each disaster Mother Nature threw at us, I believed that my work would benefit the world as I worked through one problem after another. No one wanted to handle the big decision, and I was tired of watching the climate summits become exercises in futility. So, I took matters into my own hands.

Cloud seeding wasn't my only initiative. PLaNT also stood for something else: Population Lessening and Neutralization Technology. In addition to precipitation control, I bioengineered a substance to be active in the water supply. A waterborne virus, if you will. PLN35 was part virus and part chemical compound engineered within the virus. It would reach its end life in five days and disappear. Until then, those who took it in a determined amount of substance per weight would simply go to sleep about thirty hours after their encounter with the water and never wake up, eventually dying within a few hours of falling asleep. An inactive compound immunized those lucky enough to have encountered a preponderance of them. The event was designed for total randomization, and there was no telling the percentage of people—and only people—who'd be affected. My estimates ranged from 20 to 40 percent. I couldn't tell Maya any of this. We were three days into the storm with another two to go and five days beyond that for the virus to die.

I stayed quiet, and with the uneasy silence on the phone, I knew my few words had been too much.

"Nate, what have you done? Are you responsible for this?"

I couldn't honestly answer.

"You're a madman. You're killing innocent people!"

"It's for the good of the world, Maya. I want future generations to have a better world than us. Don't you see? How else can it be done?"

"With hope and determination," Maya said, then the line went dead.

I disconnected the phone with a press on the red spot. It was beginning to get dark, and the soft shades of gray crept into my living room. I sat on the couch and contemplated, with great sorrow, my conversation with Maya.

I texted my neighbors, Ted and Joanne, an older couple of survivalists I suspected were seeking refuge from the storm in the underground bunker, asking them if they could look after Rex tomorrow. I'm going away for a few days. They loved Rex, had watched him when I'd traveled in the past, and I figured they'd agree. Of course, Joanne typed back, *You're going out in this storm? Don't you know what might happen?*

I texted her back, *Yes, I was aware, but my trip was unavoidable.*

Put him on the porch. We'll bring him in when he dries.

Brush him with latex gloves and long sleeves, I suggested. I didn't know if the virus was still active once it was out of the water supply.

My phone buzzed at about five a.m. the following day, waking me from an uneasy sleep. It was Maya.

Max arrived home safely, and we are following your instructions. I can't condone what you did; I don't want to know whatever it was. I won't tell anyone because your intentions were good, even if you wore blinders to the consequences. Don't contact me anymore, I can't bear it.

I brought Rex to Ted and Joanne's the following day, dressed only in a short-sleeved shirt and jogging pants. No hazmat suit, no respirator. I was going to accept the consequences of my actions. Like the supervillain of my teenage years, I'd unleashed my plan to protect future generations from hunger and want. Unlike the villain of the Marvel universe, I did not step through a portal to exclude myself from my goal. I would accept responsibility for my actions; if I fell victim to it, so be it. When I returned home, I turned off all my electronics. I wrote letters to all those who needed to know the truth in case of my demise. The following day, I stepped out into the sunrise. The cloud seeds we'd scattered to lessen the storm's intensity seemed effective and cut the storm's length from five days to three and a half. I left a report for the CCAC, recommending the seeding be used in future storms. I also admitted my role in the deaths in the Northwest and instructed the CCAC to destroy the containers holding PLN35 before they could be unleashed again.

I was growing tired and achy but fought off the desire to sleep long enough to check Maya's Instagram one last time. Her post was short and sweet, and I could sense her hope for the future.

Reneé Jasmine Miller arrived in this world at 4:45 this morning, delivered at home amid the storm by her proud father, Max, weighing an estimated eight pounds three ounces and nineteen inches long. Heart emojis accompanied the text.

The picture posted along with the post was of Maya holding the baby tightly in her arms, tiny hands wrapped around Maya's pinky. She had pink, bowed lips and a shock of black hair. I swore I saw a dimple on her cheek, just as her mother had.

I looked upon the new baby with a sense of jealousy, understanding that I could only do what I did because, like the antagonist in that superhero movie, I had no one to risk losing. I wondered if, when he snapped his fingers, he condemned his minions like he'd condemned the rest of the universe.

I realized then that it didn't matter what the supervillain had done; he was just a character in a movie. He felt no remorse for what he'd done. I did, and that's what separated us.

I set the phone on my nightstand, turned out the light, and waited for whatever fate had in store for me.

Raymond and Ruby

Ian Inglis

Raymond Thorley hated the heat. He always had. As a youngster, he'd sweated and struggled through every summer, and despite his best efforts to keep out of the sun, stay indoors, and take two or three showers a day, nothing seemed to help. When his discomfort continued into adolescence, he sought medical advice. The doctor explained that it was his metabolism and that he would simply have to learn to live with it. Dutifully, he drank plenty of water, ate salads and fruit, avoided alcohol, and wore light cotton clothing. But again, it made little difference.

And now, as an adult, there was something else: a simmering anger that enveloped and alarmed him. He seemed to be in a permanent state of emotional turmoil and tension. He visited another doctor who mentioned something called "the heat hypothesis": the belief that rising temperatures might increase aggressive tendencies and violent behavior. It was a compelling argument: globally, temperatures had soared in recent decades—and were continuing to rise, year on year—and with them, the incidence of mental health crises, suicides, road rage attacks, fistfights, and physical assaults. While Raymond acknowledged the possibility, there was an additional, more worrying, element of his confusion that he kept to himself: much of his frustration and antipathy was directed at Ruby.

They had met at the golf club's annual dinner dance and had begun an untroubled relationship based on mutual companionship rather than physical passion. Within six months, they were married. His occasional overnight sales trips and her shifts at the museum meant that their time together was limited, and the marriage proceeded for several years along a comfortable, if uneventful, path. But now, she, too, was displaying the same quarrelsome tendencies as her husband. He had noticed the change in her eighteen months ago, when he was diagnosed with persistent asthma caused, he was told, by higher pollen concentrations in the atmosphere and longer pollen seasons. Soon, she began to blame him for things over which he had no control. She corrected and contradicted him. If things went wrong, it was all his fault. He became her scapegoat, the source of her unhappiness, and the target of her increasing hostility. He responded in kind. They sniped and snapped at each other, engineered unnecessary arguments, and found fault in everything the other person did.

"You always have to have your own way, don't you?" she declared.

"What do you mean?"

"You know very well what I mean! It's as if I don't exist any longer. When I meet people, it's always, 'How's Raymond? Oh, poor Raymond, he's so brave. Do give Raymond our love.' Never a thought for me! And it's only asthma. It's not as if you're about to drop dead!"

"Oh, for Christ's sake! The asthma's hardly my fault. Can't you think of anyone but yourself?"

At the weekend, Ruby forsook her customary Sunday morning lie-in and with it, the only time in the week when she might permit a brief sexual encounter. When Raymond went down to the kitchen, he looked out through the window and saw that his wife had paused from her weeding and pruning and was speaking on her mobile phone. She had taken off her faded denim shirt and was wearing a white vest, a straw sunhat, and a pair of yellow shorts. Shears, secateurs, and a garden fork lay on the parched lawn next to a small mound of soil and clippings. She came into the kitchen, hat in hand, deliberately avoiding his gaze and complaining about the continued hosepipe ban.

"I hope it cools down for our walk," he said.

"What walk?"

"Over to the south bay... the old lighthouse."

"You've said nothing about that to me."

"We talked about it last night," he protested. "Don't pretend you've forgotten."

"No, we didn't, Raymond," she said with an exaggerated sweetness. "You think you mentioned it, but you didn't. In any case, it's far too hot. And you don't like the heat. Remember?"

He studied her carefully as she made no attempt to mask her triumphant expression. The face he used to think of as pretty and full of mischief was mean and hard. The warm, gentle lilt of her voice that had charmed him in the past had turned to an annoying noise that reminded him of commercially manufactured muzak. He saw pettiness in her eyes, smugness in her thin smile. She inadvertently brushed against him but said nothing. It was as if she barely noticed him. As his resentment increased, he understood, with a swiftness that startled him, what he wanted to do, what he needed to do, what he was going to do. At that precise moment, he decided to kill his wife.

Over the next few weeks, he found it difficult to conceal the feelings he now had for her. It was as if a dam had burst, releasing a flood of hidden emotions: he hated being alone with her, he detested her superficial conversation, her perfume repelled him. He told himself that the animosity he felt had nothing to do with his asthma or the climate; he simply wanted to reclaim his life. He remembered a story in the newspapers in which a discontented wife had added poison to several bottles of gin on the supermarket shelves before buying one as a birthday gift for her husband. Her hope was that police would automatically view his death as one random casualty among several engineered by a deranged serial killer. Unfortunately for her plan, her husband spat out the gin after the first mouthful. In addition, the fact that the seals on the other bottles had clearly been tampered with alerted supermarket staff, who immediately removed them before any more could be sold. Finally, and definitively, her actions were caught on the store's CCTV system. But the basic strategy was, Raymond believed, sound. All he had to do was conceal Ruby's death among others.

But not among other murders: he knew that the husband is always the first suspect, whatever the circumstances. He required a catastrophic accident or unpredictable turn of events in which Ruby would be recorded as one of a number of innocent victims who tragically happened to be in the wrong place at the wrong time. A fire, an avalanche, a flood? There had been more than enough of those in the last few years, but they were not things he could predict or control. Moreover, he knew he had to keep things simple: the greater the number of components in any plan, the greater the number of possible errors. The supermarket poisoner had been sloppy, hasty, impetuous. Raymond would learn from her mistakes. He would remain calm. Drenched with perspiration in his baking, airless office, or lying awake at night in the stifling heat, he used the time to assess the various possibilities open to him. He enjoyed the challenge. And six weeks later, he had his plan in place.

On Friday, July 23, Raymond and Ruby went up to the West End. It was their tenth wedding anniversary, and he had mentioned to several friends that they were marking the occasion by going to see the much-lauded revival of *My Fair Lady*. In the morning, he gave Ruby a small Japanese porcelain bowl depicting a traditional stylized garden. He had bought it as an anniversary gift after consulting with a couple of her girlfriends about what would make a suitable present. Following the show, and also on the Saturday night, they would stay in the hotel in which they had spent their honeymoon: he had wanted to book the same suite but her insistence on single beds made it impossible. At this time of year—the height of the tourist season and the start of the school holidays—London would be busy, busier than usual. And on a Friday evening, the always-overcrowded Underground system would be stretched to breaking point by those celebrating the end of the working week, those arriving for the weekend, those rushing to get home or seeking to escape the overpowering heat of the city. The ever-present security fears (there had been two terrorist attacks and several bomb scares in the capital earlier in the year) added to the general mood of unease. Finally, as if to confirm the validity of his plan, a sudden rise in temperatures across Britain seemed to lengthen queues and shorten tempers in equal measure.

At 6:30, they were standing on the westbound platform of the Victoria Line at Oxford Circus, waiting to make the short journey to Covent Garden. Ruby was wearing a short, floral-print cotton dress, and he a beige linen suit; even so, both were sweltering in the relentless heat. Two overcrowded trains had already come through, but only a handful of determined passengers had been able to scrap and squeeze their way into the carriages. As Raymond and Ruby waited, scores of impatient travelers, many with briefcases, shopping bags, and rucksacks, poured down the escalators onto the platform, forcing those already there nearer and nearer to the track.

"I told you we should have walked," she said.

"Did you?"

"Of course I did! This is ridiculous. But, you have to have your own way."

Raymond moved closer to Ruby and put his arm around her waist.

"Please don't do that," she said.

"I'm sorry," he said. "That's the last time. I promise."

Something in his tone made her wheel round and stare at him.

"What do you..."

The rumble of the oncoming train and the shouts and arguments of the waiting passengers drowned his wife's words as Raymond stared over her shoulder as if someone were calling to him.

"What's that?" he shouted at the top of his voice. "He's got a gun? He's got a gun!"

Those around him reacted instantly. In the already tense atmosphere, anxiety turned to fear and panic, which rippled along the platform as Raymond's cries were taken up and repeated with ever-increasing ferocity.

"A gun! He's got a gun. Run! Run!"

"They're shooting!"

"They've got guns. Run!"

But there was nowhere to run to, and the crowd turned and twisted and fell, tumbling onto the track as the train raced into the station.

"Ruby, Ruby! Hold on to me!" he cried, elbowing and kicking a path through the boiling crush of people. "No, not that way! Stay with me! Ruby, no!" He picked her up, dropped her, pushed her, dragged her, ignoring her protests, both of their screams lost in the tumult. He held her by the very edge of the platform, still shouting. "Ruby! Ruby! Stay with me! Hold on!" And then he loosened his grip and watched her fall backward, hitting the track a second before the train destroyed her. Many of the writhing, tangled masses of men and women who had toppled onto the track were dragged under the wheels of the train as it attempted to brake; others were spewed back onto the platform. As the piercing shriek of the emergency braking system amplified the human screaming, the doors of the overcrowded train burst open, hurling its occupants into the cauldron of terrified people fighting and clawing for survival. At the same time, unrelenting floods of newly-arriving passengers descending the escalators were met head-on by accelerating waves of those seeking to escape the carnage below. And all the while, the cacophony of screams and sobs continued to ring out.

"Guns! He has a gun! They're killing people!"

"Help me! Oh, please help me!"

"They have guns! They have bombs!"

"Mummy! Where are you? Mummy!"

The number of fatalities was 87. They came from 24 countries. Sixteen were children. Causes of death ranged from multiple injuries and heart attacks to suffocation; some people were literally crushed to death. A further 91 people suffered serious or life-changing injuries, including broken bones and the loss of limbs. Many more survivors, Raymond among them, were treated in the hospital for shock and minor injuries before being discharged. A number of knives and guns were discovered in the scattered baggage strewn across the station, and although it remained unclear whether an actual terrorist incident had taken place, it was assumed that the sighting of one or more of these weapons had triggered the subsequent chaos. At the much-delayed inquest, Raymond was one of more than 150 people called to give evidence. Like the majority of witnesses, he testified that after hearing cries that there were people with guns on the crowded platform, he feared that he was in the middle of a terrorist attack. Yes, he had repeated the shouts himself in order to warn others.

No, he hadn't actually seen anyone with a weapon. He had tried to cling on to Ruby, to pull her to safety, but they had been forced apart and had lost each other in the panic and confusion. Yes, they had gone up to London to celebrate their wedding anniversary.

The coroner thanked him for his evidence, commended his bravery, and offered commiserations for his terrible loss. In her summing-up, she regretted the unfortunate fact that the excessive heat of that afternoon (the Met Office had recorded temperatures in excess of 39°C/102°F in Central London) had led to a series of power outages which caused intermittent failures of the surveillance cameras at Oxford Circus, including a crucial period of 30 seconds just before the train arrived at the platform. She explained that in the absence of those video recordings, a verdict could only be reached on the basis of the witnesses' recollections. Furthermore, although a variety of weapons had been recovered from the scene, none of the guns appeared to have been fired, and none of the killed and injured had been shot. Two years after the inquest opened, and four months after she had retired to consider the evidence, the coroner announced that while she sympathized with the widely-held public view that the incident was terrorist-related, there was insufficient evidence for such an assertion. Having ruled out misadventure, accidental death, and unlawful killing, she was, therefore, legally obliged to record an open verdict.

In the immediate aftermath of what quickly became known as the Oxford Circus Stampede, Raymond found that he was variously regarded as a hero, a victim, a reluctant celebrity. Unlike many of the other survivors, he declined to appear in any television documentaries or to give press interviews; rather than draw attention to himself, he wished to divert it. When friends and colleagues broached the subject, he would apologize and explain that he found it too painful to revisit. A word out of place, an unguarded comment, a tiny variation in his account of events could undo all that he had achieved. It was essential to say and do nothing that might attract attention.

He was slightly surprised that he felt no guilt, no remorse for the deaths and injuries he had caused. He hadn't known these people, and he had nothing against them. If he had carried out his plan on any other day, 86 different people would have died alongside Ruby. They were collateral damage, nothing more. He was not a bad person. He had accomplished what he set out to do—what he *had* to do—in a workmanlike and efficient way. He had succeeded. Against all the odds, he had succeeded.

And there were unexpected advantages. After trying unsuccessfully for years to lose weight, he shed more than three stones in a few months; the doctors told him that if he could maintain the new weight level, his asthma would almost certainly disappear. He was able to dispense with the inhaler he had been obliged to use and soon began to feel physically stronger. His golf improved. He took up swimming. He became wealthy: the money from Ruby's life insurance, plus his share of a wildly generous compensation fund, would have permitted him never to work again, although, of course, he did. And, after a decent period had elapsed, he began to be invited to rounds of dinners and parties, where any number of attractive women made it clear, in a cautious and deferential way, that they were interested in him. He traveled, at first motoring through Europe in his newly-bought BMW, then on long-haul flights to Central America, Australia, and Thailand, where, to his surprise, he remained unbothered by the tropical climates. Shortly after the open verdict had been announced, he gave up work, explaining that the disruptions to his life were deeper and more permanent than he had anticipated. The company understood perfectly; they gave him a full pension, an unexpectedly large lump sum, and wished him well. On the day of his retirement, he gave a short speech to his assembled colleagues, thanking them for their support and friendship. The men queued up to shake his hand, and many of the women had tears in their eyes as they kissed him and fondly murmured their goodbyes.

That evening, he placed the last of Ruby's clothes into two large black plastic bags to be taken to the charity shop in the morning. At the back of her wardrobe, he found the Japanese bowl he had given her. He decided he would keep it. Having it on display would serve to show people that he still remembered her, still missed her, still loved her. Smiling, he went into the kitchen, opened the refrigerator, poured himself a glass of fine white wine, and wandered out into the garden, its shrubs and borders revived by the unexpected thunderstorms and torrential downpours of the past fortnight. He turned to look at the purple-gray towers of cumulonimbus clouds gathering and swelling in the west and felt the first drops of warm, heavy rain on his face. He was content. He was at peace. More than that, he was happy in a way he had not been for many years. He raised his glass to the setting sun in a silent toast.

RISE

Melody Cooper

On a bright sunny day, the brown hands of a young Black woman worked in the soil of a vegetable garden ripe with beans, summer squash, and sweet corn.

"Many plants are sensitive to heat waves, just like the elderly and people with health issues ..." The voice belonged to Kim Harrison, a nineteen-year-old with short natural hair and a face free of makeup. She continued, "... especially if they've been subjected to stressors like pollution, pests, disease, drought, frost, poverty, racism, medical disparities, police brutality—" She stopped as something stirred in the earth. Was it a worm? Four thick worms poked up from the dirt ... No. Not worms. FINGERS. Joined by a fifth, they rose up until the hand of a young Black man desperately reached up—

Kim startled awake in bed in a dimly lit bedroom, her face, neck, and chest bathed in sweat. She looked at the air conditioner in her window. It was dead.

"The power's out again!" She struggled to get out of bed, leaned against the wall, shifted her body to navigate to another window, hauled it open. The sounds of the street in Bed-Stuy Brooklyn poured in of honking car horns, distant sirens, a dog barking, someone yelling. The clear sky was gray with a hint of light. Kim picked up her cell from the night table. A red banner of "SEVERE HEAT WARNING" topped the weather screen. Current temperature at 6 a.m. was 100°F.

Several blocks away, sunrise could be seen from the historic Brooklyn Bridge, where golden light spread across the span's stone double arches framed by diagonal suspender cables. Morning rays lit up the borough's skyline as if it were tinder and a fiery harbinger of the deadly heat that would soon arrive.

A few miles away, a cane tapped on wood boards. It stopped as Kim leaned against it for balance due to her multiple sclerosis, an affliction that she refused to let define her. Dressed in shorts and a sleeveless T-shirt, she wiped sweat off her face with a bandana and looked over a garden filled with withering kale and ripe cherry tomatoes from whose vines drooped wilted leaves. She wore a silver necklace set with three seeds: squash, corn, and bean. She lowered herself to a garden seat and worked with her hands in the soil, pulling weeds out of the vegetable bed. Set to one side of the bed was a cell phone on a tripod that Kim faced as she spoke.

"Okay, first off, this live cast is from the land of the Lenape. Unlike the incomplete story of the sale of Manhattan by Native Americans to the Dutch, the Lenape were displaced by European colonialism that included forced migration to Oklahoma. Performative land acknowledgment is not enough. The government should give their damn land back." She took a moment to switch gears and settle into a more affable demeanor that was as genuine as her indignation. "Good morning from Brooklyn. In this unbearable heat, I need to keep it short. So, for today, one tip: the best time to water your garden is in the morning and after sunset to prevent evaporation." She lifted a hose and watered the bed. "Water the soil around your plants well and deeply, then give them an overall shower of water. Make sure you stay hydrated, too. Close the windows in your apartment most of the day. Open them at night to let the cool air in."

"Unless the humidity is so damn bad the temperature doesn't go down," said Elaine Winship, Kim's seventy-two-year-old grandmother, her voice tinged with the lilt of a Trinidadian accent. She leaned in to join her granddaughter's live cast. Elaine was spry, full of energy, sweet, and cute, but don't mess with her. "If you lose power, be on the lookout for signs of heat stroke. You feel faint, nauseous, have a headache? Get in the shower under cool water. Before your ice melts, wrap it up in wet washcloths to put on your wrists and neck. Your groin too. Put it right up in there."

Kim suppressed a chuckle and added, "You heard Grandma Elaine."

"And check on your neighbors. 'Cause you know the city don't give a damn about any of us. Be smart."

"Be safe," Kim added and turned off the live cast. Elaine poked her in the arm.

"Too hot to be out here. Your MS hates the heat. Get inside." She gave her sharp orders out of love, but Kim still bristled.

"In a minute." Kim stood with the help of her cane. Even at average height, she towered over her grandmother. Elaine shook her head disapprovingly.

"You're getting worse."

Kim drew in a deep breath to keep her annoyance in check. "No, I'm not. I can't sit inside all day, Grandma. A little exercise is good. Five minutes."

"Three." Elaine reached up and gripped Kim's face in both hands. "You still having those dreams?" Kim didn't respond, and that was all the answer Elaine needed. She sucked her teeth and pulled Kim's face down, so she could give her a kiss. Then added, darkly, "Something's coming."

"Weird dreams don't always mean something bad's going to happen."

"No. But check your phone. There was an alert. Big storm coming. Tonight we should pick what's ready and secure what we can. You'll probably lose half of it but we should try." As Kim looked to the skies, which, for now, looked only partly cloudy, Elaine dug into a bag and pulled out a large conch shell. "For protection and luck." Kim shook her head and decided to pass. She grabbed her phone out of the tripod so she could read the alert. It was a major advisory for a hurricane. Fear crossed Kim's face and she immediately headed to a special, lush area marked by a brightly colored, hand-painted sign: Leo's Garden.

Far above her, a peregrine falcon released an alarm call. Brooklyn hosts a large urban population of them, and Kim looked up to see the bird of prey swoop overhead. From the falcon's point of view, Kim was a small brown figure in the middle of a large rooftop farm. An ominous rumble came from far away to the southeast, from which a massive, dark storm approached New York.

Inside the apartment building, Marva Harris paced in front of her laptop that sat on the dining room table. She wore a simple sleeveless cotton sundress to keep cool. The power was back on, and a small air conditioner worked overtime in one of the room's windows. Still, her forehead bore a sheen of sweat.

"I'm not going to argue with you about this." She was agitated as she spoke into her cell phone to her husband, Kevin.

"You want me to pay up." Miles away at borough hall, Kevin climbed the wide stairs that led up to six ionic columns at the top of the north facade of the large Greek Revival-style building. He wore a suit and tie even in the heat. "I told you already, he can wait a few days. I'm focused on what we discussed ... the community." He stepped inside the building and strode down a hallway to stop outside an office. He checked his watch. "You're supposed to be here, backing me up."

Marva stood at her desktop computer, aggressively typing into a New York court form as she tried to control her anger, and said, "You have no right to demand a damn thing. You're supposed to put your children first. Your son is in Hell. There have been twenty-two deaths there already this year."

Kevin's voice cut sharply through the phone, "It's a lesson he'll never forget."

"What are you trying to prove? That he was with the 'wrong' kind of people? They weren't criminals."

There were two light knocks in the doorway. Marva turned to see Kim leaning against the doorjamb. Her shorts and T-shirt were covered with dirt. Marva made a face and put up a hand for Kim to stay where she was and not make a mess in the room. Kim mouthed, "Dad?" Marva nodded and balled up one fist to show how angry she was with him. Kim rolled her eyes and waited.

At Borough Hall, Kevin paced in the hallway as he added, "It's not just about him. It's about our family. And my reputation."

Marva was furious but knew she had to maintain some kind of control in front of her daughter. She turned away from Kim. "I'm hanging up now, Kevin. I have to make some calls to the court."

Kevin was in a sparring mood. "So, you get an online law degree and suddenly think you can move mountains?"

Marva took a beat before she fielded this insult. "You do what you need to do, and so will I." She tossed her cell onto the table and glanced at Kim. "Probably not a good time, Kim." Kim was not to be deterred and stepped into the room.

"We need to talk about Leo."

Marva held up her hand to Kim and went back to the form on the laptop. "Believe me, I'm doing all I can to—" Both their phones buzzed loudly with an emergency notification. They checked their home screens.

"Oh my God." The info shook Kim and she immediately started scrolling on social media, looking for answers as she asked, "Mom, has a Category 3 hurricane ever hit New York?"

Both women had the same look of dread as they simultaneously said, "Leo."

On an island in the middle of the East River sat a prison complex behind miles of fencing topped with razor wire. The blue and white Welcome sign outside the Rikers main building masked the frightening truths within the controversial facility. For one, it was not a prison to hold convicted criminals. It was a jail built to hold defendants while they awaited trial. This meant that 85% of over ten thousand detainees in Rikers had not even completed the due process of their trials to be found guilty or not guilty. And yet, it was the most notoriously dangerous jail in the country. In one recent year, there were over five hundred incidents of prisoner self-harm, seventeen deaths, and forty guards were suspended. There were over four hundred fires, traditionally an indication of unrest and a badly run facility. Ninety percent of those jailed were Black or Brown people. Human Rights activists were constantly accusing Rikers of egregious actions, like abuse of detainees and the smuggling of drugs inside by corrections officers.

Within the walls of this infamous jail was Leo Harris, Kim's twin. Tall and lanky, he was a perennial jokester who always tried to get by based on his father's reputation. He was funny, a great friend, and harmless. But he and a group of new acquaintances had gotten into it with two cops who were looking to harass young Black men in the neighborhood. Whether it was racism or just a need to meet a quota, the end result was Leo in jail with his angry father refusing to bail him out.

He slept face up on a narrow bed in a tiny cell. The room was dark as water dripped onto his face. The wet hand of a young Black woman desperately reached down to him. He opened his eyes. His face was dry. The hand was gone. He let out his sister's name as soon as he sat up.

"Kim."

The sky beyond Rikers roiled with a front of dark clouds.

As Kevin Harris continued to wait outside the office that had a Borough President plaque beside it, Marva arrived looking ready for business in a sleeveless column dress. She immediately addressed Keith's satisfied smile.

"Don't get it twisted," Marva said. "I'm not here for you or the community. I'm here for Leo. All we need to do is—" Lucas, the borough president's assistant, stepped out of the office. Young, white, and overworked, he looked panicked.

"Sorry, but she can't see you this morning," Lucas explained. "We're in a state of emergency with the storm upgraded to Cat 4 and headed right for Brooklyn."

Kevin couldn't hide his shock. "What? Cat 4 now?"

Marva stepped in. There was no time to waste. "That's why we're here. What about—"

"What about the poor, Black, and unhoused residents?" Kevin interrupted. "What plans do you have to protect them?" Kevin was a powerful constituent and was determined to handle this the way he wanted to.

Lucas looked somewhat offended. "The plans in place are for everyone, Mr. Harris."

Kevin pressed, "Really? On day ten of the heatwave, the city's done nothing to prevent brownouts or to add more cooling centers to the poorer and Blacker neighborhoods."

This put the assistant on the defensive. "Simply not true. The climate crisis is affecting everyone. And that hurricane will hit Brooklyn Heights and Borough Park just as hard as East Flatbush."

"And what about Rikers?" Marva asked. Kevin took hold of her arm.

"We don't need to get into—"

"Yes, we do." Marva yanked her arm out of his grip.

Lucas assured them, "You don't have to worry about prisoners getting out of Rikers."

Shocked, Marva stepped up to the assistant and seethed, "Our son is awaiting trial on spurious charges in that god-forsaken prison that should've been shut down years ago. It's on an island in the direct path of the hurricane. So you tell us what protocols you have in place to protect or evacuate 12,000 prisoners from Rikers before the storm hits. And think before you speak because we're going to the press and social media with your answer."

Lucas blinked and frowned. "I'm sorry. Why is your son even in Rikers?"

From inside the office, the borough president called out, her voice sharp and tense, "Lucas! Get in here!"

Lucas paused in the doorway before saying, "Look, Rikers is on lockdown, and we, uh, we think they'll be safe." Lucas hurried back inside the office. Marva and Kevin stood in stunned silence. Marva looked at her husband, tears filling her eyes. Kevin looked like the rug had been pulled out from under him as it dawned on him how powerless he actually was. He adjusted his tie, looked at his watch. He could not meet his wife's eyes. Without another word, Marva stormed off.

In a dim Rikers hallway, Leo stood at an old-fashioned, beat-up pay phone, holding the black receiver in a tight grip. He'd called his sister because something wasn't right and he was worried.

"I'm telling you they're not evacuating us. They're putting everyone on lockdown and the guards are leaving. I'm scared, Kim. I heard it got pretty bad here during Sandy. And that wasn't even a Category 1. Mom's gotta get me the hell outta here."

Kim had Leo on speaker so Elaine could hear while she sat at the kitchen table eating pepper pot and peas and rice. Kim paced behind her as she tried to reassure her brother.

"Mom's been on the phone all morning and she went down to Borough Hall with Dad."

"The hell with him."

Elaine sat forward. "Leo..."

"No. He's never bothered to hear me out on what happened. He trusted the cop's version over mine. And he's supposed to be this great social scientist? I want nothing to do with his sorry ass."

Elaine picked up the cell phone and held it gingerly as if she were taking Leo's hand. "They say we need to evacuate Brooklyn, Leo." There was silence on the other end.

Kim leaned over her grandmother's shoulder. "Leo?"

"I heard you. Go."

Kim took hold of the phone. "I'm not going anywhere." Marva and Kevin walked in the apartment door and right into the kitchen. "It's Leo. They're leaving them there to drown."

Marva spoke into the phone, "No one's going to drown, Leo. We just posted your bail and we're only half an hour away."

Leo cradled the receiver so no one nearby could hear. "Mom, the guards are all gone."

Kevin piped in, "What?"

"Yeah, Dad. Surprise. They've abandoned us. It's just me and a few guys here in the hallway because we asked to call our lawyers. They locked down everyone else already and left us out here." The family all exchanged looks.

"Leo, listen to me very carefully," Marva said. "Until 7 p.m., it's legal visiting hours there, and your lawyer can see you at any time. There has to be somebody left there in charge. You stay right where you are. I'm coming to get you."

"But the storm..."

Kim stepped next to her mother to add, "It won't hit for another six hours. We're coming." Mother and daughter took hands. Marva scooped car keys out of a bowl on the counter. Kevin stepped in her way.

He met his wife's gaze directly, held out his hand, and said, "I'll drive."

Elaine nodded. "Finally." Kevin turned to Kim.

"You stay here with your grandmother."

Kim protested, "But—"

Elaine touched her shoulder. "He's right." Kevin looked surprised. "I'm your mother-in-law, but I'm not an idiot."

"Don't wait for us to come back," Marva insisted. "You get on one of the buses evacuating. There won't be many of them. Promise me."

Reluctant at first, Elaine and Kim agreed in unison, "Promise."

On the rooftop, as the sun began to set, a stiff wind picked up while Elaine and Kim quickly worked to pick vegetables and then tie down what they could. Kim stopped and looked over the farm with dismay.

"Time to go," Elaine said as she dug into the bag she had earlier and handed out the conch shell in it. Kim took it this time and carefully placed it in Leo's Garden as a long, loud rumble of thunder was heard in the distance.

Sea Burial

Lee Nash

"Today we brought Wolf through the door. How strange to leave your house as a twosome and return as a threesome. Names are important: he'll need to be free-spirited and strong.

"I'm planning a virtual 'sip and see' for our bushy-tailed babe, an official introduction to his alabaster world. Not that it's snow-covered. Nevertheless, our cities are slowly blanching: roofs and roads, clothing, and the few vehicles in circulation, most are blinding white. Everyone has their allotted patch to paint to ensure our boroughs stay as cool as possible. 'Reflect' is the mantra we live by. Reflect on what we can do to reduce calefaction, to throw off the sun's fierce rays.

"Soon, I need to register Wolf's birth and organize vaccinations at a local clinic. Malaria and dengue fever are mandatory jabs, as well as DTP. To survive, let alone flourish, there's a strict protocol to follow. We avoid the top-security, high-risk hospitals; they're concerned with controlling infectious diseases and the influx of trauma injuries and mental health cases. I don't mean to sound alarmist and don't regret bearing a child.

"As parents, we have an increased water ration. Our taps don't gush, they dribble. We're accustomed to this restriction; the meager flow encourages us to save dwindling resources. We keep clean the Gallic way—*toilette de chat*—and if we're desperately cruddy, we take a Navy shower. Baths are luxury events, and swimming pools for private use are being phased out.

"A young couple living away from their immediate families, we qualify for furlough. Both of us work in NGOs: we strive to regulate the critical surge of refugees and increasing immigration demands. I spend my days listening to heartbreaking stories, filling in residency forms, and attempting to relieve disoriented and anxious people. Some places on the globe are too sultry to inhabit; there's a slow, steady exodus of heat-exhausted humans to our relatively shaded doorsteps. The black spots from Bangkok to Kuwait City are being drained of their citizens, barring the uber-rich and, sadly, the chronically poor."

"It's our cub's first continuation day. This evening, we're strolling in the park to christen his tri-wheeler buggy. It's in standard-issue UV-protection bioplastic; petrol-based polymers are banned in children's toys and clothes, and comestibles packaging. We pass almost incognito, me under my parasol and Fox under his. He dislikes carrying his flare umbrella, and his macho streak frustrates me. The AIMA (air impurities alert) is orange, so we don't exceed the maximum outdoor exposure limit of two hours. There are plenty of trees for cover. Planting is big business and the streets are breathing libraries. In leaf, they act as organic ventilators; the branches are pollarded to stop them from becoming invasive. To relieve the town council and as our civic responsibility, we've adopted a tree to monitor and are duty-bound to report anything unusual like disease or vandalism. We're at liberty to collect its produce, and chestnuts are a popular choice. They're nutritious and tasty—Saint Hildegard was right."

"We have a lodger. This is causing considerable stress. Wolf, five and a half, and his sister Birdie, eighteen months, share a room and bedtime is a game of chance. We're not alone in this predicament (or privilege, depending on your point of view) of providing temporary shelter to a displaced migrant. Although government subsidies aren't generous, they act as an incentive. If residents do their part, the situation won't deteriorate. If it does, the economic and social infrastructures are in danger of collapsing.

"In the spirit of solidarity, we've learned to adapt. Privacy and intimacy are sacrificed for the benefit of society and the environment, and as recompense, we experience a foreign culture. It sounds easy, romantic even.

"Harmony is from Bamako, Mali; I couldn't ask for a more considerate permanent guest. Character aside, the daily routine is altered and draining. Sharing your quarters with a stranger is ... let's say they aren't a stranger for long."

"Our children and their classmates are homeschooled. Special guardians trained in the syllabus shoulder a portion of the tutelage; the teachers give group lessons online. I process the bulk of the appeals at the global crisis center via teleworking. If my colleagues or I are obliged to travel, it's a pre-dawn start and only the morning shift, while the temperature is bearable. In my absence, Harmony helps with childcare and cooking. Mindful of her challenges and the burden to acclimatize, when she's not learning languages and studying for a food sustainability diploma, she's experimenting with permaculture. Every household, including our modest apartment, is rigged with an indoor kitchen garden providing a percentage of the family's diet. This season, we're cultivating lettuce, radishes, and Pink Ping Pong tomatoes."

"We're three again. Harmony moved on to a job at *Les Restos du Cœur* and lodgings in Paris. She's used to torrid extremes, so is confident she'll adjust. Wolf is a lanky teenager, and beneath the hormonal angst lies a self-reliant and intelligent individual. Birdie's a creative soul, ever engrossed in artistic pursuits. As for my marriage, Fox has changed. His passive-aggressiveness wasn't noticeable before. The cracks are invisible fissures—microscopic tears in photovoltaic cells. I doubt they can be fixed. Hardship alters personalities or shows their true colors.

"As a youngster, I imagined my adult habitat would be powered by vast arrays of solar panels or wind farms, their acreage spanning rural landscapes or skimming municipal skies. Who could have foreseen the complications, the greenwashing? Ironically, since the polemic over the nuclear waste 'burial' sites, we're as obsessed with saving power as we once were about gender equality or banning trophy hunting."

"Prudence, unlike her predecessor, is unfaithful to her baptismal epithet. As fate would have it, she, too, is from Bamako. As a qualified nurse, she won't have difficulty finding employment. I've resigned myself to the domestic tension. She has eyes for Fox and it's mutual. I'm immune to his gaslighting."

"*Plein hiver*. We're amusing ourselves with an addition to our menagerie. The tortoise is making the acquaintance of a gutter cat, a Dachshund, and a cockatoo. I'm warming to robotic animals. A mechanical purr doesn't knit the bones, but we don't have the wherewithal or time to look after other sentient beings. Provided you charge their batteries overnight, e-pets are a canny invention; to economize, they occasionally sleep.

"Nobody misses zoos now. Wildlife reserves have closed the gap, at least where it's not unbearably hot. There are aqua parks with motorized dolphins and killer whales called Keiko and Tilikum in memory of their captive ancestors. Heartsick and accountable, we mourn the rhino."

"Today, Prudence sits for her French competency exam. Fox has taken her to the train station, and I'm nervous when they're together."

"It's spring, and a violet gladiolus is unfurling in my window box. I stroke its exquisite striated petals; the velvety texture is fragile yet firm. I wish Fox had left earlier so I could have grieved during the dark half of the year. I steel myself for tomorrow; the cracks became crevices, became a split. Strangely, though I'm numb and disappointed, I don't blame or hate Prudence. And I refuse to hate Fox.

"I have to make Wolf and Birdie my priority. At sixteen and twelve, they have the maturity to cope, and outwardly, they're philosophical and calm; inwardly, they're hurting and confused. I have to attend to myself. After volunteering to open my home, I'm left with a broken one. It doesn't seem fair. Staring past the cheerful blooms, nothing seems fair, and if my sight could penetrate the distance with telescopic precision, in whatever direction I turned, nothing there would either."

"We're the terrible trio. I hired a lawyer, and the divorce is pending. 'You've joined the queue,' he told me flatly, eyeing a precarious stack of files, sweat beading on his forehead despite the whirring ceiling fan."

"There's a quality to his presence—a dignified, unflustered grace. He's yet another environmental asylum seeker and hails from Orai, a bustling metropolis in Uttar Pradesh. Conditions are intolerable from March through the first week of June when temperatures average 45°C. With humidity levels climbing to 50%, urban existence has become nightmarish. He flashes me a grateful smile as he leaves, and my heart lightens."

"Rajeev's application was successful, and our patience was rewarded. Relieved, I invite him to celebrate Wolf's eighteenth continuation day. The event brings out our inner clowns. Birdie attempts to blow chocolate dust over our *forêt noire*; it's a fail and she gets a fit of the giggles. Rajeev will have to take us as we are."

"We're four. A different combination. The gladiolus is bursting, and I swear it's a deeper hue this year. I'm not ready to accept Rajeev's proposal, but neither should I drag my heels. Wolf's enrolled in a robotics engineering degree; Birdie's immersed in studies for her *baccalauréat.*"

"It's official: we're relocating and are mustering our forces to fly south like cranes. Not by airplane, though. We're hardly VIPs. We'll go by TGV. Rajeev secured a contract in the Camargue at the former saltworks of Salin-de-Giraud. The maintenance of a restoration project that's captured the world's attention. They created a buffer zone to mitigate the effects of storms and the rising water level. We're transferring, or in French parlance, mutating.

"We've found suitable accommodation near the site. There's an allotment and I'm eager to feel my hands in the fertile earth. Wolf is relishing his independence. He's designing an e-octopus, complete with artificial papillae and squirting ink. There are issues with the ink-jet device, and I'm grateful he's doing his own laundry.

"Birdie's making friends, among them magnificent wild horses. She's into photography and baking *patisseries*. We'd like to keep her.

"I do think of my previous life, but don't dwell on it. Sometimes, standing on the shore looking out to the cool Mediterranean blue, I sense what must be peace."

"My parents lived to meet my second husband; unfortunately, they didn't have the opportunity to get to know him. They'd hoped to find a natural gravesite in woodland; plots were exorbitant, so they settled on resomation—or put prosaically, water cremation. I'd wondered what to do with the calcium phosphate powder (their mortal remains) until the funeral director matter-of-factly remarked that relatives often add it to their flowerbeds. Their posthumous mission is to nourish a rosa rugosa tolerant of the sandy soil and squalls around these coastal parts.

"Safe in our cozy nest, I have to force myself to watch the distressing news reports. Forest fires, flash floods, and scenes of misery are commonplace. So many lives are sinking as the loss of littoral systems becomes our undeniable reality. Civil servants are constantly redrawing the maps.

"I gather my courage and venture out to the small plot to do what one person can: care for what's in front of me. I tread in the mud and endure it; fresh shoots will appear. Rajeev is patient and attentive. I learned his name means lotus flower."

I pause, breathe in a salty draft, and roll the paper tightly like an ancient scroll.

"Did it help?"

It did. A turning of the page, it's a memoir of the precarity of our times. For a moment, my mind wanders to ocean mining, pollution, and extinction. I picture the research vessels bravely setting sail.

"I'm glad you mentioned me." He winks. The breeze is picking up.

I feed the message into the glass bottle. He screws the lid on and hugs me reassuringly.

The waves are at his knees already. At last, he stops wading. "To the future!"

My application is in progress. He hurls the past to the sea with all his strength.

Symbiosis

Brian Brennan

I've seen a lot in one hundred and fifty years, one hundred as an organic and fifty as a digital. In 2206 we banished excess carbon to the point that it was finally worth the effort to plan for a future. All 160 million humans working together. Symbiosis, as we came to call it, which so many initially saw as the moral and spiritual death knell of our species, had been successful. The necessary first step so that we could work together on the monumental task of resuscitating the suffocating sphere we had so unloved. Through Symbiosis, we were changed forever, but we still existed. My grandfather, who was an early campaigner for organized Symbiosis, would say, *"What is adaptation if not coming through the other side of horror with a straight face?"*

The damage done to Diqui was as bad as the ancient scionists predicted until it was much, much worse. Countless new species of microbes thrived in the heated poisons we swam in, and it made the production of food impossible as the vegetation necessary to support it died away. When the stored food ran out, we devoured the only reproducing herd animals left. Us. Only then was it called Canabalistim, a derisive, ancient term with primitive connotations, betraying a privileged perspective from a time and place that no longer existed. About the time that it became institutionalized was when the term Symbiosis started appearing in place of the ancient indelicacy.

I have accessed a piece of my grandfather's speech given right before the local plebiscite regarding Symbiosis:

"Throughout our history as a species, the moral systems we created, even as they changed, changed to support values that were believed to enable our species to continue. Our survival is the ultimate value and the one on which all the others depend. This underlying principle, survival of our species, will be unchanged, and we will continue, even as the situational considerations in support of that goal change so radically that they would be unrecognizable to any civilizations that have come before ours ... "

That was the kind of bloodless, wordy, justification decision-makers and elite families like ours repeated to each other. A lonely, dispatched prayer for absolution and a substitute truth to replace what we were giving away.

Until food production and distribution had been rationalized, no one felt safe, so coordinated efforts to recover Diqui were dependent on it. A critical early concern about Symbiosis was that it would unfairly penalize the poor, and they would come to be disproportionately represented in the Stock population—those whose was for the purpose of making more Stocks for consumption, eventually becoming food themselves when their ability to reproduce and care for the young diminished. A lottery system was designed to ensure random selection, and in theory, no one family could have more than 50% of its fertile members assigned to a facility. However, the rich could legally buy their way out of the obligation with a hefty payment to the Government or paying for a replacement.

Stock facilities, known officially as Transcendence Centers (TCs), were stood up all over the world, far from any population centers. Narcotics were given to the inhabitants to reduce resistance and anxiety and increase fertility. In a solemn, religious rite-of-passage ceremony, their Achille's

Heels were severed just before puberty to restrict mobility. Children (known as Fruit) were removed from Parents (Trees) as soon as they were born to prevent complications resulting from parents-child bonding. Eventually, they were genetically engineered to be mute, as responding to their concerns and questions slowed down production and had severe psychological effects on the TC Wardens and Minders. Each Fruit was raised in separate quarters and fed a high-fat diet and hormones to make them nutritious and appetizing and taught that they were one of the few chosen for Transcendence, the afterdeath in which the select would ascend to an eternity with Dias, the deity at the center of the Cult of Transcendence.

The lie was necessary to maintain an orderly system. *"Every society needed its myths to sustain itself,"* I can remember my grandfather saying. He told me that in ancient times, there existed animals called Kows and Pegs, and the humans who ate them told themselves that they were treated humanely and did not suffer for the conditions they were kept in, though it was common knowledge among animal psychologists of the time that their penned-in isolation from other members of their species caused severe emotional trauma, and they even developed an understanding that they were going to die as they became aware of what the anguished sounds from the other pens meant for their brief future. Still, they ate.

The primary recovery effort was the standing up of millions of carbon converters, known more commonly as Traps, all over the planet. These were 18-foot-tall tripod structures with a valve at the top and a bag all the way at the bottom. The bag is where the magic happened, where carbon was captured, or converted to harmless, and later beneficial, compounds so that Diqui could recover. The predecessor to the Chin Empire had the most advanced carbon technologies, and that is what led to their becoming the sole superpower of Diqui today. It's why we say Diqui instead of Earse as our ancestors called our sphere. It's why so many of our customs and practices in the West today bear similarities with the Chin.

A Trap needed to be stood up every 1,500 paces on the ground. It required two people, and agreement between them not to eat the other at least until after they reached their quota of installations. You didn't have to worry before or during the install; it was designed to be a job requiring two interdependents. One held the converter upright by the loose spikes and neck, and one piled the spikes into the ground. This was social as much as environmental engineering. To get people used to not eating one another opportunistically and instead relearning the ancient virtue of trust and the benefits of cooperation. But if that bond had not formed by the time the quota was met, there was nothing to prevent spontaneous Symbiosis between them.

Though it wasn't explicitly illegal, it was a definite faux-pas to eat your partner after meeting the quota. They'd call you Canabalist behind your back, and in smaller rural villages, you would be outcast and starve to death as a result. It wasn't illegal because people who failed to form social bonds were not desirable in the Diqui to come, so consumption solved at least half of a local problem. To falsely accuse one of this type of Symbiosis was seen as so evil that eventually the penalty for false accusations was, you guessed it, Stock assignment. My grandmother's people used to have a saying for when someone did something shortsighted that I think I can still probably access: "He'd eat the piler before the third spike was laid if we let him."

I remember as a child, during the Qingming Festival, the Chin Empire holiday for worshiping ancestors that was amended to include paying respects to the Stocks who sustained us, I asked why the relationship between Consumers and Stocks was called Symbiosis since the benefit went entirely to the former. The adults looked at my parents in stunned silence, which was only broken by the sound of dropped glasses breaking. I had humiliated my parents, especially as my mother was a high official at the local Transcendence Center. For her own child not to understand (properly) the nature of the relationship was unthinkable. Grandfather, seeing my mother mortified, "reminded" me that the true benefit was to the Stocks, as they were blessed from birth to have the purpose of their life directed in the sustenance of civilization. They didn't have to worry about difficulties the rest of us did—paying bills, housing, finding and maintaining employment—while we led uncertain, complicated lives, less sure of our reason for being. The challenge for us was to live lives worthy of the Stock sacrifices, protecting them to enable the Noble Chain of Being to continue.

We used words to not mean what they meant in those days, and my grandfather was a primary disseminator. Symbiosis, Transcendence, Love.

The Consumer populations rapidly improved and the reassurance of a reliable food supply blunted any qualms about the nature of our good fortune. Diqui healed, and the prospect of growing food again, and ending Symbiosis became a real possibility. By that time the fruit conglomerates that ran the Transcendence Centers had become de facto sovereign states, with the ability to replace Governments that were not pliant. They spent billions of credits funding scientific studies and advertising, claiming that the planet was not yet safe for agriculture and that ending Symbiosis would result in the loss of millions of jobs, filling the streets with the unemployed and starving, deliberately bringing to mind the dystopian nightmares of pre-Symbiosis Diqui.

Within the first generation, assignment as Stock became hereditary. It was thought less disruptive to keep Stock offspring in the TCs and not introduce outsiders anymore. Those who were not Stock no longer had to worry about ourselves or our families. There was a darker reason behind the policy change: It became known that the Transcendence Centers had started genetically altering the fruit to make them addictive, encouraging Consumer dependence not just on the nutrition but on the narcotic.

About the same time, the internal operations of the TCs were exposed on Hulianwang, the global network, when pornography between Consumers and Fruits was transmitted all over Diqui. The Fruit was an easy target because they were isolated, couldn't communicate, and had no legal protections. We'd been told that the TCs were clean and safe and that Stocks lived better than we did. We learned they lived in filthy pens, barely large enough for them to lie down in. Their waste was everywhere, and they were covered with sores. With gray-pallored, thick eye bags, their lifeless pupils floated, and their bodies were bloated from the high-fat diet and narcotics regularly injected into them. An image of a Stock spoke a million words that no rationalization could surmount, and it was no wonder that until then, we never saw any pictures of them. Big Fruit responded with all their financial and political might. The world was told that the TCs in question were anomalies, and those in charge would be held responsible and the facilities cleaned up or closed down.

One day, my grandfather appeared in the doorway of my bedroom. He explained that as a scion of a prominent family associated with Symbiosis, I could be very valuable to the cause of peace and our peoples' survival as a spokesperson. I could dampen the blazing emotions and advocate for balanced perspectives and open minds. After this, I became both notorious and famous, depending on your point of view. I still can access the lines I spoke nearly seventy years ago that went out all over the world:

"As a member of a family closely associated with Symbiosis, I was concerned when I heard the rumors about the TCs and how Stocks were being treated. That's why I was so relieved when I learned that the bad apples running those few TCs were held accountable. As a rule, Stocks live a comfortable life, as they should given their important contributions to the Noble Chain of Being. Since Symbiosis started, our communities have flourished; disease, malnutrition, and violence have been reduced from pre-Symbiosis levels; and our children can now breathe freely outside. Some Symbiosis critics mean well, but maybe they need to be reminded of the world before."

Then came a montage of old-world horrors: women being dragged away, infant head pyramids, and corpses floating down polluted rivers of fire.

Finally, back to me: *"We need to allow everyone the freedom to live according to their conscience. But why should a bunch of pampered, academic elitists too young to remember life before Symbiosis tell me what I can feed my children? What about the freedom to choose? If you want to eat grass, then do it, but keep your opinions out of my family's kitchen."*

Then the recorder pulled back for a wide-angle shot of our kitchen. Off to the left, a rack of laser-guided assault weapons, mounted between a picture of a family and the food cooling units, came into view.

The real fear was unspoken. A family like mine knew that much of what was reported was true and widespread. But implications for shutting down Symbiosis were too horrifying to contemplate. Millions of Stocks running wild, bent on revenge, and eating us as Diqui burned worse than the times prior to Carbon Capture.

Soon enough, abolitionists made contact with Stock agitators in the TCs. In New Kansopolis, near the heart of continental Stock production, over 50,000 Consumers were tortured, raped, massacred, and forced to watch as Stocks amputated their limbs and pulled out their eyes and ate them in front of them. The urban center was bombed, razed, and bulldozed over, along with most of the Consumers and Stocks there, in hopes that little of what went on would be retold by survivors. While the fruit conglomerates wanted to blunt the drive toward Stock manumission, they did not want a world enraged by Stock atrocities, fearing a mass slaughter of their valuable property and the end of Symbiosis.

Violent attacks on conglomerates brought Symbiosis no closer to an end in what the abolitionists called the "War on Canabalistim," using the ancient term for effect. Targeting just the producers seemed to miss the point that it was consumers who were critical. Without them, fruit conglomerates would cease to exist. Anti-Symbiosis radicals put an end to the system abruptly when they claimed to have inserted toxic genes into the Stock genome. Some claim it was all a hoax designed to generate terror and fear to end Symbiosis. But fear was as good as reality for their purpose.

Eventually, abolitionist forces closed in on our part of the continent a year after my appearance on Hulianwang. All my family died. I am told they were tortured and consumed. I was well known because of my prominence as a "spokesperson," so my fate would be equally grim. When the abolitionists finally boxed me in, I decided to spare myself by committing suicide. Alas, through the wonders of technology, my consciousness was removed from its dead vessel, then digitally transferred to the Net for me to serve a sentence in a virtual prison. More than a life sentence, it is an eternal sentence in eternal darkness, with steady background audio of TC victims enduring the unendurable. These are the sounds of my forever. But in the blackness, I see. Faces clearly delineated, the curved lines of the foreheads indicating fear, the lines of the mouths indicating rage, the lines of the eyes indicating grief. I was responsible for bolstering an evil system. But being repentant makes no difference. For the foreseeable future, the one—maybe only—thing most citizens agree on is that I should endure my fate in perpetuity.

Mass extermination was started in New Atlanta, the empire on the eastern seaboard, out of fear that the Stocks would poison the blood of humanity if they were not exterminated. But the Western and Northern anti-Canabalist alliance disagreed, believing that damaged genes could be eradicated with newly developed therapies. Many noticed the ultra-pragmatic nature of the anti-Atlanta alliance, fruit conglomerates hoping to recover their es and maintain something of Symbiosis, fighting alongside abolitionists who intended to liberate Stocks and end Symbiosis. New Atlanta spent as much effort on diplomacy and disinformation to break the alliance as they did on weapons of war.

New Atlanta surrendered ten years ago. Surviving Islanders (we no longer use the insensitive older terms, like the S-word, to describe them) were resettled on the Atlantic coastal barrier islands. Though it's more accurate to say they resettled themselves, invading the islands to create a safe homeland for what was left of them and displacing the Indigenous communities already on those islands.

The hoped-for Islander integration back into society never took hold. Bigoted beliefs that the genetics of all descendants of TC survivors are irreparably dangerous, despite evidence and effective vaccines to the contrary, linger on. Every few weeks, charred corpses of Islanders appear on Hulianwang after the common occurrence of flame thrower attacks against them by violent anti-Islandists. I don't blame Islanders for wanting to stay on their islands, but in responding to the horror of their own past, they have relegated the Indigenous descendants to overcrowded Isolation Centers rife with disease. Even for victims, fear trumps compassion and empathy.

The Islanders are determined to survive, and it's increasingly believed that they have been able to create their own doomsday weapons in case the Islands are ever invaded. On the mainland, genetic absolutists remain a threat, convinced that only through the eradication of the Islanders can the rest of the human species be preserved.

I think back to my grandfather's sophistoric explanation almost a century ago, presenting Symbiosis as an acceptable continuation of an evolved moral imperative behind the human drive to endure. I think about where it got us and how close people live to the edge of annihilation as a result of the aftershocks, the opposite of the conditions we actually need to endure. Ever-durable fear seems to persist and evolve with our other survival instincts, seeding our moral systems with destructive imperatives, and Diqui has the scars to prove it. I debate with another imprisoned presence here in the Net about whether humanity should be ashamed of what we have wrought or proud that, despite the horrors we are capable of, we still have maintained the possibility of further evolution. We don't agree on much, but that it's a good time to be a post-genetic Digital.

The Amuse-Bouche

Dean Engel

Cicero Krimmel was born a stone's throw from the Chesapeake Bay and loved the water. He would catch fish with poles and tackle he made himself, set crab traps, and earn money as a guide leading groups around the local waterways. He could identify most of the naturally abundant marine fauna of the area, from scallops and oysters to crabs and snails. He became quite good at collecting them for local restaurants that paid well. His life revolved around marine life and the joy that he derived from it, which included finding, selling, and eating nature's bounty.

He put off college for a couple of years and instead worked on a crab trawler off the coast of Alaska. It was there he saw and heard of the devastation to the ocean that was quickly happening throughout the world. He eventually went to California to study marine biology, then quickly finagled a spot on the legal team behind the landmark O.P.A. (Ocean Preservation Act). Soon he was putting the final nail in the coffin of the last whalers, after the Harpoon Wars of the North Pacific.

He then channeled his energies into writing a book called *The World in Balance* suggesting a middle path for conservation of the natural world and utilization of it working together in balance. So much damage had been done, but he was preaching a gospel with appeal, with a focus on all that could still be saved.

Putting his ideas into practice, he created a venture capital group for investing in the natural world, emphasizing eco-tourism, which was quite successful. He designed its administration building, which floated on the sea and housed organizations he sought out as partners.

For a while it seemed that he might be the man to bring victory to the cause. He had the knowledge, charisma, and gravitas to lead and inspire. He was well-traveled, sophisticated but down-to-earth, quite wealthy now, and somewhat of a worldwide celebrity, with high visibility and access to corporate boardrooms, charitable organizations, and policy institutes. He was appointed a Minister of Natural Resources for the Oceanic Preservation Institute (OPI), the culmination of a lifetime of knowledge, integrity, and passion. He was the right man in the right place at the right time, with a chance to make a real difference.

He was also, like many men who have attained a certain degree of wealth and status, an Epicurean. He knew how to enjoy life, to savor the things available to those with means. His hundred-foot yacht was named *Living Well* from the expression, "Living well is the best revenge." His nose for wine was widely heralded, and his taste for haute cuisine was the stuff of legend. He once hosted a party on his yacht with a hundred varieties of heirloom Andean potatoes made into vichyssoise, the cold potato leek soup, for fifty very special guests.

On his 60th birthday, he arranged a dinner date with a new acquaintance, Patricia Melton. He met her for the first time at a fundraiser for the Institute two weeks earlier. She was younger than him but not embarrassingly young. She had a BA in marine botany and a master's in public administration. She had charmed him with her talk of marrying her love of nature with a service to the public; so idealistic and pretty as she talked passionately about her dreams. Her long chestnut-brown hair framed her tan face and her large, dark brown eyes, and it seemed to him that he was disappearing into her gaze like a lost fish entering a bed of sea kelp.

They dined at the wildly popular but difficult-to-get-seated-at Café du Monde. He was on good terms with the manager, and a quid pro quo had been established. Cicero and Patricia were quickly seated with a beautiful view of the sun setting over the water.

A waiter approached the table. "Would you care to start with our complimentary amuse-bouche this evening?" the waiter asked.

"I am afraid I am not familiar. What is it?" replied Patricia.

"Tonight we have roasted swallowtail pupa, drizzled with a raspberry aioli and dusted with a bit of saffron," he replied.

"Oh, and what did you call that?"

"I'll explain," said Cicero. "And yes, we would love it," Cicero said, waving off the waiter. "So I do have something I can teach you after all," said Cicero, "as it seems they did not have such things in Pocatello from whence you came. In France, they more often refer to it as amuse-gueule, but no matter, this will be sublimely delicious with either nomenclature. An amuse-bouche is like an appetizer. Typically, quite a modest portion offered as a complementary treat to start a meal, to stimulate the appetite, and for the chef to show off. It translates as 'it amuses the mouth,'" said Cicero in his most charming voice.

"Oooh, it sounds delightful," Patricia replied.

The waiter brought the treat and they agreed it was marvelous. Cicero ordered entrees, poached branzino with a citrus glaze, huge prawns, and some fermented bean curd with a braised rabbit leg. The branzino was rare to find these days, its numbers greatly diminished. The prawns were farm-grown.

Good food always had an aphrodisiac effect upon him, and he was not so old that his rooster no longer crowed. He tried not so subtly to arouse Patricia with tales of the reproductive habits of octopi, the sex of mollusks, and other such erotic matters. Oysters, for example, can change sex and often do so more than once. "Talk about gender fluidity," he joked. "A male oyster drops hundreds of thousands of sperm balls, each containing a couple thousand or so sperm. The female then breathes them in. They enter inside the female's shell through respiratory action and she fertilizes them internally." He tried a bit of footsie with Patricia under the table, but she was not matching his efforts.

After dinner, he offered to show her around the Institute. He supposed her love of public administration got the best of her where his charms had not. Ultimately, he failed to seduce her. He turned out to be the inescapable sea kelp, and she the little minnow who did not choose to explore his bed. After a half glass of port and some dull chat, the minnow simply swam away.

The next day brought meetings on top of meetings at the Institute. The state of affairs was bad. Species extinctions, poor sanitation and water quality, exacerbated by geopolitical turbulence and disasters of a hundred different kinds, brought natural decline and despair.

Hope was difficult to maintain in the face of such staggering loss. Oysters had been around for some 15 million years and were nearly all gone now. From all of the true oysters (Ostreidae) and the Aviculidae, or pearl oysters, to the bivalve mollusks known as thorny oysters (Spondylus) and the somewhat related saddle oysters (Anomia) to just a small group, you can count on the fingers of one hand. Not quite a monoculture, but a far cry from the diversity of a century earlier. Only a few species remained, those that were left and took well to farming in a broad range of conditions. Those that required very specific conditions, like the habitat of their naturally evolved terrain, typically died off when that terrain was dead and unavailable to them. Reef decay, temperature change, contaminated water, and more all contributed to the problems.

All things pass, and finally, so did the long day of meetings. Cicero went home to his penthouse suite on the top floor of the Institute. He sat on the sofa, and his mind was full of turmoil. He was beginning to question his ability, anyone's ability, to change things for the better. His thoughts raced and his eyes furtively darted about the room. He felt unmoored and adrift. Eventually his gaze landed on the Krimmel family crest proudly displayed on his wall. The German surname Krimmel had been an occupational name for a maker or user of hooks. His family had been fishermen for several generations in the old world. Seafood always had been a cultural keystone, and food staple. The Krimmel crest was comprised of a large oak tree with a large metal hook in the center, and a sailboat appeared above the oak tree. Otto Krimmel was Cicero's great-great-grandfather. He was most famous for his fish-based sauce, which garnered quite a reputation. King Gustav of Sweden bestowed the title of Royal Steward of Sauces upon Otto, and the Krimmels became well-known and prosperous on the popularity of Otto's fishy broth. There were vague whispers in the family of a scandal that occurred, causing the Krimmel family to flee, penniless but still proud, to America.

Cicero stared at the crest and thought about seafood. He knew wars had been fought over sauces, salt and spices, and fish. Great Britain and Iceland fought the Cod Wars over fishing rights in territorial waters. France and Brazil had fought the Lobster Wars over territorial fishing rights for the spiny or "rock" lobster, present in abundance off the coast of Brazil and crawling over the continental shelf at a depth of 250 feet or more. In 1961, Brazil claimed an exclusive territory of 100 miles for their fishing rights, but the French helped themselves to the lobsters anyway. The French fishermen reasoned that the rock lobsters were analogous to fish due to their powers of locomotion, propelling themselves via walking and/or swimming, and are harvested like fish rather than crustaceans (for example, oysters), which require dragging off the seabed floor to harvest. There is no testimony on record from the lobsters. They were promptly captured and consumed.

He recalled a myriad of happy moments: sailing the coast of Patagonia, giant wave surfing in Portugal, fighting a marlin for three hours off the coast of Bimini, eating a plate of sashimi with a side of uni (sea urchin) topped with ikura (salmon roe) right on the pier in Japan, and eating a po'boy in New Orleans. He thought it harder to love this world, hard to even imagine this world without those delights, but he already knew that we were moving inexorably to that reality.

The following day brought some excitement to the Institute, and to Cicero's management team. A new mollusk had arrived. It was thought to be the very last of its kind in existence, facing the likelihood of extinction, disappearing into history, into the void of nonexistence, oblivion. An intensive cloning program had been tried but had not worked. He was a strikingly beautiful creature with dynamic coloration and rather large. Cicero needed to review his case history and options for the future. There had to be something they could do, he thought, something to keep this fabulous creature alive and well and part of Earth's genetic treasure chest. He didn't like the naysayers, those who put down every idea and every effort as insufficient, too little too late, or impractical. Some said human nature was too predictable, or too rigid, and people would never adopt new thinking, never modify their behaviors. Never, never, not, no way—he had heard it a million times. He would always think to himself that surely there was still a way forward, but all of the dour meetings, the mounting evidence, and in particular, the photos of previously vibrant coral reefs, now desolate and lifeless, hanging on the walls of the Institute, each a memento mori of the death that comes to all living things, pushed back hard on any optimism.

Then he received a call from Patricia Melton. Cicero was surprised to hear from her. It turned out she had heard about the mollusk and very much wanted to see it herself. Some pleasantries were exchanged, a date set. *Why not?* Thought Cicero. *Let her see the mollusk.* Interest in the famous and rare little fellow was good for the Institute, for fundraising, and ultimately for the little oyster's chances at species propagation. *Patricia is a lovely girl,* he thought. *Maybe something more could develop from this after all.*

Patricia arrived at the Institute in beach clothes, far less formally attired this time.

"We are dining in this time," she said in response to nothing he said but reading his mind nonetheless. "No need to be so formal now."

They sat on the classic Le Corbusier sofa and made small talk. They sipped champagne, a bottle he had been given to celebrate his appointment to the Institute, which he had been saving for such an occasion. They made a great effort to "catch up" as old friends do despite barely knowing each other.

She seemed different this time, open and friendly. He felt quite attracted to her and it seemed now that she liked him too. His chatter became more expansive and his demeanor warm and effusive. She placed her hand on his shoulder. Then a joke, some melodious laughter from her, as she touched his knee.

"Let me see it," she said in almost a whisper.

"Okay," he replied as he started to unbutton his pants.

"Ahhhhhh," she said, giggling. "Not that. The mollusk."

He regained his composure and stood up, taking her hand. Breathlessly, they ran down the hall laughing, tingling with excitement. He opened the door to the specially equipped room that was housing the sublimely unique oyster. She walked around its tank in a state of reverie.

"It's magnificent," she whispered.

"So are you," he replied, and in an instant they were panting, groping, and disrobing. He grabbed her by the hand and took her down the hall to a spare bedroom he used for late nights at the Institute.

He was a bit soft and hoped she hadn't noticed. She rolled over and kissed his nose, and stroked his thigh.

"I... understand. None of us are as young as we used to be. I've dated men... important men... before. Do you need a pill first?" she asked softly.

"I'm fine. I'll be right back. You wait right here."

He snuck out of the bedroom looking for a snack, for strength, for energy, perhaps something for staying power, for the fortification of his loins. He remembered a time in New Orleans when, as a young man, he won an oyster slurping contest at a bar and spent the night with all three barmaids working there. Oysters always did the trick. Suddenly he thought of the oyster down the hall.

He went to the specially equipped room and stared at the oyster for a full five minutes. His mind was reeling. *Absolutely not,* he told himself. But there was another voice in his head, too. That voice was passionately making its case. *You have tried,* it said. *You enjoy a well-prepared bean cake as well as any man, eaten endless vermicelli, both the noodle and the worm, since wheat had become so impractical.* But his palate grew tired. He always craved some new sensation. And the world was dying anyway, and how could anyone think that he could stop it?

Some verses from a book he read decades ago sprung to mind, the verses of Omar Khayyam:

Ah, fill the Cup: - what boots it to repeat How Time is slipping underneath our Feet: Unborn To-morrow and dead Yesterday, Why fret about them if To-day be Sweet!

The Moving Finger writes; and, having writ, Moves on: nor all they Piety nor Wit Shall lure it back to cancel half a line, Nor all thy Tears wash out a Word of it.

Oh, come with old Khayyam, and leave the Wise To talk; one thing is certain, that Life flies; One thing is certain, and the rest is Lies; The Flower that once has blown for ever dies.

He was shaking and wracked with turmoil. He fought off the urge finally and left the room. A few moments later, however, he returned with a bottle of Tabasco and a lopsided grin. He reached into the tank and held the oyster. He cut it free from its shell with a small pocket knife, the one with the Cousteau Society logo given to him as an award for conservation work. He dotted the last known oyster of its kind with hot sauce and tossed it back. And burped.

It had all happened in an instant. He swallowed it whole without a bite. Savored it with a concentration and pleasure he had never experienced. Not until moments after his all-consuming fit of passion and temporary insanity had passed did he consider the magnitude of what he had just done. He was strangely calm, aware of his heinous and foolish act, but remained somehow detached from it as if it had been someone else who committed the act while he was made to watch from afar and unable to stop it from happening. He knew he was ruined at the Institute. Unless, he thought quickly, he could make it seem like a crime. A robbery, perhaps. *First things first,* he thought, and headed back to Patricia to pound her like carpaccio before he might lose the chance.

He had handcuffs stashed in his sock drawer. His friends had given him the gift of a stripper on his 50th birthday and she left the cuffs behind. For some reason, he could never bring himself to get rid of them. He returned to the bedroom.

"Ooh Honey, yes," Patricia said at the sight of the cuffs.

"I have to tell you something," he said calmly but seriously.

"I did something... selfish."

"Shellfish what?" she asked.

"I just sent a species into extinction. I ate the Institute's prize possession," he confessed.

"Of course you did. You are such a joker. And you didn't share... you bad boy. Do you have a whip to go with those cuffs?"

Cicero rose to the occasion one more time, and then they both drifted off to sleep. It had been a very eventful night for everyone.

The Blue Ridge Mountain Tree

Adjie Henderson

The Blue Ridge mountains appear in the distance each morning as large breasts surrounded by a blue haze that doesn't darken until the sun drops behind the hills and the moon lights up the outline of the mountains in black and white. They are almost the oldest mountains in the world and are really blue or, more properly, the atmosphere around them is blue. The color is caused by a chemical released from some kinds of trees, like aspen or oak trees. The blue haze is probably a tree's way of protecting itself from overheating. Over centuries of evolution, plants had to develop sensory mechanisms to ensure their survival in one place. A tree has no choice; it can't migrate in search of food or water or a mate or social position.

A Cherokee legend tells of a big buzzard that flew over the earth. When he reached the Indians' land, he was tired and came nearer to the earth, and his wings began to hit the ground. A valley formed when his wings struck the earth, and when he raised his wings again, a mountain formed. When the other animals saw this, they asked him to return home because they did not want the entire earth to be mountainous. The mountains the buzzard formed were the Blue Ridge.

Each morning, Billy ran barefoot through the mountain paths, at peace and one with the hills. The rough paths wandered through green foliage and rocky creeks and onto rock ledges left by some ancient event. Every twist of the path was new each day. Everything was alive.

He rested on the metal couch swing in front of his trailer home and watched the dark clouds finish their daily rain trip over the mountains. Then it was hot and humid again. The heat rolled up and down the mountain paths, chilled only by the breeze over the stream coming from the forest.

"Move it, boy," said his father, arriving home for midday dinner. "Get your butt off the swing. It's time to eat."

And to his wife, with her head inside the oven retrieving biscuits, "He is strange. Takes after your family."

"For chrissake!" screamed the mother. "He's yore boy, too. Did you get the birthday present?"

"Yeah, it's in the truck."

"Good lord, what is it?"

"A tree!"

"A what?"

"A tree."

"And where will it be planted?"

"Right here, in the front yard."

"This is a freaking trailer park."

"It will make us look less like white trailer park trash, even if that is what we are."

"Get off the pot!" she yelled at the toilet, and "Move it, my sister's coming for lunch!" she yelled at the front door.

On cue, a big rusty gray van rattled right up to the trailer door, its muddy mud flaps waving in the breeze. It smacked of a Jesus wagon but was just identified by a simple sign: Church van and on the bumper, the perfunctory Honk if you love Jesus!

They ate at a card table under the awning outside the trailer where no grass ever grew. A skinny neighborhood dog prissed over and peed on the rear tire of the Jesusmobile, leaving a big, hot, muddy splotch on the bare ground.

"Mighty hot," they said when the conversation lagged. "Gonna be 95 today."

"Yep, mighty hot. Even over there in the blue mountains. They aren't really blue. Haha. Some kind of mirage."

"They are blue," said Billy, "or at least the atmosphere is blue."

His father stared at him. "You are fulla shit."

He went back to work, never mentioning the boy's existence. The sisters gossiped for a while and drank cold jug wine, followed by a lot of mouthwash for the preacher's wife.

"Happy birthday, boy," said the aunt. "I brought you a present—your own book of religious sayings. I know you are worrying about the plants and such. Jesus is gonna take care of the birds in the air and the lilies of the field. Jesus will fix the environment."

Wrapped with the book of religious platitudes was an old, smelly, musty copy of *The Secret Life of Plants*.

"And your father got you a tree from us," said the mother.

Billy named the oak tree Maria and planted it near a forest at the edge of the old trailer park. It wasn't a perfect address, probably not one a proper anthropomorphic tree would choose. It was definitely a blue-collar mountain neighborhood. Maria developed strong ties with the other trees in the forest. Her tree neighbors took care of her, and the Woman of the Forest spoke to her and watched her grow. The older trees fed the younger trees with liquid sugar from underground fungal networks and warned the neighbors that danger was approaching, sometimes using pheromones and other chemical signals. They send distress signals to other trees; carbon, water, alarm signals, and hormones also pass from tree to tree. Maria became part of the forest network.

Billy knew many of the tests in *The Secret Life of Plants* could not be repeated, but he had to know for himself. His results were certainly inconclusive, but he felt a kinship with

Maria and the trees of the forest he could not understand. Maria was his Dryad, his spirit of the forest.

The woman of the forest was a Cherokee woman who had lived for years in a rusty trailer in the woods. She knew the weather and the animals and plants of the blue mountains.

"We are the caretakers and protectors of trees; each tree and each living thing has its own special spirit that you must protect forever. When they die, we die."

Each day, the Woman of the Forest would take his hand and teach Billy about the plants and how they interact and hear and smell and speak, how they remember and touch and feed each other.

"The trees of the forest or any living being could be the work of a divine being or fortunate statistical events described by scientists. It may not matter. Living things accommodate their lifestyle, and plants do quite well in this regard. There is, of course, other stuff we do not know about.

"If all the trees of the forest form one large organism, it will be difficult for us to understand. If each tree is an independent organism, being a tree as compared with being a person should be simple. Aha, you say. It's just about time measurements. I can measure what is happening by slowing down our time or speeding up the tree timing in the frames of the same event. For plants, we people compare it to a movie run at a slow speed. It is much more complicated. It is probable that not all phases follow a simple difference in timing in concert, but rather, each individual feature may have a timing different from ours. It is a complicated problem. You must also remember that there are many species of plants, and they are all as different as the different species of animals. Their communications with each other could be as different as a dog barking at a croaking frog."

Billy became a famous botanist and studied the birth, life, and death of plants at famous universities. He gave distinguished lectures and wrote brilliant treatises. He was the scientific star of Public TV, smiling and explaining our world and becoming the darling of the pseudo-enlightened. He knew now that plants could respond to variables like light, water, gravity, temperature, animals chewing on their leaves, and signals from other plants. Each finding was fodder for arguments among the scientists.

Billy knew that there was no one in charge of our future environment, like a driver with no steering wheel racing down an empty and fallow country road singing "Wooley bully" until all were gone—the flowers, the trees, the wild herbs, the animals that needed the plants for food. There was no peace here. No matter what we knew scientifically, there was something missing in our relationship with plants. He never found the answers.

One day, he closed his books and began to run throughout the earth. He studied with Hindus in India, Buddhists in Japan, Taoists in China, and the Yoruba in Africa. He passed soldiers with no legs, women being raped, hungry children, forests with no trees, concrete farms, and parks filled with plastic bags and water bottles.

He became one again with the earth, not a world he remembered, but the earth, nevertheless. One day, he looked to the sky as he ran to the forest he should recognize. He was running home, back to the mountains.

But the trees were gone. As soon as Maria heard the loud noises of the men and their machines, she waved her limbs and sent nutrients to the younger trees. It was too late. Her network had been ripped apart. The mother tree sent pheromone warnings, but Maria felt her screams as she went down. The loud machine cut into the mother tree, and then they came for her. Maria and the mother tree began to die, strapped to a long, angry truck.

The whole area that was once a trailer park in the woods was levelled by a motorized flower killer, and the expanse was covered in black paving. There's a drive-in fast-food restaurant where Maria used to stand. The rusty trailer of the Woman of the Forest is gone, and so is she.

The afternoon rain was coming soon. For a moment, the sun made a halo around a cloud. The bright rays reflected from the pools behind the rocks in the rushing water of the creek. Billy felt the cold rain on his naked arms and legs. Then the rain ended, and he thought he saw the mountain laurel and smelled the green smell of the foothills—the smell of the wet loblolly pines, but there were no trees, only his memory. The day was still hot. A dust-covered rabbit watched him from under a remaining bush, both filled with flies and gnats. A lake had formed in the hole left by constant digging. From a distance it was lovely in such a barren place. There was a remaining rocky outcropping that baked in the constant sun. Billy sat on the hot rocks eating his lunch and had thoughts of jumping in the lake water. But as he moved to the edge, he saw the large pipes spewing soapy water and probably sewage from the new housing above into the lake.

Parts of the mountain slopes were treeless meadows, shrubland, or muddy soil crisscrossed with deep tractor tire tracks. Remnants of trees, woody detritus, and branches were remaining in the bare soil of makeshift roads that meandered up the side of the mountain. The hills were almost bare except for monotonous tree stumps like pimples on the earth's surface.

When he ran past the waterfall, he was almost home. The endless stretches of soft blue haze in the distance were gone forever. The mountains were no longer blue.

The Captain of the Fleet

David Poyer

The sky was still dark that morning as Francis Pickett, lurching after several wake-up nips from the pint bottle in his foul weather jacket, rolled down the pier toward *Miss Clearice*. "Need a crew," he howled, turning heads all along the waterfront. "Who wants to make a lick?"

But the men looked away, back to greasing blocks, chipping rust, painting, mending nets. Even the loafers idling and smoking on the front bench of the marina office suddenly found their boots more interesting.

St. Edwards was home for the Chesapeake Bay menhaden fleet. Pickett had once been its senior captain, directing the six huge Zeta Protein trawlers that had annually pulled in fifty thousand tons of the oily, bony pogies for livestock feed, fish oil, cat food, and antirust paint. Before he'd been fired, of course.

Pickett halted before the liars' bench. "How 'bout you, Denny?" he asked a grizzled fellow in a leather coat and watch cap.

"Ain't goin' out with you no more, Cap'n Pickett. Not after you slap' me that last time."

"Hundred cash, my man. Just to tend the winch."

"Ain't, Cap'n. Back's too stove up today."

"Mickey, how 'bout you? You like a drink. I'm the only wet boat out of here."

His only answer was a shake of the head, hunched shoulders.

"Well, to hell with you all," Pickett snapped. "On my own again, I guess. Line my pockets, not yours. Lazy scumbers." He hawked up an oyster, spat at their feet, and staggered down the pier.

He was far out on the open Bay when the sun rose. It burned the horizon tangerine and salmon, gilded the gentle waves the color of a whelk's pearly insides.

Miss Clearice chugged across that polished steel surface all day as Pickett hustled back and forth between the pilothouse and the huge drum that rolled up the net he trailed astern. But all it brought up were oyster toads, sharks, weakfish, and scores of quivering, scarlet-hearted jellyfish. The fish flopped about on deck, gasping, drowning in the air. "Nothin' but trash today," he muttered, stomping on a sand shark's head, then scraping the bycatch overboard with an old coal shovel.

Around one, he glimpsed the Zeta fleet on the horizon. The black-hulled ships corralled a half-mile circle. Within it, workboats were towing the huge purse seines shut. Tiny silver fish surged and struggled, churning the surface into foam and flashing fins. Shading his eyes, Pickett muttered, "Seems like there's less every year." He thought about steering closer, pecking along the edges of the school, but the last time he'd done that, they'd turned the firehoses on him.

He forked Libby's corned beef from a can for dinner, then tossed the empty overboard. "Stay out tonight, damn it," he muttered. Nothing waiting back home, just the leaning house on rotting pilings, stilt-tilted, gradually sliding into the slowly encroaching Bay. Some said the rising water would take the whole island soon. Erase it overnight in some horrendous storm. He didn't believe it. The news was all lies anyway.

It was against fisheries regulations to trawl at night. He checked his phone, the app that showed where the fisheries cops and coast guard lurked. Then snapped on the big halogens and aimed them down into the water.

An hour after dark, the winch groaned as he hit the controller handle. "About goddamn time," he muttered. When he hauled the dripping net in, the woven nylon, black so the prey couldn't see it, disgorged a tumbling flood of glittering catch. The tiny fish flipped and boiled like live mercury. He was shovelling them toward the hold when he halted, staring. Amid the flood of fish lay a dead orange cat.

He frowned, puzzled. Pulling up unexpected things wasn't uncommon. Old anchors. Abandoned crab pots. Once, he'd brought up a shell from the old Navy range down Tangier Island. But the cat seemed familiar. All the cats on St. Edwards were orange, with flat faces, stupid, and slow from inbreeding since the island had been a haunt of picaroons.

He seized it by its stumpy tail, cursed, and flung it back into the Bay.

He slept too late the next day, so he just reached under the bunk and pulled out the gallon of Senator's Club he'd bought in . He stayed in all day, taking a snort now and again, and finally forced himself up as the sun declined. "Might's well hit 'er again tonight," he muttered.

Two hours later, out by Turkey Reef, a human body tumbled out of his net. "Holy shit," he muttered, jumping back, almost falling over a barrel of diesel. He recognized the long jaw, the scarred pale trawlerman's hands, the staring brown eyes. The Baltimore Ravens cap. "Euey," he muttered. "Eustace Simmons."

Shaken, Francis yanked the throttle back. The Detroit clattered to a halt. *Clearice* drifted in the dark. He collapsed on the barrel and lit a Camel, contemplating the corpse.

They'd worked together, friends at first. Until his mate threatened to tell the company Pickett was selling on the side to Zeta's biggest competitor, Oleum Products. Called him a thief, even when he'd offered to split.

"You won't rat on me, Euey," Francis had told him, and grabbed a bait knife.

Now he remembered the cat, too. Tray, the wharf mouser. Francis and the other boys had tormented the ginger tom, smearing grease on his fur, setting him on fire, finally drowning him in a bag. Just for fun.

He shook his head, confused. "Don't get it. Tray, then Euey. Should be rotted, crab food. How come they look so fresh?"

He didn't say it aloud but wondered: *And why the hell were they coming back?*

At last he weighted the corpse with a chain and rolled it back over the side. Hands shaking, he went to the pilothouse and tilted the bottle again. Then put *Miss Clearice*'s helm over and headed home.

That day, only just asleep, he dreamed he was back in the Coast Guard, but he'd fallen overboard. He was floundering in the wake, trying to swim after the vanishing cutter. Then, somehow, he was back at school, and Miss Morris was threatening to tell his dad Francis had put his hand up her skirt.

When he woke at last, he'd pissed his sheets. He lay in the wet for a while, head pounding, then reached under the bunk again. The gallon was getting low. "Might's well finish it off, get more in Reedville," he grunted.

He kept drinking all day, waking on and off. Finally, he staggered out down the little main street to bum a wedge of stale cake at the Island Bakery. Then wove down to the harbor, taking a hit off the dregs now and then, not bothering to hide the jug. The loafers by the office didn't look up as he staggered past. He heard them laughing behind him and turned to flourish a finger.

The first lick that night, the motor whined under a heavy load. When the fish spilled out, among them lay a middle-aged blonde in green rubber waders and a cable-knit sweater. Francis shuddered and squeezed his eyes shut.

"Candy," he moaned.

His second wife. She'd helped aboard *Clearice* after Euey had mysteriously vanished. But in a fit of rage, when she warned him he was about to run into a weir, he'd clubbed her with a winch handle and pushed her over. Seconds later, he'd spun the wheel and gone back, but she was gone.

What was going on? How were these animals, people, *coming back?* He smoothed her eyes closed, and tears stung his own. "I'm so sorry," he muttered.

Then he rolled her, too, back into the Bay.

The next morning, when he made port for fuel, the harbor master was waiting on the pier. His boyhood pal, Russ McLean. "Russ," Francis muttered.

McLean caught his line and made it off. "Doin' any good, Frank?"

"Maybe a half a ton. Not much goin' out there these days. Not like it was when I went out with Dad."

"Yeah, we all gotta scratch harder these days. But I got to talk to you, Frank."

Francis bent to adjust a fender. "Suit y'self."

"You been drinking too much, Frank. Tour people complained you tried to run 'em down in the channel comin' in. And Billy says you owe him fourteen hundred now for fuel. Diesel I 'spect you're trading for booze in Reedville."

"Do you remember Tray, Russ?"

"What?"

"The cat we killed."

"The cat *you* killed," McLean said. "We tried to stop you. Poor creat're was still alive when you threw the sack in the water. Cruelest thing I ever seen. Anyway, I gotta report you. Mayor says town don't need a captain plays chicken with the tourists."

Francis vaulted the gunwale and tigered him with two hands to the chest. McLean stumbled back, almost falling off the far side into the harbor. "Oh, *I'm* cruel?" Francis growled. "You're the ones who dared me to do it. I ain't afraid of your threats. Ain't afraid of nothing, man or sea or sky. Put that in your lousy *report*."

"Don't curse the Bay, Frank. Waterman should know better'n that." McLean started to swing at him, then stopped. His fist dropped; he retreated down the pier. "No more line handling when you come in, Pickett. And no more free wharfage. You just lost your last friend."

"I never needed no so-called friends!" Francis yelled after him. "And y'all can go screw yourselves, hear?"

McLean just waved as he left, not even looking back.

That night, Francis went out again. The wind was rising, but so what? If this was a curse of some kind, he'd outlast it. He'd never yet let man nor woman nor fish nor company get the better of him. "Bring it on, show me what ya got!" he yelled, aiming down the channel as dusk fell.

His first pull that night yielded a bounty of shiny, flapping menhaden, along with dozens of blues. Unusual; the bluefish usually lurked below the schools, preying on them. He threw the biggest in the cooler; he'd sell them in Reedville in the morning. "All right," he exulted. The curse was broken. "In your ugly face, Chesapeake Bay." He gave the sea and sky the finger, grinning.

The second netful came up even heavier. The winch motor strained, whined, close to burning out. Francis danced on the reeling deck. "No h'ant'll beat me," he slurred, staggering, nearly falling overboard, until he caught himself on the davit.

When the net dumped out on the wet, slicked deck, a body sprawled amid the tons of struggling fish. Francis gasped. His own face stared up blindly. A crab crawled over it, then jabbed a claw into one open eye. The live Pickett choked and gripped his throat, staring down.

Then, somehow, the deck lights went out. Even the moon vanished, leaving him anchorless in the black.

Francis came to swimming furiously in the freezing dark. Above, below, to either side, other bodies threshed the infinite Bay. He swam desperately, propelled by a mindless and terrible fear.

From below, cruelly toothed jaws snatched at his legs, barely missing. A horrible crunch grated as they tore apart someone else. The school swerved, all at once, all together, and thoughtlessly yet still terrified, Francis wheeled with them, mouth gaping like a gaffed rockfish.

The gray light of dawn filtered down, illuminating tiny ures drifting. He snapped at them, swallowed. Yet even as he ate, he was still ravenous. And still consumed by that terrible fear that he, too, was prey.

Then he slammed into something strange. It yielded, yet somehow held. Around him, men and women in robes, uniforms, dresses, expensive suits struggled and fought, but it was useless. They were lifted up, up, choking, gasping, dying, into a region where each breath was scorching fire.

Into blazing, glaring light.

The Circle City Run

Tom Sterling

Three... two... one.... We're outta here!

I empty my dustpan into the trash can, grab a bag of ice, and fill a shopping bag with snacks from the damaged item shelf. My buddy, Gary, scoops the pile of cardboard boxes he's been cutting up into the recycling bin. Thirty seconds later, we're racing across the Food Lion parking lot to an old wooden dock, where Tyrone and James are waiting in James's twenty-one-foot Carolina Skiff.

"Sup fellas," says Tyrone.

"A pack of Oreos got stepped on today," I say, shaking my head. "That's two Saturdays in a row. There were some dented Coke cans, too, and a smashed bag of Doritos."

"It's hard to find good help these days," says Gary, winking.

"Hop in, guys," says James, grabbing the engine's tiller handle. I move the ice, cookies, and Cokes into a cooler on the floor of the boat. Once we're seated, James twists the throttle, and we cruise slowly along the edge of the parking lot past McDonald's. He pulls out onto Hall Highway, where disconnected power poles, dead pine trees, and the skeletons of old houses line both sides of the road, now a waterway. The rusting roofs of a few dead cars poke out of the salty water where the curbs used to be. Branches and wooden planks float listlessly along both sides of the road, forming small islands of debris where reeds and Virginia Creeper vines have taken root.

"Careful, dude," cautions Tyrone as we cruise down the street. He grips the bow of the boat and stares through the water at the faded yellow lines on the asphalt road three feet below us, watching for obstacles.

"Relax! I've got this. It's high tide," says James. "Oh, and coming up on the right is my uncle's old house. The roof fell in a couple of weeks ago."

"Can you believe this is where the rich folk in town used to live?" I ask, staring at gaping doorways and broken windows. "They should have built their houses up on poles."

"Poles don't do much good when your whole yard is underwater," says Gary. We all nod.

"There it is," says James, pointing to an old Cape Cod set back among the dead trees. The red brick wall on the west side of the house has pulled away from the corners and now sways precariously in the air, looking like a mild breeze might blow it over. The roof lays straight back as if it's on some giant hinge. The two dormers that used to face the street now point straight up at the sky. We ooh and aah and say, "Cool," but the place mostly just looks sad.

We continue cruising, and Gary points to a crumbling pile of boards and bricks on our left and says, "Governor J. Millard Tawes used to live there."

We finally reach the end of the road and arrive at the old, abandoned McCready hospital where my grandfather was born. The boring part of our tour is over. The sun is shining, and the water is calm and clear. It's time for some fun!

"First run goes to the navigator," says James. "Legion Library Run?" he asks as Tyrone pulls a life jacket over his bright, white T-shirt, kicks off his sandals, and places his feet into the rubber bindings of the bright blue water skis. Tyrone nods and sits on the gunwale, swinging his long, thin legs one by one over the side. There aren't any sea nettles in sight, so I hand

him the bright yellow tow handle, and he drops into the water.
I feed out the line as James creeps the boat forward.

The rope goes taught, and Tyrone gives Gary and me the
thumbs-up sign. "Hit it!" shouts Gary, and I record on my
phone as James twists the throttle. Tyrone leans his body
backward and slowly stands on the skis. The boat picks up
speed and planes on top of the water once Tyrone is all the
way up.

James steers west toward the abandoned town of Crisfield.
Back in the '40s, long before I was born, the ocean water
levels started rising until they reached a point where folks had
to pack up and move. Low-lying areas were the first to go,
but every year, the Chesapeake Bay took a little more until
finally, Crisfield became just a big, empty ghost town. The
government will probably begin some massive cleanup one
day, but the flooding happened all over the country. A small
town like ours will be way down on their priority list. We're
on our own.

We cruise in a long, wide circuit around a tiny island,
where snowy white egrets and colorful great blue herons sit
in nests along the rusty metal roof of the deserted American
Legion building. James skims past Wellington Beach and steers
through a long line of white and orange buoys. The buoys hold
signs saying Condemned, No Fishing, Polluted Waters, and
Boats Keep Out.

We enter what used to be the old boat harbor, avoiding
submerged poles and debris. Cattails and reeds along the edge
of the inlet sway in our wake. Tyrone leans side to side in the
narrow harbor, spraying plumes of water high in the air with
his skis. We burst onto Brick Kiln Road and pick up speed in
the shallow water before taking a fast, whipping loop around
the old Family Dollar store.

Tyrone finally releases the rope and makes a long, straight
glide over to a long, metal wheelchair ramp leading up to the

abandoned library's front doors. He flips out of his skis when they touch the ramp, casually strolls to the doorway, and peers in the window.

"Nice job, Ty!" I yell, pocketing my phone, slow-clapping a few times, and winding in the tow rope. "See any books about global warming in there?"

James pulls the skiff up next to a rusty handicapped parking sign beside the ramp.

"That's all just fake news," says Tyrone, grinning, as he wades down the ramp, hands the skis to Gary, and climbs in the boat. "Top that run, white boy!" he adds, pulling off his life jacket.

"Way to stick the landing, Ty, but get ready for me to show you how it's done," says Gary, grinning back. "Condo Crashdown Run!" he calls out to James.

James steers the skiff toward deeper water. Gary drops over the side, and I feed out the line. The rope pulls tight, Gary gives a thumbs-up, and James floors it. I record as we race west past the old shell of Handy's crab-picking house and take a long, slow turn toward three side-by-side condominium buildings standing empty at the water's edge. James threads the needle through a bulkhead wall and races along a long wooden walkway toward a narrow strip of water between condos two and three. Gary lifts the ski rope handle high in the air, shifting his weight and zigging and zagging around mooring poles as we approach the buildings.

We blast in between the condos, and James twists hard on the tiller, sending a wall of water over rows of abandoned cars and accelerating past the gaping doorway to condo two. We take another hard right, narrowly skim by condo one, and race through more rows of poles. Gary whips back and forth between the exposed pilings, crouches down, and leaps over a 4x4 sticking out from the walkway.

James speeds off in a long loop and turns back toward a submerged swimming pool in front of condo three. He throttles to maximum speed and steers the boat toward a homemade plywood ramp we nailed onto the dock a few weeks ago. James points the skiff between two poles at the last second and heads out to deeper water. Gary squats and angles himself toward the ramp. He releases the handle and leaps just as he hits, flying high into the air and forming an X with his skis, like a snow skier, before splashing down in the center of the pool.

James cuts the throttle and motors slowly over to the ramp. With skis in hand, Gary climbs out of the pool and wades over to the boat.

"That was awesome, brother," says Tyrone. "Spectacular run!"

"And I recorded the whole thing," I add, smiling and holding up my phone.

We pull out the snacks and soak up the warm sunshine. The cookies and ice-cold Cokes hit the spot.

"Are you going to go today?" I ask James.

"No reason for me to ruin a perfectly good boat ride," says James before popping another Oreo into his mouth. "It's all you, man."

"Alright, alright, alright," I say, doing my best Matthew McConaughey impersonation. "There's only one possible way for me to top those two runs."

James stares at me. "Are you talking about—"

"Yep," I interrupt. "I'm doing the Circle City Run today."

"No way!" says Gary and Tyrone in stereo.

"If not now, when, dudes? If not me, who?" I say, loosely quoting some old poet my mom likes named Hillel. I'm not sure the man said dudes, but I think McConaughey would.

I don't have Tyrone's quick turn ability and can't do the wild acrobatics Gary does. My skiing superpower is endurance, which I'll need to complete the Circle City Run. At least, that's what I think I'll need. I'm not 100% sure because no one has ever tried it. Endurance is needed because parts of this run take place in less than two feet of water. I can't afford to fall onto the asphalt, and not just because it might kill me, which it might. If we have to stop, we may have to get out of the boat and walk back to deeper water, which would suck.

I picture the run in my mind. We mapped it out in history class one day on an old, laminated, pre-flood map of the town. On the map, someone had scratched out "Crisfield" and written "Circle City" underneath. No one knows why, but it sounds cool. We'll cruise past the city dock and across Somers Cove, then wind our way through town, following old street signs sticking out of the water at intersections. We traced a path past houses, churches, and straight down Main Street. It'll be a blast, IF I can stay up without falling, that is.

"Are you sure you want to do this?" asks Gary as I clip my phone into my chest harness and slide into the water. "We're still not sure it's even possible. If you want, we can ride out to Old House Cove and circle the chimney a bunch of times instead."

"I want to try it," I say, leaning back and gripping the tow rope handle. When the rope pulls tight, I press record on my phone and give a thumbs-up to Tyrone, who shouts, "Hit it!" The boat lurches forward, pulling me against my skis. I tighten my leg muscles, keep the skis in front of me, and rise as if standing up from a chair. The boat picks up speed, and cool mist sprays my face as I skim the water's surface. I relax and enjoy the ride, cutting back and forth and taking short jumps over the boat's wake.

We motor past the city dock and race through the narrow entrance to Somers Cove. As we do, I cut over next to a small island on the right wrapped in tar-coated wooden bulkheads. This part of town used to be a lot bigger, and my mom said her grandfather used to have an oyster-shucking house here.

I stay behind the boat once we're in the cove. James has his work cut out for him, so I hang back and let him do his thing. When the marina shut down, out-of-towners abandoned their boats and left them tied up at the docks. Most of them sunk or came loose from their moorings, and now, years later, the entire harbor is one giant tangle of sunken boats, sailing masts, cables, ropes, and garbage. Gary keeps an eye on me while navigator Tyrone uses his height and sharp eyes to help James avoid obstacles.

We wind our way through the wrecks and motor toward the southeast corner of the cove. James steers through a section of road that washed away and cruises into a wide, flat field full of marsh grasses. The boat takes a hard left, but I head right and lean into a wide arching turn. I skim through reeds and grasses as I go, knocking clinging periwinkle snails down into the water. I barely miss skiing through a raft of hidden black ducks, but at the last second, the ducks leap into the air, avoiding me and almost scaring me out of my skis.

We make it to Somerset Avenue, zipping past the middle school parking lot where flagpoles and streetlamps rise out of the water. The school roof peeled away years ago when a line of huge water spouts ripped through town. Dead mimosa trees lean onto the rusty bus stop canopy.

James follows Somerset past a mud-caked End School Zone sign as the waterway turns north, and we hit our first obstacle. An enormous pine tree fell over up ahead. The top of the tree rests precariously on sagging phone lines, and vine-covered branches dangle down, blocking most of the road.

Tyrone points at a large branch, and I'm shocked when the boat turns toward it and disappears behind a mountain of vines. I try to follow behind, ducking and twisting to stay on my skis. The boat's wake rolls the tree branches back and forth, catching against the rope and digging into my legs and arms. Tyrone and Gary cheer when I burst out on the other side, bleeding from my scratches and trailing long strings of Virginia Creeper vines behind me.

Next, we sail through my favorite section of town, where rows of old Victorian houses sit peacefully atop solid brick and stone foundations. Paint peels from the old clapboard siding, and the tall pecan and magnolia trees that once decorated the front lawns have long-since collapsed into the brackish water. Otherwise, the sturdy hardwood houses stand intact, and I sometimes dream about moving into one of them, installing solar panels on the roof, and using the wide, wraparound porch as my boat dock.

We have a plan for getting past the second obstacle. Years ago, when the flooding got bad, folks piled sandbags across the street between the Baptist church and the old Masonic Temple, thinking they could keep water out of Main Street. The bags didn't help, and no one ever bothered removing them. One day, we waded here after school with shovels and prybars and dug away a section of bags wide enough to get the boat through.

As we approach the sandbag wall, I briefly think about trying to leap over it, like Gary, but instead, I stay behind the skiff. It's a long walk back from here. The roar of the boat's Yamaha engine echoes off the brick walls as we race past.

What happens next feels like something right out of a nightmare. James turns left down Chesapeake Avenue, and I notice that the corner of the cemetery wall has fallen over. I decide it'll be fun to ski among the marble and granite tombstones sticking out of the water. An old joke pops into my head as I ski through the opening in the wall. *Why do they put walls around cemeteries?* I think, grinning.

A Speed Limit 25 sign suddenly looms on the road between me and the boat. I lift the tow rope at the last second and avoid it. I turn to look ahead and barely keep from slamming into an open coffin floating in the water a dozen feet away. Skimming past, I see bones scattered across the top of a dark suit.

Coffins are floating all over the cemetery. Trapped air must have ripped the boxes up through the wet soil. Most of the coffins are closed, and they aren't hard to avoid, but several are clustered around the gate, blocking off my exit.

I ski past the gruesome log jam to an older part of the cemetery, dodging statues and rusty, wrought iron fences. I don't see a way back out to the road, and the end of the graveyard is flying up fast. I'm just about to let go of the handle when I spot a small gap between the wall and a row of dead trees. I squeeze through the opening, scraping my elbow on the side of the corner column. Gary and Tyrone applaud when I pop out onto the road, jump the wake, and fall back behind the boat.

Because people are dying to get in, I muse, smiling and remembering my joke. I'm happy to be leaving the cemetery behind.

We turn left down First Street and hang a sharp right onto Main Street next to the old Mount Pleasant Church, another building standing above the waterline. My dad told me his grandparents got married there.

My arms are tired, so I hook one through the tow rope handle, relax my legs, and dead-ski behind the boat to rest. The square, brick buildings of Crisfield's downtown district loom up ahead. As we cruise through downtown, the wake stretches out in a wide "V" and splashes back off the brick walls, crisscrossing past me in a diamond-shaped grid of harmonic ripples. I see the red and gold McCRORY'S FIVE AND DIME sign and wonder what life might have been like before the water ruined everything. I think it must have been pretty good.

We round the corner, and James points the boat toward deeper water and the setting sun.

My Circle City Run is over.

The Island

Mary Ethna Black

A woman in expensive beachwear—floppy hat, designer sunglasses, espadrilles—descends the stairs from a waterfront villa. She's old enough to be a grandmother—straight-edged gray bob, improbably unlined face, stiff hips—and is helped onto the launch by a tanned teenage girl in board shorts, her granddaughter perhaps? The woman sits in the prow and holds on to her sunhat. The girl puts a picnic basket on board, then casts off from the jetty. Turquoise waters curl from the prow as dolphins weave in and out before them. Around the headland, to drop anchor in a sheltered bay. The girl gets off first, carrying the picnic basket and a spear gun. As the woman swings her legs over the side, she overbalances and her kaftan dips into the shallow water. The girl holds out an arm and together they make it onto the sand, laughing. The woman lays a towel out on a waiting sun lounger and takes a magazine from her beach bag. I can see Jamie Oliver on the front cover, that chef who was famous in 2020. Such a perfect day.

This is how it used to be.

Fast-forward to 2065.

Harp

Grandma was determined to bring us to this island, so let's hope we don't get killed. The weather patterns are messed up, and the ocean can change quickly, so I'm on guard. Gentle waves can rapidly churn up into a freak storm, so I watch for any changes, ready to get back to shore. If a storm brews, I'll collect Grandma and take the Travelor down to deeper waters. When we're hovering 100 meters down, feeling the pull and suck of the turmoil on the surface, I like the motion, but Grandma doesn't. She says it makes her want to throw up. Grandma worries about the mining gear, how long the oxygen generator will hold, everything. I don't. What's the point?

She came here with her own grandmother for a picnic, and she's been planning this for weeks. A picnic for the two of us, which is weird but kinda nice. When Grandma was young, families lived in houses, children went to school in big buildings, and people ate cows. I've got old surfing videos and a small dried-up tin of surf wax—I like the smell. I've built myself a board and worked out how to use it. I'll pretend I'm battling to get my place in the line-up, imagining there are lots of us instead of just me. I've made a new stun gun, the first time I've tried this one. Hope it works.

I'm gonna catch us a fish.

Alice

Here we are, the first two people to set foot on this island in decades. The ocean stretches all the way to the horizon, and the blue sky is devoid of clouds. Just like it was that day, I came here with Grandma and we sunbathed on loungers, slathered in sunscreen. Those were the stupid, senseless, wonderful days. I watch my grandson amble across the sand with his surfboard. All young people are beautiful, and he doesn't know it.

"Was there really a hotel here, Grandma?" Harp hollers back.

"Yes, darling. Do be careful."

Be careful of what... I doubt we'll get any sharks. He's already on his board, paddling out. I catch his faint words.

"Will do."

This is a good spot for our picnic. I'll sit down under this palm tree and read my magazine, or rather my collection of tattered pages. See? Here's Jamie Oliver standing over a bonfire on this very beach, the white sand dimpled with the footprints of his family and friends. There's a recipe for grilled fish and salad to the side of the page and most of the writing is still intact. That's what I'll cook today.

"Hey, Grandma! Look at me."

I hold my breath as he paddles out, and I'll worry until he returns to shore. That's what grandmothers do, for we know what dangers lurk in the deep, or just around the corner. Concentrate, Alice. Ground yourself. I stare at the rime of faded plastic debris and white sand around my feet, like hundreds and thousands, those sprinkles we used to put on cakes. I pick up some bigger pieces and imagine what they once were. This was the corrugated top from a tube of toothpaste, that was a white plastic tie that might once have held an Amazon package. All that disposable stuff—we kept using it even when oil was running out, and plastic was destroying the world. So many thoughtless years of sandwich bags, disposable straws, and takeaways. Fun years.

These days we get just about enough nutrition, but our food is extracted from plankton and seaweed. We collect the raw materials, check the settings on the food machine, and press a button. Meals eventually emerge—*hamburger, spaghetti carbonara, pancakes*—but these are approximations of the real thing. Food is about survival, not about taste, flavor, or company.

Carelessly delicious food, how I miss that. Jamie's recipe for a good picnic is simple food cooked in nature for the ones you love. Of course, he had a whole team in place for that magazine shoot: hair and makeup, cameras, food consultants, and I couldn't make anything quite as wonderful.

We'll light a real fire. I've worked out how to repli-
cate every impossible-to-find ingredient in Jamie's recipe for
grilled fish. For me, a Last Supper. For Harp, a meal to remember... I fold the magazine pages carefully and move the
picnic basket further into the shade. No trace remains here
of the luxury resort I visited as a child. No holiday makers
creating TikTok clips, no beach hawkers, no music blaring. It's
arguably nicer now, just the beach, the sea, the sun... and the
radiation. I check my monitor, automatically. I'm constantly
worrying about something. Folks my age check their monitors
frequently. Harp does it automatically; he may be thirteen
now, but he acts much older. He piloted the Travelor here;
the technology is simple: a metal double-cased sphere, add a
third layer to dive deeper.

Flipping my bootees off I dig my feet in, once more a
young girl on a beach holiday, and let grains of sand and plastic
flow through my bare toes. There is a kind of beauty in this
multicolored mix. Here is one perfect, curled shell amidst
the rainbow selection of faded plastic pieces. There is the
entrance to a burrow. Crabs survived species collapse, but
even they must hide from the sun. I bet this is the home of
a sand crab.

Alice and Harp

"Got one!" Harp calls, "And it looks fine, no obvious
bumps!"

Alice has a flash of concern about blood in the water but
steels herself to say nothing. She waits at the water's edge,
gutting knife and hand scanner ready. Harp hauls his board
the last few meters, the occasionally thrashing fish carefully
stored on top.

"Strange," Alice says as she passes her scanner over the fish.
"Radiation and plastic are both low."

"Guess it's our lucky day!"

"It is almost sad to kill a fish like this."

Harp shows off his knife work, but Alice pretends not to notice, a game they happily play with each other. He makes a pile from the pieces of wood scattered around—not much left after the winter storms—and maneuvers a sun-catcher overhead. As the flames subside into embers, they prepare salad. There is dill, nothing short of a miracle when the seed took in the permaculture box, tomatoes, and high-iron spinach.

"How long will the fish take?" says Harp.

"Nearly done."

"Data think?"

"Jamie says fish shouldn't be overdone, but I find that microplastics change the cooking time."

"This fish doesn't have much."

They eat side by side. The juice and seeds of the tomatoes burst out as they bite, the fish is soft, the salad slightly grainy. Delicious. Afterward, they perch under the scrawny palm tree and pick over the fishbones. There is a gentle hiss as the plastic shifts on the shoreline. The sand crab pops out of his burrow and wrestles with a large blue piece, trying to drag it down, expending energy pointlessly. Harp bends down and gently lifts the piece away, only for the creature to tackle the flattened handle of a dental pick. Clearly a very dense crab.

"Now, Grandma, tell me a story."

Alice

"Once upon a time, there was no plastic at all."

Harp always likes to hear the old tales. He knows them by heart, but I always start at the beginning, our little ritual.

"Grandma, skip the stuff when you were growing up and go to the bit when I was young."

I wonder why, as the earlier stuff is more interesting. He must have his reasons.

"When you were born, there were many more of us small-time miners. We lived connected in floating pods gathered together into villages and you had friends to play with. Each family group mined a patch of plastic deposits and sent mechanical gatherers down to the ocean floor to work the seams of plastic that had settled there."

"Big machines, right?"

"We left the really big ones to the corporations; we were guerrilla miners. We pressed the plastic particles into brics, then remotely steered the brics to dock at collecting pads. It was a happy enough life, a better life than the ones who stayed on the land. There, only the super-rich could live safely while everyone else had a miserable time. At sea we helped each other out with intel and weather warnings or medicines if we had any.

"We were fortunate."

"You could say so."

"Go on, Grandma."

I pause, knowing what he will ask next. Our little game. Markets, I bet.

"How did we trade after the markets failed, Grandma?"

"We were networks of small communities operating off the main commerce grid. We chose places just ahead of the big reclamation companies. They tolerated us because we offered semi-processed brics to feed into their supply chains. Post-capitalism with a local face, they called it. As the pickings grew slim, we designed better solar-powered pods that could stay further out and dive when the upper surface got choppy. For a long time, raw plastic sold for a reasonable price, in some years very good indeed. Bartering brics for food and other supplies was easy, and the market functioned well. And your mum is really good at bargaining."

"Yes, she usually gets her own way," Harp says and snuggles a little closer beside me, no longer the tough guy.

"There were many deposits in those days, after the oil had failed, and base chemicals were scarce. Vast dumps on land kept the big players busy for years and they mostly left us alone while they competed to grab territory. While they fought it out, the small underwater deposits were left to us. We were nimble, not greedy. When all the high-value urban dumps were exhausted, the big companies turned to the thick layers under the sea."

"After the Great Amalgamation," said Harp, "emerged the Big Six. And the worst of all was Transmine."

I nearly add *Amen.* When I was a girl, we went to Sunday School and recited prayers aloud. Harp has the same tone of voice: perhaps this is his Bible story and Transmine will become his Satan.

"There's change coming."

"People are getting sick."

"Oh God, does he know? Best carry on with the story. I don't want to talk about me."

"Plastic infiltrates everything: our food, our water, our bodies, even our ability to have babies. You're the healthiest child anyone has ever seen. A miracle, never been ill. Perhaps it's luck, perhaps something more."

I kiss him, and he pretends he doesn't like it.

"Stop it, Grandma!"

We both know he does like it.

"We've survived by staying one step ahead of Transmine [A.1] , going further out, always one small step ahead."

"They're coming," says Harp. "Last month, I saw a set of explorer drones."

"Yes, darling, they're coming, but not today. Today is just ours."

Harp falls asleep first. I watch him for a long while, such a beautiful boy. I wish he had been born in an earlier time when life was simpler, safer. I know what Transmine will do to a healthy child. Experimentation: kept alive to extract what is useful from his organs, his skin, his cells. AI controlled, Transmine exists to further itself. I've never discussed these things with him. At first, he was simply too young to know, and more recently, I didn't want to, but I bet he's found it out some other way. Up to his mother now, not me. I don't have long left.

I have plastic sickness. Residue builds up in our food and water. It alters our genes, disrupts hormonal signals, and over-rides cell repair. The last stages are unpleasant... vomiting, bleeding, rapid mood changes—that part is something to do with brain function—but apart from a little nausea, I don't feel too bad. I have the skin changes, though. I'm nearing the end, and I'll just be a drag on him.

I sit for a while, remembering, watching the glint on the darkened sea, hearing the waves shush. What I would give for some proper dessert, something like... chocolate pots. Oh yes! Jamie has a great chocolate pot recipe. I can recite it exactly: two cups of heavy cream, three-quarters of a pound of dark chocolate (coarsely chopped), four large egg yolks, three tablespoons of dark rum, and three tablespoons of unsalted butter (in my experience, any kind of butter works fine). It sounds like a dream now, but I remember the rich smell of the chocolate, the creamy weight on my tongue, the taste...

What the hell, best to leave when the party is at its peak. I wash the tablets down with a gulp of filtered water. Guess that's my dessert. The stars rise in a strangely pink sky. They have never looked so beautiful. *What do they see?* Two people, one old and the other young. And the remains of a picnic.

Harp

I've been awake since dawn. I stroked Grandma's hair for a while and talked to her, told her we could go for a stroll along the beach together. I picked her up and carried her—she was light, barely a feather in my arms.

Grandma got sick a few weeks ago. She tried to hide the vomiting, but in such a small living space, that's impossible. I saw the marks on her back when she was changing for bed, the same ones I saw on the others. When you get the sickness, you die, and it's not an easy death. We keep a bottle of Blue Peaceful for when things get bad. Families can take the tablets together if they get ill at the same time. I didn't want to know about what was happening to Grandma, and she didn't want to talk about it, so I didn't ask, and she didn't tell. But two of the tablets went missing. I know because I counted them.

Adults are so stupid sometimes. They think I don't know about what Transmine might do, but I've picked up bits and pieces listening to them whispering, so I know enough and can imagine the rest. I must stay alive, duck, and dive. Grandma says that; she likes rhyming stuff. *Liked*.

The waves are moving more, and some clouds are coming up. A storm is on the way. I'll gather up our things, take the useable stuff, like her scanner. I know I should salvage the lot, but it doesn't feel right. Her potions box, for sure. She's always trying to get me to take some weird stuff, so it may come in handy. I should say she *was* always trying to feed me weird stuff 'cause she won't be doing that anymore now, will she?

Grandma always told me to get out there and find adventures. An area I've never been to, where maps don't exist anymore. Somewhere out there are Mum and the others. Two months ago, I picked up the tail ends of a video message from 300 miles away, so I'll go back to our pod to pack up the mining gear and then head out. It'll be slower by pod than Travelor, but it means I can bring everything with me. Mum left plenty of stores, and if I can't find her or if I get sick, then I have the pills, just in case. But I won't need them, you'll see. Who knows what I'll find? Last week I saw a turtle, and that fish I caught was healthy. Plastic levels are going down—no more being made, and the old deposits are mostly processed. The ocean is an amazing place; it seems to be waking up again. Perhaps the world will fix itself.

Bye, Grandma—s*ee you later, alligator*—time to go. We're off on an adventure, me and Jamie.

The Island

The not-very-bright crab wrestles with another piece of plastic, then gives up and retreats into his burrow. The wind wipes away two sets of human footprints that intertwine along the beach. Sightless, Alice keeps guard over the picnic spot until she breaks down into tiny particles and is swept away. The island, deserted once more, waits.

Harp sails on.

When the Water Starts to Rise

Jennifer Gryzenhout

It's happening.

"If the river's going to flood, it'll be after a lot of rain," Mom had said. "You'll see the water start to rise up from the edge of the riverbank and flow over into the backyard. You might get a call or an alarm, but maybe not. Keep an eye on the water, notice if it starts to rise. If I'm not home just call me, I'll be on my way."

Where's my phone?

"It probably won't happen," she'd said. "The chances are slim, but still, we should take precautions. We'll just carry on; you'll go to school, and I'll go to work, and I'm sure everything will be fine."

Just because of the rain?

"No, it's not just that. There'll probably also be other reasons, like a weather pressure system or snowmelt. I'm only trying to protect you, to prepare you. Just in case. Of course, a lot of rain is no guarantee. The water has nowhere to go when the ground becomes saturated, so it flows over."

But what about the cat?

"Never mind the cat, he'll get himself out. Cats don't like water."

What about Mrs. Dean next door?

"Get yourself out first, everyone for themself. Someone will come for Mrs. Dean. We can't worry about every neighbor.

You can call nine-one-one to send someone to her, but only after you've left the house."

There's been no alarm.

"I wouldn't keep your books on the ground floor if I were you. We've got to take precautions. Let's keep that ground room empty, keep garbage there, keep things there that you don't care if you lose. If you want to keep your books there on the shelves, that's a chance you'll have to take, but I wouldn't if I were you. The water can rise quickly. You'll have no time to lose."

Maybe we should move.

"Yes, of course we should move. We can try to sell, but really, these days, who's going to buy a house in a flood plain? Only someone who doesn't read the news might do such a thing. This house was your grandpa's from a time before the water was a problem. But sure, we can try to sell. We can't move until we sell, though. We can't afford it."

Phone, charger, laptop... wait, where's the cat?

"We'll keep the valuables upstairs. The water probably won't go that high. But if you see the water rising and I'm not home, leave the house and get to high ground. You don't want to be caught by it. The water can pull and swirl; it's stronger than you think. What's more important: your books or your life? Leave it all behind."

But she's old, Mrs. Dean, she can't walk very well.

"Close the doors and the windows, make sure the house is sealed off if you can. If the water is coming up quickly, please, just get out, don't wait for it to flood. Too much rain, too much bad weather, it doesn't even need to be a perfect storm anymore. If there's too much water, the ground will be soaked like a sponge, totally drenched. It won't be able to absorb anymore."

You can't predict it, though, can you?

"The river will flood, of that they're sure. Not if, but when, is the question. That's what we get for staying in a house in a flood plain. We should have bought that house on higher ground all those years ago, but who would have thought?"

So much rain.

"The water can rush and rise quickly, reclaiming the land and the house and our things, but don't let it take your life. You must save that. You've seen the videos online? Will you remember what to do when the water rises?"

C'mon, Mrs. Dean, let's hussle.

"I have to go to work. If I'm not home just call me, I'll be on my way."

Why aren't you answering your phone?

Wildfire

Nicola Billington

It's coming closer. Joelly wrinkles her nose. She can smell the smoke now; it's the cause of the heavy darkness in the sky, at three in the afternoon. The wind has changed direction, bringing it ever closer. Most people have left town, but her father is refusing to go.

"I've only got a couple of months left, pet," he said to her the day before. "You need to get out while you can. You've got your life to live."

There was no chance of her leaving him to die.

He's contributed to it, of course—all those years digging coal out of the ground. And he's paid the price, his lungs shot, riddled with the disease that pays the pension for a life spent in a mine. She doesn't blame him, not in the least. It was work that was available and a source of pride for those who went underground every day, armed with pick hammers, screwdrivers, pliers, steel bristle brushes; it was skilled work, essential work, and no thought for the consequences of taking fossilized rocks out of the earth to burn. It wasn't her father's fault. He didn't open the mine or own it. He was paid a wage for sacrificing his health but no share in the profits.

A knock at the door. A young man, a stranger outside.

"You have to get out now. The fire's heading this way—it's likely to be here within the hour. There's a bus leaving in twenty minutes, just outside the General Store. Grab what you need and come with us." He doesn't wait for a reply, is on his way to the next house.

Joelly climbs the stairs. The air is thickening, making it difficult for her to breathe. She opens the door of her father's bedroom, seeing his emaciated body through a haze.

"Come on, Dad," she says. "We've got to go."

"Not me," he says. "It's no use."

She gives him the ultimatum: either they both go, or they stay here together and take their chances. He's not going to waste his daughter's life. She helps him into his clothes: trousers now hanging off his hips, the belt with too few holes, a shirt, a cardigan. Even though the temperature is rising. He's so weak, he can barely stand. She half carries him down the stairs, beginning to panic that they'll miss their chance of escape.

At the door they pause to have one last look at their house. Joelly darts back in to collect the photograph of her parents' wedding that stands in pride of place in the center of the mantelpiece.

"Are you not going to lock up?" he asks. She hasn't the heart to tell him there's no point and takes out her key for the last time. If she were on her own she'd reach the bus in two minutes; it's harder trying to get her father there, but it's as if the bus is waiting for them. As soon as they embark, it rumbles into action, and her father stumbles as he tries to claim a seat.

No one speaks. The bus gathers speed, heading away from the flames, but to where? She looks out of the window, past her father: empty roads, hoardings advertising luxuries that you can't live without—they will succumb to the flames. Her father has fallen asleep, the rattle of his breathing getting louder. Until it stops.

First Can on Mars

V. M. Sawh

I can hardly believe it when the water pouring through the hotel lobby soaks my shoes. I mean, you would think that the exclusive Pearl Regency Hotel had tsunami-proof doors; they certainly *charged* like they did, but nope. Which means I get this nasty wave of what looks like toilet water, and smells like hot ammonia, that turns my tennies brown. I yelp like a 12-year-old and leap up onto the imitation leather couch, careful to keep my Hermes handbag from getting wet. They don't like it when you get them wet. Such a pain in the ass to get cleaned. Last time, I'd dropped a venti caramel macchiato in one because my boyfriend (at the time, don't get me started) wanted a sip. I was driving, and he was supposed to be holding my purse, but I tried to answer a call that came in through the dash, and my fingers slipped because the cup was condensated or whatever. I'll just order a new bag this time.

Point is, I'm trying to take better care of my stuff. Sure, Daddy's the Buck Goldberg, y'know, the inventor of MyPoint, the biggest social media platform in the entire world—we can afford to just get a new bag, is what I'm saying—but that's not the point. We value stuff right now. It's *consciouscore*, and if you're not on trend this year, then what are you even doing?

So I actually save my Hermes, thank god, but Lucinda doesn't make it onto the helicopter before the tsunami waters catch up with her. It's kinda sad, really. I don't have to fake the tears when I post my reel. One thing I'll never forget is there was like this bright red soda can that washed in right when the waters busted the doors down. Bobbing and bouncing right along like a little boat in a bathtub. It made me think that like, even with all the water around, you could still be thirsty, right? Anyway, the stupid soda company's an official sponsor, so I have to remember to hold it up in all my shots. Don't wanna piss off the backers. Nobody who makes any real money does. I mean, sure, you can be a MyPoint activist, but Daddy says the real activists/anarchists/*losers* aren't even on the site. It makes me snort every time I think of them texting each other on their poor-people Android phones in their run-down, stank little apartments. What did open-source do for anybody? Can't charge for it. The closed ecosystem is where the money is. That's how we paid for our spaceship.

I've got the new holographic lens on my Pointphone and it's alright, all things considered. The signal is weak out in space—which doesn't make sense, by the way, because we're closer to the satellites—so I have to wait while it's buffering before I can post to the Earth audience. That sounds so weird to say, but it's true. I get to be the first live-streamer on Mars—if we ever get there, anyway. I've been so bored on this trip. The astronauts are nervous and sweaty all the time, like their careers depend on all this working out. Mine doesn't, but I wouldn't be sweating even if it did. When you have unlimited money, you can afford to take a few risks.

My soda sponsor wants to be the first product on the new planet, and I'm down for it. They're paying me like how-much-ever hundreds of millions of dollars. I don't worry about the money; worrying is for poor people like Lucinda. Nice lady, but always going on about the damn ocean, saying how there's no more fish or reefs and how we're all doomed. *That's* what poor people think about. They don't have access to the lab-grown fish or meat. We brought that stuff with us on the trip. Part of me does feel kinda bad that her whole country got crushed in the tsunami, but it's not my fault all her people lived in huts and boats by the water. Earth is so last century anyway. People there are always whining about taxes and the rich. They don't even appreciate how much effort it takes to be a leader. You have to decide what's going to be good for your brand, but there's always going to be somebody who gets all pissy about what you do. Those same activist guys went nuts when we cleared the Amazon rainforest for our manufacturing plants. Because they don't think *strategically*; Daddy taught me that. When you don't think strategically, then whatever happens affects you the most. You want to be behind the tsunami, not in front of it. That's how you benefit.

So we finally touch down, and all the scientists are bouncing around the surface like happy toddlers. All I wanna do is puke. There's nothing here. *Nothing*. It's a big red desert. Oh, look at that rock. There's another one. Can you believe it? Another big stupid rock. Why did I agree to do this?

I can't even drink the sponsor's soda while I'm here. Something about the carbonation and the atmosphere; apparently, it will explode my lungs. So I hold the can awkwardly up against the side of my helmet. There's a reflection that blocks part of my face. I sigh. What's the point of taking all that time to put on my makeup when the glare from the Mars sunset is gonna block half of it?

I reset and try again. Works better. I wanna pour it out—the gravity's weaker here, so it'll look all slow-motion-y—but the scientists freak out. They're always freaking out. They freaked out about the whales dying off, the monkeys burning alive in the rainforest, and even *bugs* disappearing. Who gives a crap about bugs? I mean, *really*—there's not even anything alive on Mars. That's why we're here! We get a fresh start. So what if I pour it out? Honestly, what's the worst that could happen? The sand gets wet? Like guys, Mars is a big planet. We just got here. They're like big parents, always trying to control us, telling us what we can and can't do. Daddy says it's because they don't like freedom. That's why we came out here. Away from the governments and watchdogs of Earth that don't do anything but complain.

Mars means freedom to do what I want. So I pour the soda out and watch it form little sealed bubbles as it captures up globules of Martian sand. Looks kind of neat, so I set up my reaction face, and paste it alongside the globules for the thumbnail. I label it: FIRST CAN ON MARS... YOU WON'T BELIEVE WHAT HAPPENS!

Views cross a billion before the end of the first day.

Heh. I can't believe there's even a billion people left alive on Earth.

Oh well.

I begin setting up for my next shot. "Hey guys, be sure to like and subscribe to my channel..."

The empty can bounces along the surface behind me, so I kick it out of sight.

Contributors and Judges

Benedict J. Amato ("Lookout Point") is a retired educator, writer and journalist. He participated in educational collaborations with a Long Island, NY newspaper and has written articles and columns for various Long Island magazines. An avid sailor and reader, Ben has gained insights into the boundaries between today's fiction and tomorrow's facts. He and his wife live in the Hudson Valley of NY and Southwest Florida. His Facebook address is: https://www.facebook.com/ben.amato.1

Douglas Arvidson ("Blue Cassandra") has published his short stories internationally. His story "The Rifle" took first-place honors in a competition sponsored by the Women's Institute for Culture and Education (WICE) in Paris. His novel, *A Drop of Wizard's Blood*, won the 2017 New Mexico-Arizona Book Awards, while his novel *Brothers of the Firestar* was selected as a Book-of-the-Year Finalist by Fore-Word Reviews. He now lives on the Eastern Shore of Virginia. See douglasarvidson.com.

Tabitha Bast ("Deluge") lives in Bradford UK, works as a therapist, and writes a personalized feminist blog on positive masculinity (https://theboysarealright.substack.com/).She has had nine short stories published since 2018, most recently "Finished Symphony" in *Oluwale Now* (Peepal Tree Press, 2023).

Clare D. Becker ("Dislocation") is the pen name for a former teacher who has collaborated on both written and filmed oral history projects. She lives in the Boston area, where the sea has started tickling the land. She is working on a set of linked stories and finds that catching the ironies of history, as well as the present, can be instructive, perturbing, and sometimes amusing.

Kitty Beer ("Don't Ask"), from Cambridge, Massachusetts, has written a series of novels about climate change entitled *Resilience: a Trilogy of Climate Chaos*. Her most recent book is *Marriages and Other Dilemmas: Collected Stories and a Memoir*. Currently she's publishing short stories, the most recent of which appeared in the literary magazine *Constellations*.

Nicola Billington ("Wildfire") worked as a pianist and teacher in London until 2020, when she wound up her private teaching practice and relocated with her husband to Corbridge, Northumberland UK. She now divides her time between music and writing and has recently started a Substack newsletter, the Good-Tempered Pianist, about practicing and playing the piano. She attends two writing groups and their encouragement and support has given her the confidence to send out her work.

Mary Ethna Black ("The Island") is a doctor and writer from Northern Ireland. A medical globetrotter, she has judged silver salmon in Alaska, and raised two children with the oarsman who saved her life from pirates.

Brian Brennan ("Symbiosis") is a writer from Springfield, Virginia, retired from his former occupation as an information technology executive providing services to the federal government. His work has been or will soon be published in many literary journals including Yale University's *The Perch* and *Isele Magazine*. He has also published history through the George Washington University Press. He is currently marketing his upmarket crime fiction work *Throughline*, and his historical thriller *The Emigrant*. Look for him on X @brian-booklover.

Paul Briggs ("American Mangroves") is the author of four science-fiction novels, one of which, *Altered Seasons: Monsoonrise*, was a Finalist (Science Fiction), in the Foreword INDIES Book of The Year Awards. He learned to read and write when he was two, has a master's degree in journalism, and has worked as a layout editor, copywriter, scopist, and audio transcriber. See paulbriggs.com.

C.B. Buzz ("My Dearest Daughter") lives in the Pacific Northwest with his two dogs. He works on a farm but has always dreamed of writing epic fantasy and sci-fi stories. An avid reader, C.B. Buzz is also an all-around nerd who enjoys video games, DnD, and late summer nights.

French speaking, born and raised in the Swiss Alps, **Catherine Chaddic** ("Landslide") escaped gender inequality by embarking on a thirty-year adventure around the world. A passionate writer, obsessed with freedom and fairness, she retired on the Eastern Shore of Virginia where she draws upon rich experiences to unburden her vivid imagination into works of fiction and creative nonfiction. New to publishing, she hopes to release this year her humor-filled stumble into life's jungle.

Lee Clontz ("Leave No Trace") is a writer, distance runner, amateur guitarist and technology enthusiast from Decatur, Georgia. His past lives and passions include journalism, programming, blogging and parenting. His goals are to run the Boston Marathon and to publish his first novel.

Jim Coleman ("Collateral Damage") is a resident of Ridgely, Maryland, via western Pennsylvania. While he has been writing stories of some sort or another ever since the day his mom brought home some blank newsprint for her bored eight-year-old, this is only his second foray into the world of published fiction, his first being in Secant Publishing's previous anthology, *The Year's Best Dog Stories 2021* ("Nellie and the Big Dog").

Melody Cooper ("RISE") writes fiction, TV, and film. Her work includes "Sundown" in *African Ghost Short Stories* by Flame Tree Publishing and the comic book OMNI from Humanoids. Melody recently returned from Antarctica and has been invited to work on her speculative novel about climate change at a Bellagio Residency in Italy.

Andrea Dejean ("Bitter Almonds") is a writer and translator based in France. Her work has appeared in over a dozen literary journals. Her first novel, *Sphinx*, was issued in October 2021 (Middle Creek Publishing & Audio). Her second novel, *Terra Firma*, is forthcoming from another independent press.

Cindy Diggs ("Awakened") lives in Machipongo, Virginia. She spent her career as a Licensed Mental Health Professional writing clinical papers for her profession, and years writing anything but clinical papers as a hobby. Now that she has the time, she is looking forward to dusting off all those old personal writings and creating some new ones. She recently had a short story about childlessness selected for publication on the website of World Childless Week.

Dean Engel ("The Amuse-Bouche") has written short stories, poetry, and a play that was staged by a small community theater group in Chicago. He works for a manufacturer by day but is also an avid gardener and birder whose writing often reflects his interest in the environment and natural world.

Karly Foland ("Adaptive Solutions")is a U.S. Department of State Foreign Service Officer with a master's in International Psychology and a bachelor's in International Studies. Originally from Omaha, she has spent a decade in Africa, Asia, and Europe, and lives with her husband and the two cats they rescued from Morocco.

Jennifer Gryzenhout ("When the Water Starts to Rise") is a writer from Canada living in Amsterdam, The Netherlands. She teaches creative writing and English literature, holds an MFA in Creative Writing from UBC, has fiction published in *Ink Tears* and *Avalon Literary Review*, and is the recipient of a Pushcart Prize nomination. Currently she is writing short fiction and a novel.

Adjie Henderson ("The Blue Ridge Mountain Tree")is a scientist and previously a Dean for Graduate Sciences. She published two hundred reports on basic research, from genetics to standards for environmental controls. She has made many public appearances related to science and published 26 short stories, none of which have to do with the credentials above.

Ian Inglis ("Raymond and Ruby") was born in Stoke-on-Trent and now lives in Newcastle upon Tyne. His short stories have appeared in numerous anthologies and literary magazines in the UK and US, and his debut collection "The Day Chuck Berry Died" was published by Bridge House in Autumn 2022.

Olaf Lahayne ("Beyond the Timberline") lives in Vienna, Austria, where he works as a scientist at the Technical University. He has published newspaper articles, a non-fiction book and around 150 short stories from pretty much all genres in anthologies and magazines. Five collections were also published separately as e-books or print books.

Jessica Marcy ("In Times of Change, Root Down to Rise Up") is a writer, filmmaker, and Pulitzer Center Reporting Fellow. Her work has appeared in National Geographic, Maryland Public Television, The Washington Post, NPR, MSNBC, and Kaiser Health News. She holds a master's in journalism from Columbia University and an MFA in film and media arts from American University.

Maura Morgan ("PLaNT Man") is a writer of both fiction and nonfiction, covering a range of topics including travel, history, speculative and historical fiction, and short stories. She graduated from Drexel University with a Master of Fine Arts degree in Creative Writing. She is working on an historical novel.

Lee Nash (she/her) ("Sea Burial") writes poetry, fiction, and creative nonfiction. Her work has been featured in diverse journals including *Magma*, *Slice*, *Southword* and "The Best Small Fictions 2019," and has won or been placed/shortlisted in international competitions, including Bath Flash Fiction Award, the TU Dublin Short Story Competition, and the Bridport Prize.

Martin Phillips ("Planet Suite") grew up in London in the 1960s. He graduated from the Institute of Education of London University and taught English in schools in London and Devon. He was English Adviser to Devon County Council for 15 years. He won first prize at the 2020 Yeovil International Literary Festival, second prize in the Anansi Archive Short Story Competition in 2022 and was longlisted for Bridport Short Story Prize in 2021 and the Henshaw Press Short Story prize in 2023. He has an MA in Creative Writing from London University's Birkbeck College.

David Poyer ("The Captain of the Fleet") is a retired naval officer and educator, as well as a novelist and playwright. He lives on the Eastern Shore of Virginia with fellow writer Lenore Hart. See https://poyer.com/.

Cedric Rose ("Brownian Motion") is a librarian, journalist, and writer working in Cincinnati, Ohio.

A. A. Rubin ("Noah's Great Rainbow") roams the multiverse like Cosmic Cain, jumping the variegated planes of reality across the dimensions of space and time. A member of the SFWA, his work has appeared in *Love Letter to Poe*, *Cowboy*

Jamboree, and Ahoy Comics. Follow him @TheSurrealAri, or visit his website, www.aarubin.com.

B. E. Saunders ("2100, Remnants of a Thriving World") is English born but is now living in Tasmania, Australia with her partner and children. Though she has traded her itchy feet for settled roots, her time travelling the globe still feeds her stories and motivates her studies for a Bachelor of Natural Environment and Conservation.

V.M. Sawh ("First Can on Mars") is a multiple-award-winning author and proud supporter of independent artists and authors. His "Good Tales for Bad Dreams" series of dark fairy tales is available on Amazon and via the Toronto Public Library's "Best in Ontario" collection. It has received awards and critical acclaim from Australia's Chrysalis BREW and the Ontario Writers' Conference, among others. His story "Till Death Do Us Part" was longlisted for the Iridescence Award by Kinsman Quarterly, a literary magazine highlighting fiction of cultural significance by authors of color. See https://vmsa wh.my.canva.site/

Tom Sterling ("The Circle City Run") was born in the small town of Crisfield on Maryland's Eastern Shore. He moved to Northern Virginia and worked as an engineer in the defense industry for forty years. Tom writes a collection of short science fiction and fantasy stories describing ordinary people thrown into extraordinary situations. The series is called *Postcards from Earth* and can be found on Amazon. Tom is retired and lives in Fairfax, Virginia, with his wife, MyPhuong. See https://tomsterling.com.

K. M. Watson ("Desert Fish") lives in Maryland's farm and horse country near Sykesville with her husband and quirky rat terrier mix. Raised in a military family, she has moved and traveled most of her life. She briefly pursued a childhood dream of becoming a marine biologist and worked on board a research ship, but turned to science writing and teaching instead. Outlets for her work include Discovery.com, the University of California, and Alameda News Group. Later in her career, she lived in Baltimore and taught in high-poverty schools. She loves exploring the natural world. Follow her work on Facebook at KM Watson writer.

P. H. Zietsman ("Blood") is a South African writer. The Monster Becomes Knight, a poem appearing in the *Best New African Poets Anthology 2017*, was his first published work and has been selected to appear in the 10th-anniversary issue of *Best New African Poets*. He is currently working on bringing a novel to life.

Judges

Karen Gravelle has authored seventeen nonfiction books for children and teens, including perennial bestseller *The Period Book* and *What's Going On Down There?*, both of which have been translated into multiple languages. She has also written two adult books, a graphic novel for older elementary school readers, and a middle school novel set on the Eastern Shore of Virginia.

Philip Wilson owns and operates a 43-year-old treasure of Virginia's Eastern Shore, the Book Bin in Onley. He became a bookseller after serving for more than twenty years as a professor of medical, scientific, and British history, primarily at Penn State. He also makes time for assisting students in the Learning Resource Center of the Eastern Shore Community College.

Ron Sauder is owner of Secant Publishing, LLC, located in Salisbury, Maryland. He was the publisher and editor of *The Year's Best Dog Stories 2021*, which won a Silver Medal in the 2022 national IPPY Awards competition. Secant Publishing is a small, independent publishing house on the Eastern Shore of Maryland, with a special focus on regional authors and books. See secantpublishing.com.